Sadie
and the
BAD BOY
BILLIONAIRE

Sadie and the BAD BOY BILLIONAIRE

EMMA ST. CLAIR JENNY PROCTOR

Copyright © 2023 by Jenny Proctor and Emma St. Clair

All rights reserved.

No part of this book may be reproduced in any form or by any electronic or mechanical means, including information storage and retrieval systems, without written permission from the author, except for the use of brief quotations in a book review.

If you have questions, email Emma@emmastclair.com

To all of the readers who send us raccoon videos. Never stop.
#banjo4eva

Also, to all our pelican friends who don't get the credit they deserve.
Just keep swooping.

CONTENT WARNINGS

This is a light romcom, but these are topics that are touched on in the book:

- Death of parents (past)
- Divorce & ugly family stuff (past)
- A brief tense scene involving a gun
- Talk of pregnancy & infertility (epilogue)
- Attack pelicans & Shakespeare-loving parrots
- Making fun of boat shoes & yachts

Spoiler alert: No one dies. There is no sex in this book. You will get a happy ending with no cheating and minimal angst.

ONE

Sadie

I'VE NEVER MET an anthill I didn't want to kick. Literally or figuratively. All the anthills. All the kicking. Is it curiosity? Some inherent need in me to stir things up? I haven't been through enough therapy to know.

The thing I've learned, though, is that if I'm going to kick anthills, I need to be ready to jump out of the way. And though I excel at kicking, I'm not the best at jumping.

I learned this the hard way when I was six, visiting Gran on Oakley Island like my sisters and I did most summers. Growing up in the Midwest, I didn't know about fire ants and the way they don't start biting until they've swarmed, a tactic that maximizes their impact. I have the scars on my ankles to prove it.

I still remember Gran rubbing cream on the angry, pimple-like bites the ants left behind, all while lecturing me on respecting nature and staying out of messes I knew would only cause trouble.

The memory of my grandmother, who died a little less than two years ago, makes my throat tighten. But those aren't emotions I can handle right now.

The point is: even if fire ants are the insect version of Satan's minions, I can't seem to leave them alone. At least not the figurative kind.

A fact evidenced by what I woke up to this morning.

My phone is lit up with notifications for missed calls and texts from my main contact at the government agency where I often do contract work. And by contract work, I mean light hacking and things the government needs done ... by someone a few steps removed from their *actual* employees to give them a solid amount of plausible deniability.

Dread tightens my belly. I *immediately* know why Agent German is calling me.

Don't get me wrong. I might be a trouble-making anthill kicker by nature, but I've definitely learned to be careful. Most of the time I'm better than careful—I'm invisible. Especially when it comes to my online activities.

But this time, with the digging I did this week ... I wasn't careful enough.

Before I can even begin to get through the notifications, my phone rings in my hand.

I swallow and clear my throat. "'Sup, German." Even though alarm bells are going off in my head, I answer my agency contact the way I typically do. Mostly because it exasperates him and I love hearing the sound of him sighing into the phone. But also because I'm still clinging to the hope that this is all just a big misunderstanding.

"What did you do?" he demands.

"You'll have to be more specific. I do lots of things."

There are muffled noises, and I'm pretty sure I'm hearing him cover the phone while muttering a long line of curse words I've never heard from German before.

I really *did* kick the wrong anthill this time.

"You weren't supposed to go any deeper into their system. Just a cursory glance—enough to give us what we needed for basic intel. But you couldn't do that, could you? You had to go deeper."

His accusatory tone triggers a sense of indignation I can't tamp down. If it were any other situation, I might feel guilty. But in this case, the network they had me mirror to pull the requested data seemed shady from the start and immediately piqued my interest.

By interest, I mean disgust and a sense of vengeance. Because in addition to the other unsavory activities I uncovered, there were clear things to indicate the slime in charge of the organization had ties to human trafficking. I didn't even hesitate. A deeper dive into the network was completely necessary, even if risky.

A chance to expose scum who treat human beings like property? Not gonna just sleep on that. Nope. The intel I turned over should be enough to shut everything down as well as expose other key players.

You're welcome.

But a *thank you* doesn't seem to be forthcoming. At least not from German.

"Sounds like you know exactly what I did," I say. "Why'd you even ask?"

He ignores my very practical question. "There was a reason we asked you to keep it light. You screwed up, Sadie."

No regrets. Even though I knew going deeper and accessing servers remotely meant more chance I'd leave some kind of trail.

"What's done is done," I say. "Next time I have a chance to get you important information—"

"You'll walk away unless it's what we've asked you to do."

Or not. I make zero promises when it comes to something like this. Most of the time, the work I do involves white-collar crime. Data, codes, account numbers, information I can't decipher out of context, and I normally don't try. I do my job, and I do it *well*.

Get in. Get the information I'm asked to retrieve. Get out.

But once I realized what I'd discovered, it felt too big of an issue to ignore. I couldn't *know* human trafficking was happening and not work to expose it.

Still, I shouldn't have gotten caught.

The fact that I did irks me just as much as German's flat, compassionless tone.

I hate getting caught. And making mistakes. I may not be the obvious type-A perfectionist my older sister, Merritt, is (both she and my younger sister, Eloise, would laugh at the comparison), but I *despise* screwing up. Especially when it's in front of an audience.

German breathes one of his trademark sighs into the phone. "And now I'm on my way down with a team."

A shocked laugh bubbles out of me. "A team? Overreact much?"

"You better hope it's an overreaction. Now, what we need for you to do is—"

"Sit tight and not so much as log on to anything at all. Got it."

"No," German says. "We need you to get some physical distance from your current location."

"You mean my *home*? The place where I *live*?"

I glance around my fairly new apartment. It isn't huge or

fancy but I chose it for the location in Midtown Atlanta and the fact that it's in a 1920s style bungalow, broken up into four apartments. Mine is a thousand square feet of details you don't find in new apartment complexes: scarred but gorgeous hardwood floors, high ceilings and thick crown molding, a wall of exposed brick. I glance at my desk with all my monitors and fun toys set up exactly how I like them.

"For now, yes," German says. "We'll reevaluate once we get to you."

My gut twists, and I feel a cold prickle of dread as the seriousness of the situation hits me. They say teenagers have this innate sense of feeling invincible, which is why they do so many dumb things. I'm not sure I ever outgrew that. I feel especially invincible when I'm safely behind my computer screen. But that feeling is gone now.

"German, am I ... in danger?"

"Hopefully this is all just precautionary," he says.

"But you said I need to leave my physical location. Does that mean these men—the ones I uncovered—they know where I am? Who I am?"

He's quiet for a long moment. *Too long.*

"Don't lie to me, German."

Another sigh. "Yes. Whatever you did left a digital footprint that we have reason to believe has been traced directly back to you."

"Not just the United States government," I say. "*Me.*"

It isn't hard to imagine the nature of the men I uncovered. I'm willing to bet whoever they are, they're scary. Powerful. Cruel.

I close my eyes, remembering the exact moment I clicked too far. I have a dozen different ways to keep myself safe online. But this one particular firewall—I could tell it was set up to keep people like me out. There was a work-around, an application vulnerability I could expose, but it meant disabling the proxy server I was using to stay invisible.

I should have known better, but something told me it might be worth the risk. When I turned over the information I uncovered, it felt like it *was* worth it.

"Don't freak yourself out over there," German says dryly, offering me exactly zero comfort. "We're already acting to take care of things. If you do what I ask, you'll be fine."

"*Acting* to take care of things? That feels like vague government speak."

"It is vague government speak," German says. "I'm not at liberty to discuss the details, but let's just say we're hoping to eradicate the threat before it has time to reach you specifically. We would very much like this to become a non-issue."

Okay, so I'm taking this to mean they're taking down the big baddies who are doing big bad things before anyone tracks me down. It's a reassuring thought. Bad guys in jail is what we all want. If I had a hand in that, I still have no regrets.

"Okay. What am I supposed to do?" I ask, sobered enough to stop joking with German.

"You've got family on Oakley Island, right?"

Weird how I was just thinking about Gran, and now German's bringing up the island. I didn't know he even knew—but then, I guess it's his job to know things.

Both of my sisters relocated to Oakley after Gran passed. At first, it was just to fulfill parts of the will, which required one or more of us to live there while renovating Gran's house.

The fact that both Eloise and Merritt *stayed* has everything to do with Jake and Hunter, the island locals they inexplicably fell in love with, then *married*.

I'm still wrapping my brain around those particular events. I understand sweet little Eloise falling for a small-town guy—especially a steady and objectively hot man like Jake—but Merritt getting back together with her first teenage love? I did *not* see that one coming. At least not until I saw her and Hunter in the same room. Those two are ridiculously in love. Who knew my stony-hearted sister is actually a big softie? I mean, she has a pet raccoon and a small pack of dogs. *And she likes it.*

The thought of seeing my sisters sends a sudden burst of longing right through my heart, but ... I can't *really* go to Oakley, can I?

"If I'm in danger, I'm not going within ten states of the people I love," I say.

I'll hop in my car and head west, in the opposite direction from Oakley. I've always wanted to see California. Though ... I'd probably be better off *flying* west. Since my house is within walking distance of a MARTA station and so many restaurants and shops, I've been eking out the last bit of life from the ancient Honda I've had since high school without worrying about replacing it. It's definitely on its last leg. Or last wheels? The AC doesn't even work, which makes it not the best choice for road trips.

"You're not in immediate danger," German says, and I want to believe him. Because the *other* reality isn't one I want to consider. "This is more of a formality."

"You just said they know who I am," I fire back. "You're bringing a team all the way to Georgia to babysit me as a formality?"

German hesitates, then clears his throat, like he recognizes the contradiction in what he's telling me. "Look. This isn't a spy movie. You did screw up, and your actions did put you at risk. But it's unlikely that anyone will actually track you down."

"Then why have me leave home at all? Atlanta is a big city. I can just lay low here, stay off the internet for a while."

"Because on the off chance they do track you down, they'll probably be looking for your hard drive," German responds. "If someone breaks into your apartment to trash your equipment, we'd rather you not be there. We're just taking every precaution, Sadie. Get out of Atlanta. Go see your sisters and stay offline. This will blow over in a couple of weeks."

The tension building in my chest eases the slightest bit. "Fine. But for the record, if this were a spy movie, my character would be played by early 2000s Sandra Bullock."

As for who would play the heavily sighing agent on the phone, I'd cast a Hemsworth to play his part. Probably pre-Miley-Cyrus Liam over Chris. I've never seen the man, but his voice is deep and rumbly. In short, it's never a hardship to hear him talk. Even if he is about as fun as a log stuck in knee-deep mud.

Have I wondered a time or two about what it would be like to meet German in person? Speculated over whether he's the exact combination of sexy-tough-grumpy that's my personal catnip? Most definitely. And I'm imagining it again right now.

Clearly, the man himself is only imagining business.

"We're also trying to avoid any situation that could lead to legal problems for us," he says. "And we don't want any of this information to go public."

"Ahhh. So, this is really about you covering your butt. Are you worried I might sue the government? Or … wait, is it more about not wanting people to know you hired someone like me in the first place?"

German won't answer my questions, but I don't need him to. I mostly keep things above board when I'm online. I don't steal. I don't cheat. But I *could*. And the people who hire me know that better than anyone.

At any rate, I'm much happier with the idea of going into hiding because the government doesn't want bad press or legal troubles than I am because bad guys want to take a baseball bat to my computer desk. Or worse—to *me*.

As predicted, German acts like I haven't said a word. "Leave the phone we issued you in your current location as well as any electronics that could trace back to you."

"Can I take my personal laptop?"

"Sadie," he says sternly. "No computers. Leave everything behind."

"Geez, fine. You don't have to make me feel like an idiot for asking," I mutter.

The beat or two of silence sounds very much like German wordlessly assuring me that I am, in fact, idiot enough to stick my nose where it doesn't belong and get caught doing it.

And fine—maybe this time he's right.

"I'll see you in Oakley tomorrow. Possibly two days, depending."

I bite my tongue to keep myself from asking him *depending on what?* But why ask? German won't tell me.

And honestly, I'm feeling better and better about things. If I were really in trouble, German wouldn't wait two days. He would take me into protective custody immediately and set me up in a safe house somewhere. He definitely wouldn't send me to hang out with my family.

That better be the case. I'm fine dealing with the consequences of my choices, but I'm not about to put my family at risk.

So, yeah. I'm going to take him at his word that this is overkill.

"I assume you'll be at your sisters' bed and breakfast?" German asks.

I almost correct him and say that Gran's house technically belongs to me too, even though Lo and Jake are the ones running it with support from Merritt and Hunter, who handled the renovation.

They actually invited me to visit this weekend, for the grand opening of the bed and breakfast that was always our grandmother's dream. I should be there. Of course, I should be there. I *did* say the reason I relocated from DC to Atlanta was to be closer to Oakley—even if I've only visited once since the move.

But instead of making the trip, I made excuses, going on and on about how I have to fly rather than drive the four or so hours it takes to get there because my car is unreliable. And if I did try to drive, it's May, which means humidity, which means having no AC in my car is even worse than usual. And flying is such a pain and getting shuttled from the airport in Savannah to Oakley is a pain, and … yeah. I'm not sure my sisters bought any of it.

But I'm not about to admit the real reasons I didn't want to go. First, how do I explain how incredibly emotional I am at the thought of seeing the bed and breakfast open? Don't get me wrong—it will be amazing.

But it feels so *final*. Like Gran is really gone, and we're all moving on to new things. Maybe I'm not in touch with my feelings or maybe grief really does take on different shapes and come in various sizes, but I'm not sure I've fully come to grips with Gran's death.

Somewhere shoved deep in my belly, there's a ball of guilt and sadness and regret and just plain loss. I miss her. So much. I had a feeling that going this weekend would have that complicated ball of feelings shooting out of me like some kind of rogue cannon blast.

I'm just not ready.

I guess now I have to be.

The second reason I've been avoiding Oakley is a lot sillier—silly enough that I don't want to admit it out loud. Because it has everything to do with a man who I think is technically a billionaire and is absolutely a thorn in my side whenever I set foot on the island.

Every time I visit my sisters, Benedict King pops up like he's in one of those old music boxes and I'm the one turning the handle. Only, instead of jester clothes, the man is forever dressed like he's headed to the yacht club in khakis, a polo, and boat shoes, armed with the kind of smile that comes from thousands of dollars spent at a high-end orthodontist.

I shouldn't be so bothered by Benedict, but there's just something about him that gets under my skin. Like a very attractive parasite.

"It's a little creepy how much you know about me when I know so little about you," I say to German, pushing thoughts of Benedict out of my mind. "Is German even your real name?"

I'm rewarded with another sigh.

"It's called a background check," he grumbles. "I'm in the business of knowing your business." He pauses. "You know, you really should start going to bed earlier. It's bad for your circadian rhythm to stay up all night and sleep most of the day."

Okay, now that's just downright *creepy*.

"Kidding," he says a moment later while I'm still busy peeking between my blinds to check for white surveillance vans outside.

"I certainly hope so," I mutter.

"Don't get into any trouble before I get to you."

"Me? Trouble?"

"I mean it."

"Hey, German?" I say before he can hang up.

"Yeah?"

"This means we're going to finally meet in person."

"Yes." His tone is clipped. Which only makes me want to mess with him more.

"What's your favorite color, so I can make sure to pack accordingly? Are you more of a casual guy or should I dress up?"

"Sadie?" German says. "Respectfully, shut up and get out of town."

TWO

Sadie

HONESTLY, it's probably good I'm making the trip to Oakley now. This is what I tell myself on my flight and then on the Uber ride to the island. Over and over, I think this like a mantra or a prayer, as if repeating it will keep me from the mild panic leftover from German's call. Or the bone-deep sadness that almost swallows me whenever I think about Gran.

It sort of works.

Eloise and Merritt will be stoked that I'm here, even if my reason *isn't* the opening of the bed and breakfast. I'm still debating what I want to tell them about my change of heart, but that's a problem for Later Sadie. And if I don't mention it, they'll assume I'm here just to support them.

Despite my onslaught of emotions regarding Gran's beach house, I can't wait to see the finished product. I've only been back once since Merritt and Hunter's wedding, but Eloise has spent months blowing up my phone with pictures of all the work.

Meanwhile, I have been happily *not involved*.

Not that either sister has needed my help.

Marriage has been good for Eloise. She seems more grounded, focused. Plus, she just finished her master's degree, even if opening the bed and breakfast is keeping her from any actual academic literary stuff. As for Merritt, she has a new business to run and a new stepdaughter. They both have a lot on their plate, but they're doing it. Juggling everything. And they're doing it without me.

It's a little weird, honestly. Having been the constant buffer as the middle child, I'm not used to Eloise and Merritt being so close. But finishing the bed and breakfast, that's something they've done together.

Not that I'm jealous, exactly. It's just one more change.

As I expected—or maybe as I feared—standing on the front porch of Gran's fully renovated and honestly *stunning* beach house hits me right in the feels, with all the subtlety of a wrecking ball.

I drop my bags and simply stand there, breathing as I will my emotions to settle back down where they belong. But they don't want to recede. Instead, they're clambering up my throat, making my vision blur as I sway on my feet.

"Dramatic much?" I mutter to myself, but the normal smart-mouthed edge to my voice is muted. The emotional weight of this is more than I expected, even though I knew it would be a lot. More than I want to admit, definitely more than I want anyone to see. Especially my sisters.

Even though I like to pretend I don't have roots anywhere, my roots on this island are deep. Seeing this house—*Gran's* house—like this, all shiny and polished and perfect, just the way she would have wanted—

"The place looks great, doesn't it?"

I spin around at the deep voice rumbling behind me. And then promptly trip over my luggage, tumbling forward into the perfectly pressed, pale purple button-down stretched across the stupidly firm chest of Benedict King.

Because of course I do.

The very last person in the world I would ever want to see me emotional—or clumsy—is the man I'm currently pressed against like a fitted shirt. The only upside is that for the few seconds my face is hidden from view, I have time to school my features and steady my breathing. My wildly beating heart, though, I can't even begin to steady that.

Ben's arms—bulging with muscles I'd like to ignore—wrap around me, tightening against my back. I swear, I can feel his surprise that I'm not shoving him away. If I didn't need to compose myself, I definitely would. When I'm steady on my feet again and sure any trace of my sorrow is tucked away, I wiggle out of his embrace.

Or attempt to.

Ben loosens his grip but doesn't let me go, instead sliding his hands to my elbows, creating a respectable distance between us while still keeping me close. Close enough to smell his masculine scent, which has a faint note of sugary sweetness. Like he's managed to manufacture a signature cologne that makes him smell like a sexy cupcake.

What am I thinking? He's a billionaire. He probably *did* make a signature scent.

I make the mistake of meeting his gaze. His blue eyes, fringed with thick lashes only a little darker than his dirty blond hair, search mine. A smile plays around his unfairly full lips, but Benedict King will *not* smile at me. He'll smirk. And then he'll say something flirty and ridiculous. I've encountered the man enough times to know his modus operandi. Usually, I'm composed enough to give it right back to him.

Clearly, today is not that day.

"You cut your hair," he says, and I abhor the little thrill I get knowing he noticed.

"How observant, Mr. King."

Before, I've always made jokes about his name, calling him Benedict Arnold or Eggs Benedict or Benedict Cumberbatch. Calling him Mr. King seems a little bland by comparison, but I'm running out of Benedicts.

"I like it," he says. Lifting a hand, he gives a strand of my shoulder-length waves a gentle tug.

Another tiny pulse of something I'd rather ignore zips through me.

"Don't even think about it," I say, pushing away from him and holding up a finger in warning.

He pushes his hands into the pockets of his chinos. "Don't think about what?"

"Flirting," I say as I wheel my suitcase toward the front door. "No lines about me tripping on purpose so I can fall into your arms or anything else cheesy and completely not true."

"Oh, I know you'd never fall into my arms willingly," Ben says as he follows behind me. "That's one of the things I like about you. You're a challenge. And I like challenges."

Ugh. I don't *want* him to like challenges. Or to like me. And yet I can't ignore the way his words make my skin prickle with heat.

"But for the record," he continues, "I was only going to ask if you were okay."

I roll my eyes. I've had enough interactions with Benedict King—he owns Oakley Island so he's been very involved in the renovations of Gran's house—to know that he's a shameless flirt and, from his reputation, a total player.

Still, a tiny voice in my head whispers something about how I, too, like challenges.

I ignore the voice.

I glance over my shoulder at the front lawn as I knock on the giant double front door, only hesitating when my eyes catch on the sign affixed to the freshly painted white siding. *Genevieve's Bed and Breakfast.*

Gran would be so proud of this place. So proud of the three of us, though my sisters did the lion's share of the work. I blink back sudden and very unwelcome tears, wishing my time alone on this porch hadn't been interrupted.

Especially by *him*.

Benedict reaches around me and opens the door, his arm brushing against me as his low voice rumbles, "You don't have to knock, Sadie. It's a place of business. You can just walk in."

Goose bumps break out across my skin, and I frown. Benedict King does NOT deserve my goose bumps.

"It's not technically a place of business *yet*, is it?" I say as I follow him inside. "They aren't open until—"

"Sadie?!" Eloise barrels into me, cutting off my sentence and pulling me into an enormous hug. "What are you doing here? I thought you couldn't make it!"

"Surprise?" I hug her back long enough to appease my excessively affectionate little sister, then shrug out of her grasp. "Change of plans," I say.

She eyes me curiously. "Did something happen?"

I wave away her concern, hoping she doesn't see just how close she is to the truth. "Is it really so hard to imagine I would rearrange my schedule so I can be here to celebrate this enormous accomplishment?" I motion around the front room of the house which does, as expected, look completely amazing.

Eloise's gaze turns shrewd. "Yes, actually. I know you love me, Sades, but I also know how married you are to your work."

If she were Merritt, this would be an intentional guilt trip. As it stands, it's just sweet Eloise stating a fact. One that absolutely floods me with guilt.

"How's your car?" she asks. "Did it make the trip okay?"

My gaze skirts to Ben. I don't love the idea of him knowing my car is a pile of garbage, not when he probably has a dozen different cars at his disposal. "I flew, actually."

"You flew? But that was probably ex—"

"Not expensive at all," I say, cutting her off. "My work schedule cleared up last minute, and I got a great deal."

Lo looks like she's going to argue, but she doesn't say anything else. I have a feeling if Ben wasn't also standing with us, she might.

"I'm really happy to be here for the grand opening," I say, and at least this much is the truth.

"Speaking of ..." Ben steps up beside me and hands Eloise an envelope I never even saw him holding. Is the man some kind of magician, pulling paperwork out of his fancy dress shirt?

"Your final occupancy permits came through. You're good to go."

Eloise grins as she takes the envelope. "Jake will be so relieved! He's made so many phone calls to Savannah, each one more frustrating than the last. I thought those little veins in his forehead might completely pop." She looks at me, still beaming. "We've got a full house this weekend. Booked out completely because of the opening and the

Flower Festival. Without the permits, we'd have had to cancel everything." She frowns as realization seems to hit her all at once. "Wait—a full house means I don't have a place to put *you*."

"I wave a hand. "It's fine."

"No, it isn't." She taps a perfectly pink fingernail against her lips. The color matches the enormous flowers all over her sky-blue dress. "You could sleep on the couch at mine and Jake's place, but honestly, it's not very comfortable."

"What about the other half of the carriage house?" I ask.

"Naomi is living there right now," Lo says. "She's helping out at the bed and breakfast for us. We thought housing sounded like a nice perk so Liam can be close, especially when he gets out of school for the summer. If you'd waited until next month, our house would be done, and we've got a gorgeous guest room, but we still don't have water." She points at Ben. "I bet there's something *you* could do about that, actually. We can't live in the house until there's water." She puts the paper from Ben down on the check-in counter behind her and props her hands on her hips. "I bet Merritt and Hunter wouldn't mind you staying with them. Want me to text her?"

I can't think of anything I'd like less than staying with *either* of my still very newlywed sisters and their enthusiastically affectionate husbands. They're all in that disgustingly annoying phase of being starry-eyed and all over each other.

I mean, I'm happy for them. But no walls are thick enough to entice me to stay across the hall from either of their bedrooms.

"Don't text Merritt," I say, quickly enough to make Ben's eyebrows go up. "I'll just get a room at the place next to Ned's."

"It's all booked up too," Ben says. "The flower festival is this weekend. Everything is booked."

"In Savannah then," I say through clenched teeth, wondering if that's close enough to Oakley to make German happy. I'm out of Atlanta, at least. I suppose that was the whole point. Maybe I can rent a car? Or borrow Lo's car?

"You could always stay on my boat," Ben says.

Eloise beams. "Yes! That's perfect! The boat is great!"

Oh hell no. I take a few steps backward, wheeling my suitcase with me. "Actually, I think I might get seasick sleeping on a boat. But it's fine. I'll find something in Savannah. Don't you worry about me."

Ben steps close and wraps his hand around the handle of my suitcase, his fingers brushing against mine. "Sadie," he says, his voice calm and soothing in a way that annoys me simply because it *is* calming. I might expect him to treat me like a petulant child right now, but there's a sincerity in his voice that's catching me off guard. "I won't be staying on the boat with you, if that matters."

His eyes dart to Eloise, who frowns, and he gives his head the tiniest shake. Which means … he normally *does* live on his boat? I've been on it once before, the night Eloise and Jake got engaged, but I don't remember thinking it was Ben's permanent residence.

Also, it's more than a little off-putting how Ben and my sister can communicate with no words.

I don't like it.

"You remember it," Ben says. "It's comfortable, spacious, and large enough that seasickness should not be a problem." His smirk returns in full force as he raises a brow. "Especially when it's sitting stationary in the harbor."

Right. He has a point there. But still—I don't want to

accept anything from this man. It feels like losing a point in a rousing tennis match.

"I don't think so."

"Please. Your sisters are married to two of my closest friends which also makes *them* my close friends. Let me do this for them, if not for you."

Closest friends? I narrow my eyes at Eloise, who only shrugs. What has been happening? While the cat's been away, it seems the mice have done their fair share of playing. Or … *bonding.*

"Come on," Ben says. "It's perfect."

I frown, but he's making it difficult to argue, even for *me.* "I'll be alone?"

"More or less," he says. "The boat is staffed, so you won't be entirely by yourself, but it's a minimal crew when we aren't actually at sea."

Annoyingly, I'm already aware that I'm going to say yes. And not just because a boat *on* Oakley Island sounds better than a hotel room across the bridge in Savannah. Introvert though I may be, I do actually like my sisters. If I'm going to be here, I'd rather be closer to them than not.

But I'm also going to say yes because Benedict King has made me feel something *besides* annoyance. And that fact is strangely hard to resist.

THREE

Benedict

I REALLY NEED to stop seeming so eager. I'm practically a Labrador retriever waiting for someone to throw me a stick.

The stick, in this analogy, is a smile from Sadie. And they are very hard-earned.

My count so far today is two. Once when I tripped over a rope on the dock at Oakley Marina and almost pitched right into the water. The way she laughed—until she saw me watching and immediately stopped—made me wish I *had* fallen in. What's a little water if it means making Sadie smile?

The second is more of an evil grin right after we step aboard *The Oakley*, a name which is, admittedly, confusing when we're actually docked *in* Oakley. Call me a sentimental fool, but I like to be reminded of the home I love whenever I'm not here.

"Your yacht is flying a pirate flag," Sadie says, pointing to the black flag sporting a skull and crossbones.

I grin. "Yes. I like to keep a sense of humor when it comes to my boat."

"It takes a sense of humor to call this thing a boat, Mr. King," Sadie says, eyes gleaming. "I don't know if you've noticed, but this monstrosity is a *yacht*."

I push my hands into my pockets. "It floats. It's a boat."

She snorts, but her gaze rakes over *The Oakley*. Is she impressed? Bothered by the lavishness? I try to shove down the ripple of worry. Because if I admit how much I care what Sadie thinks of me, I'll have to also deal with *why* I care. Why I want her smiles. Why I want her to see past the stuff in my life and see *me*.

Why I'm feeling like a total simp. *Ugh.*

Sadie shakes her head. "I love how rich people find such quaint ways to describe their expensive toys."

Okay, so *not* impressed. To some people—Sadie clearly being one—my wealth falls into the negative column. It isn't going to make it easy for me if I want to get to know her better, but generally, I prefer this reaction over the other.

I learned from a very early age how it feels to be wanted only for what I have or what my last name is. From friends at school, to women, to my own father, who got cut out of my mother's family wealth when they divorced. His attempts to get at the money through me have failed, but it doesn't stop him from trying.

More than once, I've wondered what it would be like to give it all away. Or *most* of it. I do like nice things, though I could absolutely live with far less. The only thing that's stopping me is this island.

I love Oakley. The place. The people. The history. And so

long as I own it, it won't be overpopulated, overbuilt, and overpriced. It's not unusual for sleepy coastal towns to morph into luxury tourist meccas, becoming so expensive that families who have spent generations living there have to move away.

Not on my watch.

Even if very few people know exactly what it costs me personally to preserve Oakley. I'd rather they not know. It allows me to maintain my image as the carefree billionaire with a bit of a playboy reputation.

This image is, maybe unfortunately where Sadie is concerned, a little *too* believable.

"If it's too much, there's a Best Western just across the bridge," I say. "I'm happy to drive you over."

Sadie's shoulders drop the slightest bit and something flits across her face, but then her expression turns saucy and she rolls her eyes. I'm left wondering if I imagined the passing moment of vulnerability.

I don't think I did imagine it, but I'm unprepared to deal with it, so I steer us back into familiar waters. Which, for us, feels a little like paddling a canoe through a sea of snapping crocodiles, but with Sadie, I'll take whatever I can get. "Maybe they'll have a free breakfast with one of those waffle makers."

Sadie levels me with a look. "Like you've ever seen the inside of a Best Western. Or any hotel with a free breakfast."

"You might be surprised. I'll go anywhere for a free waffle."

She blinks at this, then shakes her head again. I'm not sure if she realizes how often she does this around me. A subconscious effort to shake me off, Taylor Swift style?

I hate to tell you, Sadie. I'm not a man who is easily shook.

"I think I can manage your *yacht*," she says, "even if it pains me to do it."

Her response makes me supremely happy. Grinning, I reach for her suitcase and haul it toward the doorway that will take us below deck.

She follows closely behind until I turn and offer her my hand. "I know you've been here before, but I'm guessing you only saw the pool deck. How about a full tour?"

She stares like my fingers hold a bomb she's unsure how to defuse. But then, to my surprise, she slides her palm into mine. An electric energy hums along the surface of my hand and up my arm. I do my best not to visibly react and hope she doesn't notice, even while another part of me hopes she feels it too.

"I don't know. I'm supposed to be back at the bed and breakfast in an hour for the party. Do we even have time to tour this massive *boat?*"

Despite the thickness of her sarcasm, there's a curiosity in her expression that makes me think she *would* like to look around, and that triggers a reaction inside my chest that feels much larger than the situation calls for.

But that's how it always is with Sadie. I meant what I said when I told her I like a challenge, but it's more than that, too. I'm not interested just because she isn't interested in me. There's something about her. Something that makes her different—that makes me want to impress her more than I've ever wanted to impress anyone.

And I'm afraid I'm not hiding it well at all.

"We'll start with your stateroom," I say, giving her hand a tiny squeeze, taking it as a win that she hasn't jerked away from me yet. "Then we'll see how far we get. Because you're right—a proper tour might take a few hours. Days, even."

I don't miss the way her lips twitch, like she really wants to smile. I'll count it as another point for me. I lead her to the largest stateroom, save my own, the one right next door to mine. Not that it will matter since I already promised Sadie I wouldn't be sleeping aboard.

A knot of dread forms in my stomach as I think about leaving the boat and going home to the cavernous mansion I inherited from my mother when she passed away. The one I generally avoid by sleeping on the boat.

The house originally belonged to *her* parents, as did the rest of Oakley Island. It's a gorgeous property—right on the water—but it's never really felt like a home. It's more like a museum full of ancient, expensive things that probably should have meaning to me but *really* don't. I'm reluctant to sell it though, for the same reasons I won't sell *any* of Oakley. I like the island just the way it is. I don't want millionaires crawling around its shores looking for development opportunities. And only millionaires could afford to buy my house.

Which ... I realize that sounds pretentious. But it is what it is.

Sadie drops my hand when I reach the door, and I grin at her to hide my disappointment. Such a casual touch to care about, but with her, all the little things matter.

I wheel her suitcase into the room, leaving it at the foot of the king-sized bed. It sits between two framed oil paintings I bought from Merritt. If Sadie recognizes her sister's work, she says nothing as she takes in the room. Despite everything being top-of-the-line, the feel of the room is bright and inviting, meant to invoke comfort, not intimidate with opulence the way these kinds of boats often do.

To our left, the balcony doors are open, letting in the cool breeze coming off the harbor. Leandra must have opened them. I texted my chief stewardess on the way, asking her to make sure the room was ready and aired out. It's been a long time since anyone else has slept here, and I wanted it to be fresh and perfect for Sadie.

In the fading afternoon light, the water is a deep navy blue, melting into the darkening sky. Sadie moves to the open doors as though drawn to the sea.

When she steps onto the private balcony, something in her posture relaxes, and I can see her take a deep inhale. I do the same, smelling the salt air as well as a faint hint of her perfume, or maybe it's her shampoo, as the breeze stirs her golden waves, exposing the line of her neck and shoulders. I'd like to brush the rest of her hair aside and kiss her right there at the top of her spine.

Bide your time, Ben, I tell myself.

But a big part of me already feels sure my time will never come. Not with Sadie.

I'm debating whether I should join her on the balcony when she comes back in and shuts the door. She locks it, then unlocks it again, frowning.

"The lock works?" she asks, looking up to meet my gaze.

"Of course, it works. But the balcony is private. No one is going to come through that door."

She nods even as she crosses the room and checks the lock on the door leading into the hall. "And this one works too?"

I lean casually against the wall, shoving my hands into my pockets so I don't do something dumb like reach for her hand again.

"Is there a reason you're concerned about the locks? This is Oakley Island, Sadie. You could sleep with your valuables spread out on the street corner in the middle of town and no one would mess with them. If anyone *did* mess with them, they'd only be gathering them up so they could carry everything door-to-door, looking for the person who lost their stuff."

She glances up at me, then blinks in surprise, as though

she didn't realize how close we're standing. But she doesn't back away. Instead, she turns, leaning against the door to mirror my position.

"I'm not worried about being robbed, Mr. King."

Leaning closer than I have any right to, I murmur, "No? Then what? If you're afraid I might break into your room at night, you shouldn't be."

"No?" She seems temporarily spellbound. Normally, she'd have pushed me away by now.

My heart takes this cue and begins to thump faster.

I lean forward a little more, testing her limits. My lips are as close to her ear as they can be without touching her. Still, she doesn't move.

"No, Sadie. You don't need to worry about me breaking in." I pause, drawing in a last breath of her scent, which smells like spicy vanilla. She smells sweet but with a little bite. So *very* Sadie. "My thumbprint will unlock any door on the boat."

Sadie scoffs, placing both hands flat on my chest and giving me a shove. Laughing, I trip over her suitcase and land on the bed. I catch a tiny, upturned smile before she darts through the door and into the hallway.

By the time I follow, she's peeking into my open bedroom door. Leandra straightens things up every morning, but the room definitely looks lived in. There's a half-full bottle of water on my nightstand and a charging station for my phone. The rest of the surface is covered with books, my reading glasses on top of the largest stack.

I clear my throat, feeling more exposed than I should considering how few personal effects are visible at a glance. "Can I show you the rest of the boat?"

She looks at me, then into my room, then back at me, her

brow furrowed. "This is your room," she says as she crosses her arms over her chest.

"Yes," I say slowly. "It is."

"But you said you wouldn't be staying on the boat."

"I won't be. I also have a house on Oakley."

She bites at her thumbnail like she can't quite decide how to feel about this new piece of information. Then she swings her assessing gaze my way. "Why do you stay here if you have a house?"

I rock back on my heels and offer her what I hope looks like an easy shrug. "I like boats."

"It's a yacht."

"I like other boats too. Sailboats are great. Canoes. Tugboats."

"But why sleep here rather than your house? You know that's a little odd, right?" She snaps her fingers. "Unless … you're playing into the eccentric billionaire stereotype?"

"You figured me out."

"Do you have a Batcave too?"

I grin. "If I did, I'd definitely be sleeping there. Batcaves are awesome."

There's a lull in which Sadie looks away toward my balcony doors, her expression shifting into something a little more pensive. "It's nice of you to give up your boat for me, Mr. King," she says. "Thank you."

"Anything you need, just ask." I start down the hall so I don't risk Sadie seeing the sincerity in my offer. The hallway is narrow, so she walks a few steps behind me. "Like I said. Your family means a lot to me."

It's true, and I hope Sadie recognizes my sincerity. Her sisters have become like family over the past year. It wasn't something I anticipated, but then I doubt Jake and Hunter anticipated the way the Markham sisters would barrel into their lives either. Maybe a little like the way Sadie continues shoving into mine despite her continued attempts at distance.

When we reach the door that will take us back outside, Sadie steps in front of me and checks the lock to *this* door, too. I frown. There's definitely something to this, and it makes me wonder if her unexpected appearance on Oakley isn't about something entirely different than just surprising her sisters for opening weekend.

What's spooking you, Sadie?

I don't think she'd answer me if I were to ask. But with a call to the private investigator I employ from time to time, I bet I could find out. If I want to take it that far.

Or I could just ask.

"Do you want to tell me why you're so worried about security?" I say. "Is there something I should know?"

"No!" she says a little too quickly. "Nothing. It's nothing. Just a nervous habit." She waves a hand dismissively. "Guess I've been living alone for too long."

I fold my arms across my chest, studying her. Nervous is a strange look on Sadie, who's normally the very poster child of strength and confidence. It worries me.

"I don't believe you."

She rolls her eyes. "I swear. It's nothing. It's just ..." She pauses and forces a breath out through her nose. "In my line of work, I've seen enough sketchy stuff to be ... I don't know. Cautious about stuff. I just like to make sure I'm safe."

"In your line of work," I repeat. "I thought you worked with computers."

"I do," she says. She pushes through the door and walks across the deck, pausing at the railing and looking out toward the Atlantic. This time, the tension doesn't leave her body. If anything, it coils tighter.

I follow, stopping right next to her. "Doing what?"

She turns and faces me, leaning her hip against the railing. The wind picks up her hair, fluttering a strand across her cheekbone. I make a fist to keep from tucking it behind her ear.

Momentarily, I get lost in her dark blue eyes, forgetting what we're talking about. And why my radar for trouble is flaring to life.

"I could tell you about my work," she says. "If you really wanted to know."

"I do want to know."

I'd like to know lots of things about Sadie. Though I'm beginning to suspect I know exactly what kind of work she does based on this conversation. Now, little comments and jokes Eloise and Merritt have made about hacking and spying snap into place. Clearly, Sadie does more than just build websites. Cybersecurity? Hacking?

"I could tell you," she repeats, leaning forward and blinking up at me. "But then I'd have to kill you." She reaches out and pats my chest before striding off.

I groan, trailing behind her.

"Now come on, Mr. King. Show me the kitchen. Or is it a galley? I'm prone to midnight snacking, so its location is of supreme importance. Also, is there a chef? Because this looks like the kind of place that would have a chef. I don't need to be pampered, so maybe they could take a few days off? You'd be amazed what I can whip up with a hot plate and a toaster oven."

She's babbling now, almost like she's intentionally trying to distract me. There are a thousand questions I want to ask this woman, but I know a deflective move when I see one.

For now, I let her deflect, sensing that if I push, it will lead to the opposite of what I want.

Sadie barely seems to tolerate me. Why would she tell me anything just because I ask?

Still, if she's nervous about being on the boat alone, maybe I *shouldn't* go stay at the house. The thought sits on my tongue and I almost voice it out loud, but then Sadie turns away, walking the opposite direction, and I lose my nerve. She'll be perfectly safe here with or without me, so it doesn't really matter, does it?

I make quick work of showing Sadie the main living and dining areas. In the interest of not stoking her ire, I don't show her the theater room or meditation room or the second living area with the saltwater tank housing three short-tail nurse sharks.

We end in the galley where I introduce her to the skeleton crew I employ year round. There are others if I'm actually traveling on the yacht or hosting a party, but typically, it's just Leandra, Tao the chef, and John, my first officer who doubles as security. I'm especially glad the older, ex-military man is on board considering Sadie's nerves.

I give Leandra special instructions to tend to *any* of Sadie's needs, and the white-haired stewardess, whom I've known since I was a teenager, winks at me. Nothing gets past her.

And nothing gets past Sadie either. "So, Leandra. How long have you known him?" she asks with a shrewd gaze.

Leandra beams. "I've known Benedict since he was a gangly teenager."

I groan. "Must we discuss this?"

Sadie links an arm through Leandra's. "We must," Sadie says, dragging a laughing Leandra into the dining area just off the galley.

I don't think Leandra knows any truly embarrassing stories, but even if she does, I like that Sadie is interested enough to care. While the women are gone, I pull John aside. "Will you double check locks and make sure everything is secure while Sadie is on board?"

"You won't be staying?" he asks.

I glance toward the dining room, and the sound of Sadie's laughter floats through the air. "The plan is for me to stay at the house."

More and more, I want to take back my offer to let Sadie stay here alone. I might not know *why* Sadie is concerned, but it feels wrong to walk away when I know she is. Even if that means annoying her by staying when I said I wouldn't.

"I'm happy to be extra vigilant. But ... any particular reason?" John asks.

"I'm not sure. She seems nervous but won't say why."

John nods without further comment, and a moment later, the women return and he and Leandra excuse themselves, leaving me alone with Sadie again.

"Are you going to the party tonight?" she asks.

Jake and Eloise are hosting a soiree, a reception for the vendors and sponsors of the Flower Festival, which starts tomorrow morning, doubling as an opening party for the bed and breakfast. The house will be open for tours, which is smart, because every business owner in town will be there, and word of mouth from locals is a great way to secure future business. Not that the bed and breakfast will ever lack customers. Eloise is a genius at online marketing. She's got more followers on social media than anyone else on Oakley, even Frank. Frank's TikTok is full of Oakley gossip that's only truly relevant to islanders, but he's still grown a decent following.

"I wouldn't miss it." I arch an eyebrow and give her what I hope is a flirtatious smile. "Why? Are you interested in being my date?"

She huffs out a breath. "You wish, Benedict. I need a *ride*."

Her words look like they physically pain her to say them. They probably do. This woman definitely has a way of keeping me humble.

Still, I don't need her to realize how much she's getting under my skin, so I keep my smile in place, leaning toward her the slightest bit. "I'd be delighted to have you go with me, Sadie."

"We're not going together."

"Technically, we'll be in the same vehicle, hence—we're going together."

Sadie pokes me in the arm, then blinks as though surprised by the muscles there. Which, of course, I happened to be flexing.

"Who says *hence* these days? Is that a rich boy thing?"

"Who pokes people when they disagree? Is that a hacker thing?"

She gives me a narrow-eyed look, then pokes me again before taking a step backward. "Honestly? Can you ever just smile without looking like you're up to something?"

"What am I up to?" I ask. "You requested a ride, and I said yes."

She steps closer again, close enough that her folded arms brush against my chest. "This is a fun game for you, isn't it?"

"Who said anything about playing a game?"

"Oh, come on. You think I don't know anything about you? I *do* work with computers, and I know how to use them better than most people. I'm particularly good at unearthing secrets."

Something about her tone makes me nervous, and I have to remind myself I don't actually have anything to hide. I stand by every business decision I've ever made. My mother always stressed the importance of maintaining integrity, and I've never forgotten her counsel.

"Exactly how many supermodels have you entertained on this boat?" Sadie asks. "Two dozen? Three?"

Ah. She means *those* kinds of secrets. Immediately, I feel guilty. But I haven't betrayed Sadie or anyone else. Yes, I've entertained models and heiresses and even an actress or two. I definitely wasn't involved with most of them, but knowing Sadie has read gossip implying I *was* makes me feel ... I don't know. *Squirmy.*

I resist the urge to catalog my real, not-all-that-exciting dating history for her. "Are you admitting that you googled me, Sadie? You were that curious, huh?"

"It felt more like searching for the source of an irritating skin rash, but *yes.* I googled you. And I have your number, Benedict King. So you can put that million-dollar smile away whenever I'm around because I'm *not* interested."

All I hear when she says she's *not* interested is that she has to be at least a *little bit* interested or she wouldn't have to say it. Right? Seems logical to me.

Unless she really believes everything she's read about me. Or if she buys the part I'm so used to playing. I'd be disappointed if she does. I'd expect more from someone like Sadie.

"So you've said," I say. "More than once, actually. I'm beginning to wonder if you're trying to convince *me* or convince *yourself.*"

She barks out a laugh. "Ha! That's a good one."

"I'm glad you think I'm so funny. Now, if you'll excuse me, I'm going to change before we go to the party. There might be women in attendance, and since you googled me, you know exactly how much I love to impress the ladies."

These last words leave a bad taste in my mouth, because despite my carefully crafted reputation, I have no desire to impress anyone at tonight's party. Unless we're talking about Sadie, but I'm pretty sure no amount of effort, certainly not anything I *wear*, is going to help me in that regard. These words are all about needling Sadie, and based on the way she wrinkles her nose, they landed exactly as I hoped.

Though Sadie may not care, I still choose my clothes carefully, picking the shirt that I know makes my blue eyes pop the most, spending extra time tousling my hair just right. I even spray on a little cologne. I'm a glutton for punishment, I guess.

In the mirror, I look like the man Sadie seems to think I am: a carefree rich boy.

But Sadie doesn't know me as well as she thinks she does. Not the real me beneath the obvious exterior. And it grates on me the same way it grated when I made the comment about impressing other women.

It's never mattered before if people believe what they read about me on the internet. I know the truth, as do my closest friends, which is admittedly a small circle. But for some reason, it matters with Sadie.

Maybe because she's Eloise's sister, and Jake and Eloise are the closest thing I have to family. Jake has always been like a brother to me, but extending that relationship to include his wife has been highly beneficial. Lo softens my best friend and brings out his good side faster than anyone. He's always been loyal, but now he's almost likable. This past year, my little circle expanded to include Merritt and Hunter too.

It's a believable story—that I only care about Sadie because of her connection to my closest friends.

But when I leave my room and find Sadie on the deck of *The Oakley* wearing a deep blue dress, Jake and Eloise couldn't be further from my mind.

FOUR

Sadie

I DON'T WANT to be impressed with Benedict's boat. *Yacht.*

I don't want to be impressed with his *yacht*.

But honestly, the thing is gorgeous. I'm pretty sure the mattress in my stateroom alone costs more than my entire apartment in Atlanta.

I only sat on it for a moment while I strapped on my sandals. But it practically reached up and cradled me, luring me so effectively, I almost texted Eloise to beg her forgiveness and proclaim I'd be staying in for the night. All the traveling today combined with the worry in the back of my mind has left me exhausted anyway.

Fortunately, *The Oakley* isn't anything like the *other* boat I've spent actual time on. My last (and only) serious ex, a college professor who was much too old for me, had a sailboat. He talked about it like it was a yacht the size of this one, but you could fit Justin's boat in this thing fifteen times. Still, the similarities between Justin and Ben aren't lost on me. There is a specific brand of confidence that comes from wealth, a sense of belonging, of knowing the world will open up to you in ways it won't for others. Thinking about it makes me queasy and uncomfortable. I'd rather *never* think about Justin if I can help it. Things ended so badly, that over two years later, I'm still positive I'll never be ready for another relationship. It just isn't worth it.

While I'm waiting for Ben to finish changing clothes, I pull up my texts, checking again to see if German has given any updates. He hasn't. Of course, he hasn't. I would have gotten a notification if he had. But I can't help checking anyway. This whole situation—being here, pretending like everything is fine—has me feeling completely off-kilter.

And Benedict King isn't helping. Not with his flirting and his questions and the way his gaze seems to see right through me.

Not to mention his face and his biceps and his blue, blue eyes. *Ugh.*

"Ready to go?" he says from behind me.

Tensing, I take a breath and turn to face him.

Oh, geez. This is entirely unfair.

For once, Ben has lost the preppier look of his casual daywear. He's wearing dark pants, perfectly tailored, and a light blue button-down that makes his eyes look extra blue. The top couple of buttons are undone, revealing a triangle of smooth, tan skin, and the sleeves are rolled up to his elbows.

He looks delicious. *Perfect.* Entirely *too* perfect.

I swallow against the sudden lump in my throat. "Yep. Ready."

His eyes rove over me. "You look great, Sadie," he says, no hint of teasing in his tone.

I press my lips together. He's being earnest, and I allow myself to be the same in return. "Thanks. So do you."

We stand there awkwardly staring and smiling for a moment. As though the break from our typical back-and-forth has broken us.

I follow him to the gangway leading down to the dock and let him go first, knowing (and hating) that it'll be a lot easier to walk down the steep ramp in my heels if he's there to keep me from pitching forward. Just in case.

I slip my hand into his, holding it tightly as he guides me onto the dock. We're standing close when he lets me go, close enough for me to smell Ben's cologne. It's not overpowering, which likely means it's expensive. As soon as he moves away, I breathe in deep, replacing his scent with the salty harbor air. It smells like my childhood summers.

Ben looks over his shoulder to see me still standing at the foot of the gangway.

"Are you okay?" he asks.

I hurry toward him. "Fine. Good. Let's hurry. We're already late."

The party is in full swing when we arrive, the wide lawn of the bed and breakfast populated with Oakley Island residents. Eloise explained earlier that the rest of the Flower Festival events will be geared toward tourists and people who come over from Savannah, but tonight is about Oakley's old guard—the business owners and residents who have poured their heart and soul into keeping Oakley exactly like it is. I recognize a few faces from the last few times I've been down, and still others feel familiar even if I can't connect them to a name.

Weirdly, I don't need names for this place to feel like home.

Which doesn't even make sense. I only ever lived here

during the summers. *Some* summers. Until our parents got divorced and the relationship my sisters and I had with Gran was collateral damage.

Maybe it's enough that in my heart, in my blood, I belonged to Genevieve, and Genevieve belonged to Oakley. I swallow thickly. Then I remember that Ben is beside me, watching me carefully, with none of his usual snark and bluster.

He opens his mouth, but before he can speak, I walk away.

"Sadie!"

I look up and see Merritt crossing the lawn toward me. She's wearing a loose, flowy dress in a kaleidoscope of colors and she's never looked happier. Less uptight and controlled. More loose and free and *happy*.

"Hey, Mer," I say as she pulls me in for a hug. "You look good. Really good."

She smiles, but then it takes on an edge, and I clap my hand over her mouth. I know that look. "I do not want to hear a single word about why you're so happy. Especially if it has to do with all the happy married sex you're having." I yank my hand away. "Ew! Did you just *lick* me?"

I wipe my palm on my dress while Merritt laughs. This is not my oldest sister. The queen of the control freaks, captain of the type-A army. And yet, as I watch the way her eyes sparkle, I realize it *is* her. She's *more* herself.

I'm sure she still has a planner, filled out and color coded, and spreadsheets for every conceivable area of her life. But now, it's like a door has been unlocked, releasing some other part of her she didn't feel safe letting out before. Even with Eloise and me.

Love did that. And it's fascinating to see, startling even, because the three of us did not grow up seeing love modeled in any healthy way. Not from our father who spent all our money before he left, and not from our mother who spent the remaining years of our childhood desperately seeking something she never found, even with her current husband.

As Hunter appears, wrapping an arm around Merritt's waist, the love between them is like a spark lighting them both up from the inside. It makes me happy for her, but it also *hurts*. In the same way too much sugar can make your teeth ache.

"Hey, Hunter. Oh! There's Lo. I'll go grab a drink and make sure she knows I'm here."

I'm gone before I can tell if they bought my words or know I just ditched them. Apparently, ditching seems to be the theme of my evening. I'm sure it seems like I'm trying to escape people. Really, I'm just trying to escape my emotions.

I grab a glass of rum and Diet Coke at one of the bars set up around the lawn, stepping back into the shadow of a live oak. Pressing the cool glass to my cheek, I survey the party.

Lo is easy to spot, decked out in a bright pink dress with equally bright green alligators all over it. My youngest sister's style is such a perfect reflection of her. Not because it's loud—Eloise does like to talk, but not in a way that demands attention or overtakes others. No—her happy, playful prints and dresses carry the brightness and light and quirky, unfettered sense of joy my sister seems to be stitched together with.

How she came to be this way has to be a result of nature, not nurture.

I wish sometimes I could borrow a little of her light. *Maybe a little of Merritt's steadiness too,* I think as my older sister joins Eloise. Hunter and Jake aren't far behind, both immediately finding ways to touch my sisters—their *wives*.

Though I was in attendance at both weddings here on the

island, the reality of their marriages hits me now with pummeling force. Jake tugs Eloise close to his side. Even from this distance, it's impossible to miss the adoration in his eyes. It's matched by the brilliant smile Lo gives him, rising on tiptoes to kiss him on the cheek. Hunter stands behind Merritt, looping a big hand around her waist as she leans back into his bulky frame, a satisfied smile on her face. She reaches up to touch his beard, as though even after months of being with him, she's still delighted and surprised to find him there.

I slowly sip my drink as I watch, the cold stinging my eyes and the alcohol burning its way down my throat until it simmers low in my stomach. Once again, an unfamiliar longing grabs me in its vise-like grip as I watch the happy couples. For years, I've made it clear I never want to get married or have a family.

So clear that now I'm not sure I can admit I might feel differently—not even to myself.

I pull my gaze away, skating over the other guests, most chatting or eating and drinking, with a growing contingent dancing on a wooden floor in the center of the lawn. Speakers are blasting the typical wedding fare meant to get people out of their seats. It's working. I find my hips swaying to the beat of "Uptown Funk," absolutely without my permission. I have a strict "No Bruno Mars" rule, but apparently, my body didn't get the memo.

My movements halt the moment I catch sight of Benedict in the middle of the dance floor. I can't see the woman he's with, and I'm unprepared for the jealousy clawing its way up my ribs like a ladder. But then he turns, and his dance partner comes into view.

I laugh quietly, watching as Harriett, the sixty-something-year-old diner owner, pulls Ben into a fox trot. One where *she's* leading.

For the briefest of moments, I swear his eyes meet mine. I don't know how he could possibly see me, tucked into the shadow of the tree like I am. And maybe he really doesn't because his gaze moves quickly back to Harriett. Knowing Benedict and the way he's been acting, especially today, I don't think he would have torn his gaze away. The man seems determined to push past my boundaries and encroach on my territory.

Which leaves me wondering … is he just playing? Or is he banging a battering ram against my walls hoping to *actually* gain entrance?

I don't like thinking about those questions, because they inevitably make me think about what *I* want. And I have no idea how to even begin to find an answer. Despite my efforts to keep my distance and the way I adamantly told him I'm not interested, I've always been drawn to Benedict. *Ben.*

I have a sneaking suspicion that if I were to give into the attraction, it would be like eating jalapeños. They're delicious in the moment, but regret is inevitable the moment they hit my digestive track in earnest.

I only let myself watch him and Harriett for another minute or two. Long enough to wish I hadn't watched at all. Whatever quick-step dance Benedict is now leading a surprisingly nimble Harriett in, he looks *good* doing it.

"I'd say you look like you need a drink, but you've already got one."

I startle, spilling a little of my rum and Coke as Naomi, Jake's sister, appears beside me, grinning with a glass of wine in hand.

"I might need another one now. I didn't hear you coming."

With no hesitation, she pulls me into a tight hug. I do my best not to pour my drink down her back, which is almost completely bare. Her short, dark dress is the kind you wear to impress, and I wonder if she, too, has found a decent guy.

And I'd be happy for her if she did, I tell myself. *Because I'm not some stupid sad sack who stands like a creeper in the shadows, spying on all the happy couples.*

"When did you get in?" Naomi asks, finally letting me go. As though checking to make sure it's still in place, she puts a hand to her dark hair, pinned up in a loose twist. "Your sisters told me you weren't coming."

"Changed my mind this afternoon. I decided I couldn't miss this," I tell her, the lie of omission tasting worse every time I tell it.

She turns to watch the crowd with me, bumping my shoulder with hers. "Well, I'm glad. I need a partner in crime."

"What crime are we committing tonight?"

"Hm." She takes a sip of her wine. "That depends."

"On?"

"Whether or not this dress does its job. If so, then maybe we can stay on the right side of the law. But if not …"

"Honey, if it involves a man, you in that dress will accomplish whatever you want. If it doesn't, I'm still in … all the way up through maybe light felonies." I pause to take another sip of my drink. "Who's the guy?"

Naomi lifts her wine glass, tilting it toward a tall man standing alone near the bar. Other than his height and broad shoulders, what I notice first is the fact that he looks distinctly uncomfortable. No drink, hands shoved deep into his pockets, and glancing around like he's looking for the closest exit sign.

"His name is Camden. He plays professional hockey. We've been sort of dating."

Naomi doesn't strike me as the type to fall for an athlete. But then, I guess I don't know her *that* well. And it's not like all athletes fit into the same box. Personality-wise, anyway. Physically, this guy looks exactly like a man who makes a living honing his body like a machine.

"That sounds like a very tasty kind of trouble. Where's the closest hockey team, anyway?" I ask.

"Not close enough." She sighs. "Well, Savannah does have a minor league team. There are probably at least two teams within a few hours' drive. But no, Camden happens to play for a team in the mountains of North Carolina. Have you heard of the Appies?"

I shake my head. "I don't follow sports of any kind."

"Even so, if you're on TikTok—"

"I hate social media. That's Eloise's thing." I've seen too many things in my work to be interested in leaving any kind of online footprint.

"Right. Anyway, their team has a big following. He's here temporarily on a hockey sabbatical."

"Is that a thing?" I ask.

She laughs. "Definitely not a technical term. It's basically a mental health break."

"So ... are you going to put him out of his misery?" I say, watching the big man shift on his feet, running a hand through his hair. "He looks like he's ready to bolt."

Naomi sets her wineglass on a nearby bench. It's still half-full. "I'm nervous."

I turn, studying her delicate features. At times, I can really see the resemblance between Naomi and Jake. Other times, like right now, there's barely more than a hint of similarity. One thing I've never seen in either of them is nerves.

Jake on his wedding day, maybe. But Naomi? Never. Which tells me she must really dig Mr. Hockey player.

Leaning in, I rest my head on her shoulder. "Nerves are a good sign."

"Yeah? They don't *feel* like a good sign. I feel like I'm a planet out of my orbit. Or like, if I try to talk to him about things, I might end up vomiting on his shoes."

"Let's try to avoid any vomit. Though, it would be a good litmus test for whether he's a keeper. If you puke on his shoes and he sticks around, that's a good man."

"Valid point."

"But seriously, your nerves are a good sign," I tell her. "You care. That's no small thing."

She draws in a deep breath. "You think so? With Liam, dating is just so much more complicated."

I feel slightly guilty that I hadn't even considered Liam, Naomi's ten-year-old son. But then, most of the time, I see her at adult functions. I've only met her kid a handful of times. I can only imagine how infinitely more difficult dating would be with a child in the equation.

"Does Camden like Liam?"

She lets out a little chuckle. "Yes. Except now Liam's into hockey."

"Is that a bad thing?"

"It is when Liam wants me to drive him to practice in Savannah a few times a week." Naomi straightens her shoulders. "How do I look?"

I make a show of sweeping her brown hair back off her face and brushing invisible lint from her shoulders. "You look like the kind of woman worth fighting for."

"Let's hope it doesn't come to that," she says.

And with that confidence, Naomi throws her shoulders back, marches across the lawn—somehow not sinking into the grass despite sky-high heels—and straight to Camden. I expect her to tug him onto the dance floor or maybe just hug him.

Instead, she reaches her hands behind his neck and pulls his mouth down to hers. Right in front of everyone. Practically the whole island. Frank is even filming for his famous TikTok channel, which I've yet to see.

"Go, Naomi," I say, watching what might be in the running for longest PDA ever.

"Enjoying the show?"

For the second time tonight, I startle. This time, it's Benedict sneaking up on me.

I swat at him. He doesn't budge, coming to stand shoulder-to-shoulder with me. "I'm not into watching people make out. I'm just happy for Naomi. She deserves this."

I see Ben nodding through my peripheral vision. Even though I refuse to turn toward him, it's like the man is a beacon for my attention. I need to get that fixed *quick*.

"She does. And Cam seems like a good guy."

"Cam? Y'all are on a nickname basis now?"

"*Y'all?* My, how the South has gotten to you."

My sisters and I all grew up in the Midwest, with no strong accent, but every summer, without fail, a little Southern always slipped in. By the time we left Oakley, we were always y'alling along with everyone else. I guess it happened a little faster this time. Less than six hours and I'm dropping y'alls.

Ignoring Ben's ribbing, I ask, "Was that the Carolina shag you were doing with Harriett?"

I swear, I feel the force of his grin like a tidal pull. Still—I keep my eyes straight ahead. Naomi and Camden disappear, but now Merritt has pulled a reluctant Hunter onto the dance floor. Eloise and Jake aren't far behind. That same stupid feeling of missing out rears its ugly head. I have a feeling it's like a hydra—cut off one head and two more grow back in its place.

"Down here, we just call it the shag," Ben says. "Wanna give it a whirl?"

I do. And it shocks me—the sudden pulse of *want* reverberating in my chest. It's as though my heart is a chapel bell, and Ben's question just yanked on the pull.

"No." It comes out automatically. And doesn't sound authentic at all.

Benedict chuckles and leans closer. "If it bothers you so much, you can tell everyone I forced you. Or that you lost a bet."

"Still no."

But I want *so* badly to say yes. Though I spend most of my waking hours with my butt parked in a chair, I love dancing. And it's been way too long since I've done it. My limbs are practically screaming at me to get out there.

Leaning so close his breath tickles my neck, Ben says the only three words that could possibly make me cave. "You scared, Sadie?"

He's barely finished the question before I'm dragging him under the lights. His laughter, a rich and throaty sound, makes me tighten my grip on his hand. As we step onto the dance floor, I ignore Merritt's shocked then smug look and Eloise's delighted one.

"Teach me," I demand, spinning to face Ben.

His eyes gleam. With mirth, I think first, because of course the man is happy to be getting his way. But his expression is less amused and more ... something else. Something that makes my cheeks hot. I can't quite name it, but it's genuine and makes me feel alive.

"See if you can keep up, Sadie girl," he says.

And then we're moving.

Ben is good at leading. But he still seems surprised—and happy—over how quickly I pick up the basic steps. I'm pretty good at imitation, and despite myself, I watched a good bit of Ben and Harriett while talking to Naomi.

"You sure you've never done this before?" Ben asks as we spin closer.

"What? Does it surprise you to know I have hidden talents?"

"Oh, I'm not surprised at all that you've got hidden talents," he says, giving me a smirk. "Feel free to share those with me any time you want."

I make a face. "Keep dreaming, Mr. King."

"Oh, I will." His darkened eyes catch mine for as long as the dance allows. "I do."

A few steps later, Ben shifts us into a new, more complicated set of twists and spins. I'm determined to keep up with him, but I find even more than that, I'm doing this for the rush.

A kind of happy glow unfurls in my chest. Familiar but a little rusty too, like it's been too long since my heart muscles have been stretched.

Somewhere in the middle of the first song, I forget about what I'm trying to prove, forget about my very real intent to keep Ben at arm's length.

I'm lost in the beat and the adrenaline high and the feel of Ben's hands on my hands. On my waist. Every so often, on a place they have no business being. Like when his fingertip grazes my cheek or my collarbone, or he gives me a quick and totally unnecessary squeeze low on my hips.

Whatever, I tell myself. *It's just one dance with the bad boy billionaire. It won't ruin me or my sense of practicality and self-preservation.*

But one song turns into two, and I forget who Ben is and why I'm so set on maintaining a high hedge of distance between us. This dance has taken an electric saw to my shrubbery.

I'll have to worry about it later.

Right now, I'm chasing something elusive, an emotion I've almost forgotten how to feel. My skin is aglow, my muscles are singing, and my gaze is fixed firmly on Ben.

If I thought he was attractive before, this Ben is nearly irresistible. His hair is a wild mess, his eyes are sparkling, and every touch is like a brand.

When the current song abruptly ends, I'm shaken out of my Benedict King haze. I stare at him for a beat. His eyes are wide, his chest visibly heaving as he catches his breath. I suspect I'm mirroring his expression.

What just happened?

My gaze is ripped from his by the sound of my sister clearing her throat into a microphone. Eloise and Merritt are both standing on the stage in front of the band, and they give me wide eyes and not-so-subtle jerks of their heads to indicate I should be up there too. Which I definitely hadn't planned on.

Though I've done very little other than offer emotional support to my sisters as they renovated Gran's place, I shake free of the moment with Ben and practically sprint up to join them.

I may not want to be on stage right now, but I definitely need to leave Benedict and whatever *that* was far behind.

FIVE

Ben

IT WAS JUST A DANCE, I tell myself. The same dance I did with Harriett not twenty minutes ago. One I've done countless times since I was a teenager and my mom forced me to take lessons—which, as it turned out, I actually enjoyed.

So why do I feel like my entire world was just turned upside down?

Holding Sadie in my arms was a drug all its own, but more powerful than that was the unbreaking eye contact. The way we felt connected through the music, the way my skin buzzed every time it touched hers—cheesy as it sounds, the only word I can think to describe it is *magical*. It's all I can do not to follow her like a lost puppy and beg for more.

Sadie has been distant since I met her—trading one mask for another depending on the circumstance and whether one of her sisters is nearby. But that dance—I was seeing the real Sadie. No pretense. No masks. Just *her*.

And she is even more alluring than I thought.

She's also one hell of a dancer. She picked up the steps quickly, her body leaning and shifting with mine, her movements smooth and graceful. We hit pause on our usual snappy banter and found a whole new sort of give-and-take. One I could really get used to.

I stare at the small stage where Sadie is now standing beside her sisters, her eyes darting from the sky overhead to the sprawling live oaks at the edge of the lawn. She enjoyed that dance as much as I did. I can tell because she's refusing to look at me now. Acknowledging that she felt the same connection I did would go against everything I've observed about Sadie so far.

I don't know why she's fighting this.

Only that she won't stop.

A tiny thrill pushes through me at the thought. After growing up watching my parents fight—both in person and by using various assets, including me—I never would have thought I'd enjoy fighting. But with Sadie ... I do. And something tells me this fight will be particularly worth it.

"We want to thank the whole community of Oakley for your support," Merritt says. "And we know our Gran—Genevieve Markham—would be grateful as well." The oldest Markham sister makes a show of welcoming Jake and Hunter onto the stage, and Sadie steps off to the side to make room. Suddenly, she *does* look at me.

When both of her sisters have men standing beside them, it's *my* eyes Sadie finds in the crowd. She looks away, quickly enough that had I not been watching her closely, I might have missed it. But I don't miss it, and I'll hold onto that moment as long as I can.

While Eloise starts discussing the renovation plans, making everyone laugh as she recounts the time she found a pelican living inside the house, I grab a water bottle from a bucket of ice sitting at the refreshment table. I move toward the side of the stage, watching Jake grow uncomfortable as Eloise talks about how much he helped while also making jokes about his grumpiness, playing it up for the crowd. I never thought I'd see my best friend so smitten, but I'm not even a little surprised it was one of the Markham sisters to do it. All three of them just have that sort of presence.

Finally, Eloise finishes, and Merritt thanks the crowd one last time. Sadie gives a tight smile and a wave, and they all file off the small stage. Sadie is furthest from me, but I assume she'll come this way with everyone else, descending the small stairs and passing right by me. Instead, she hops off the front of the stage and makes a beeline across the yard, heading straight for the house.

As though she's decided to go right back to avoiding me. *Swell.*

I'm contemplating whether to follow her when Jake stops in front of me. "Is that for me?" he asks, holding out his hand for the unopened water bottle.

"Nope. For Sadie," I say, proud that I don't trip on the words even a little.

Eloise nudges Jake with her elbow. "See? I told you he likes her."

"It's just water," I protest, watching Sadie disappear through the back door of the bed and breakfast.

"I didn't disagree with you," Jake says. "He hasn't exactly been subtle about it. He flirts with her every time she's in town."

"Flirting is different," Eloise says. "*This* is different." She looks at me, her wide ocean eyes bright under the twinkle lights that stretch across the yard. "Isn't it, Ben?"

I shrug and run a hand through my hair. "I don't know if *Sadie* thinks it's different. But I might."

"You might?" she asks, like the word concerns her.

"Does it matter when Sadie seems determined not to take me seriously?"

Eloise purses her lips to the side. "Do you like logic problems?"

"What, like word puzzles?" I ask, unsure of the sudden shift in conversation.

She nods. "Or crossword puzzles—anything that requires you to look for clues."

"You used to do them all the time when we were kids," Jake says. "Remember the book Frank kept on the counter at the barber shop? You solved half the puzzles in that thing."

Eloise brightens. "Perfect. Then you have a lot of practice already."

"Practice for what?" I ask.

She reaches up and pats me on the shoulder. "Just treat Sadie like one of those puzzles. It might take a few tries, and you might have to really dig for clues, but eventually, you'll figure her out."

I look at Jake, but he only arches an eyebrow. "Sounds like good advice to me."

Eloise nods her head toward the house, and I take that as permission to go after her sister, unsure whether it makes me look completely besotted or just desperate. I'm not sure I'm either, but I *am* sure that Sadie intrigues me more than any other woman I've met in the past year. Maybe the past five years.

Certainly, that's worth a risk, right? Worth trying to solve the puzzle?

I climb up the back stairs of the giant old house, admiring the fresh paint and newly replaced floorboards.

There used to be a screened-in porch on this end, but the thing was almost beyond repair. Eloise and Merritt decided to close it in, turning it into a sunroom with giant glass doors that lead onto the patio. When the weather's nice, it'll be easy to open the windows and let the ocean breeze blow through the house. But they'll also be able to use the space when it's too hot to even breathe outside, much less sit and relax a while.

There are only a few lights on in the house—the party is pretty well contained to the backyard—but I know the property well enough to make my way through the unlocked back door, through the sunroom, and into the kitchen. I don't see Sadie anywhere, but I hear creaking overhead, so I make my way toward the stairs.

I'm halfway up when I start to wonder if this is a terrible idea. What if she's in the bathroom? Or looking for some privacy? Or hiding from me?

What if this is exactly the wrong answer to the first clue in the puzzle?

I'm still debating, paused on the third step, when Sadie appears at the top of the stairs, having just left one of the bedrooms.

She startles when she sees me, a hand flying to her chest. "Geez, Ben. You scared me."

It's maybe the first time she's ever called me Ben. Not Benedict or Mr. King or Mr. Cumberbatch or any of the other nicknames she usually flings at me. Just ... *Ben.* I like it.

"Sorry. I thought you might be thirsty." I hold up the water bottle. "After our dance," I add.

My words sound too eager, too earnest, and I wish I could call them back. Where is my cool? My suave ability to impress women without even breaking a sweat?

Gone. That's where. Sadie has stripped away all my cool

and left me bumbling about like some pre-teen boy talking to his secret crush in the hallway at school.

Sadie drops onto the top step of the wide staircase and holds out her hand. I finish the climb, then drop down beside her, handing her the bottle. She opens it and takes a long sip before offering it to me.

It makes me ridiculously happy that she doesn't care if I drink after her. That presumably, she'll drink after me as well. Maybe some people wouldn't see this as a big deal. Maybe it's not.

But with Sadie, it feels weirdly intimate. Like she's taking down a tiny piece of the wall that's always between us or cracking open a closed door.

I take a long swig, then hand the bottle back.

"That was my room," she says, tilting her head toward the doorway behind her. "Or at least the room I slept in whenever we were here."

The overhead light isn't on, but there's a lamp at the end of the hall, sending just enough light our way that I can make out her expression, though her eyes are still in shadow. She looks contemplative, maybe a little wistful. I want to ask a thousand questions, but I'm afraid if I say too much, she'll remember who it is she's talking to and slam that door closed again.

"It's totally different now," she says. "Of course, it is. They were almost finished remodeling it the last time I was here. But I wondered if it would still feel the same."

"Does it?" I ask as she drinks and passes me the bottle again. I take a slow sip.

Sadie looks down the stairs, down into the darkness, and I think she might be ignoring my question. But then she shrugs. "It's just a house."

It's a nonanswer. An evasion—or at least a deflection. This isn't just a house—not to her. Not to anyone on Oakley.

Genevieve Markham was the kind of woman who had an impact on the island. You'd be hard-pressed to find someone who doesn't have a story about her kindness. Or her quirkiness. And the sisters spent every summer here, staying in this house. It matters.

I nudge her knee with mine. "Sadie Markham, I think you're telling me a lie."

She rolls her eyes. "Mr. King, I don't think you know me well enough to judge."

It takes effort to bite back a comment about how little she really knows about me or how I'd like to get to know her better. I've made a tiny bit of headway here, and I'd rather keep my foot in the door than have her slam it in my face.

Stick to the topic at hand, I tell myself.

"Are houses ever just houses?" I ask, giving her as much of a smile as I can manage. I can't help but think of the empty mansion I avoid like the plague—the one I'm supposed to sleep in tonight.

"I mean, I just spent summers here," she says. "And I didn't help with the renovations at all."

Her eyes lift to mine, and for a quick second, the mask slips, and she's the same Sadie who danced with me. But then she turns her face away.

"Sadie, this house belongs to you as much as it belongs to either of your sisters. As a memory, as part of you. So does Oakley."

"Pretty sure Oakley belongs to *you*," she says, shooting me a snarky smile.

I roll my eyes and take a chance, bumping her leg with mine. As I hoped, she bumps me right back.

"You know what I mean," I tell her.

She's quiet for a long moment before she shifts and stands, leaving me to miss the warmth of her sitting beside me.

"What *I* know," she says, tossing a sardonic smile over her shoulder, "is that I've had enough serious conversation for one night." She offers me a hand. "But if you promise not to talk, I'll let you dance with me again."

"You'll *let* me?"

She rolls those beautiful blue eyes one more time. I never would have thought eye rolls could be attractive, but on Sadie, they absolutely are.

"Come on. You know you want to." She wiggles her fingers in front of me. "Don't make me dance with Frank, Ben."

"Fine," I say, getting to my feet. Then I slip my hand into hers and let her tug me down the stairs and back outside.

For the rest of the night, I *don't* make her dance with Frank. In fact, she doesn't dance with anyone but me, and we absolutely tear up the dance floor. It's funny—we've never managed to have a conversation that doesn't end in some kind of verbal sparring, but when we're dancing, our bodies manage to talk just fine.

The first time we danced, I thought the connection had everything to do with Sadie finally letting me in, but as the night progresses, I start to wonder if what's really happening is that *I'm* letting go. Relaxing. Forgetting to worry about what people think of me, of the way I'm managing Oakley and the other responsibilities in my life—the ones I can't complain about without sounding like a poor little rich boy.

I may look like I've mastered the art of doing and caring about nothing, but that level of cultivation requires a great deal of effort. And is a very convenient protection against the insecurity that still rears up to haunt me every now and then.

But with Sadie in my arms, the music thrumming through my veins, I don't feel anything but the warmth of her skin under my palms. I don't see anything but her bright blue eyes and her wide smile every time she throws her head back and laughs. I definitely don't worry about optics or anyone else's expectations of me.

Could I truly solve the puzzle that is Sadie Markham?

Do I want to?

"Okay, I'm done," Sadie says as a song ends, smiling and breathing hard. She uses my arm to hold herself steady and reaches down to unstrap her shoes. "I can't dance another step."

I tilt my head toward a table where her sisters and their husbands are chatting with Naomi and Camden. "Want to sit?"

She watches her sisters for a long moment, then frowns. "Benedict, if you walk me over to a table full of happy couples like we're about to add to that number, I'll key the side of your boat." She steps a little closer. "But I do have another idea."

There's a hint of suggestion in her tone that makes my throat go dry. "Yeah? What's that?"

She moves closer still, one hand pressing against my chest while the other drops lower. Before I realize it's happening, she deftly slips her fingers into my pocket and snatches out my keys. She steps back, holding them up like a carnival prize, her grin wide.

Is this woman some kind of trained pickpocket? A thief-for-hire? Honestly, when it comes to Sadie, nothing would surprise me. I could ask for them back, but I kind of want to applaud her instead.

"I think I'll go for a scenic drive around the island," she says coyly.

"In *my* car?"

Her expression stays playful, but her eyes turn serious, holding my gaze. "I promise I'll take good care of it. I just ... need to get away."

Her eyes dart over to her sisters, and I catch a glimpse of something like longing flitting across her face.

I almost ask her if she wants company or even a getaway driver. I don't love the idea of Sadie being out this late on her own, even if this is Oakley. But it could just be that Sadie's worry earlier, all the questions about locking doors, has me feeling more uneasy than I usually would.

Either way, I get the sense that right now, she needs to be alone. Implying she shouldn't be would definitely be getting a Sadie clue wrong, if we're sticking with Eloise's puzzle analogy. And I'm quickly realizing I don't want to get *anything* wrong when it comes to this woman.

"Go ahead," I say with a nod. "And if you decide you've had enough for the night, just drive back to the marina."

"What will you do?" she asks.

"I can walk to my house from here. It isn't far. Or someone will give me a ride."

She steps forward and wraps a hand around my forearm, giving it a quick squeeze. "Thanks, Ben," she says softly. Then she disappears, leaving me to breathe in her lingering scent and wonder what happened to me tonight.

I still haven't moved when Jake steps up beside me and hands me a beer. "Guess you're not as good at puzzles as you used to be."

"Thanks for the vote of confidence. But I think I was doing pretty well there for a while."

"All the way up until she stole your car keys," Jake says, hiding his smirk behind his beer as he takes a sip.

"You saw that, huh?"

"I did. Impressive."

"We'll call it a work in progress," I say. "I've never seen a woman dance like that. *I've* never danced like that."

"The Markham women tend to make big impacts," Jake says knowingly.

"That, I already knew." I take a long swig of my beer. "But there's something going on with Sadie. Something that made her different tonight."

"You sure it wasn't just *you* who was making her different?"

I shake my head, struggling to articulate what I'm trying to say. "That's just it. Sadie is usually completely immune to me. More than immune—almost antagonistically opposed. But tonight, she seemed ... I don't know."

Vulnerable is the word I don't say. Somehow, I just know that Sadie would murder me if I ever used that word to describe her in a conversation—even one with Jake.

I look over at the table at the edge of the lawn where Eloise is leaning in, whispering something to Merritt. "Has Lo said anything?"

"Nothing except she didn't expect Sadie to be here."

Jake frowns at something behind me, and I turn, following his gaze until I see what he's seeing—two big men in dark suits standing on the wide stone path that leads around to the front of the house. Not all that strange, considering we're at a party. Even less so with the Flower Festival starting tomorrow. As I told Sadie earlier, the whole island is booked up.

But there's something about the men's body language that has me—and clearly Jake, as well—on high alert. Maybe it's their posture or the stiffness of their suits, but it looks like they're here on some sort of *official* business. Not partygoers. Not here for the festival.

No, they're clearly looking for someone.

My chest immediately constricts with worry, thinking of Sadie's off behavior today. I'm probably just being paranoid. My mind is turning them into mobsters, but they could just as easily be a pair of detectives from Savannah, or government agents from the IRS or SEC or some equally boring agency. Which, if that's the case, they're probably here for me. I keep my business dealings completely above board, but my father does not have the same scruples. It wouldn't surprise me if he's landed in some sort of trouble with the government.

Eloise appears beside Jake. "Do you recognize them?"

"Nope," Jake says. "Let's go check it out."

Together, the three of us push through the crowd until we reach them. "Hi," Eloise says, a little too brightly. "May we help you?"

"Is this the Markham residence?" the tallest guy asks.

My gut tightens—this is not about me, then. This *does* have to do with Sadie. I don't know how I know it, but I do. She was clearly nervous about something, and now there are strange men in Oakley, mere hours after she arrived, looking for the Markhams.

I'm glad Sadie stole my keys, and I can only hope she's made it safely to my boat.

"What's this about?" Jake asks, using the voice I imagine he uses when he's in a courtroom. It's firm and commanding and clearly positions himself as a man in charge. He also physically positions himself in front of Eloise.

"I'm Eloise Markham," Lo says, stepping around Jake. "Would you mind telling us why you're here? I'm guessing it's not for the party."

"I'm German, and this is Daniels. We're with the

Strategic Unit over Cybersecurity and Safety. We're looking for your sister, Sadie. We assume she arrived today?"

My stomach drops. This can't be good. Even if I have no idea what this agency is or what it does.

"I'm sorry—what agency are you with again?" I ask.

"The Strategic Unit over Cybersecurity and Safety," he says. "It's a division of the FBI."

"Never heard of it," Jake says. "Can I see some identification?"

"Your name is *German*?" Eloise asks at the same time.

German reaches inside his suit coat and pulls out a badge. I don't miss the gun strapped to his side. Suddenly, the situation seems a whole lot more serious. Jake frowns at the badge, then pulls out his phone, clearly checking the info. This is when it's nice to have lawyer friends. Or, you know, friends who can keep a cool head in a crisis. While he's fact-checking, I can't stop thinking about the disproportionately small size of German's neck compared to his body and his giant head. Or the fact that the acronym for the agency he claims to be from spells *SUCS*. Neither realization is helpful, and I give my (normal-sized) head a small shake, willing myself to focus.

Merritt steps up beside Eloise, looking every bit the older sister. Hunter isn't more than a step behind her, looking tense.

"Maybe you should tell us *why* you're looking for Sadie," Merritt says smoothly. "Government agent or not, you've just barged in on a private party. And Sadie didn't mention anything about expecting you."

"So, she *did* arrive in Oakley," German says, looking slightly relieved.

Daniels still hasn't spoken a word, and I'm beginning to wonder if he *can* talk. Or maybe this is a version of good cop/bad cop, but more talks-a-lot cop and silent cop. Just substitute *government agent* for *cop*, and there you go.

"Look, it's very important that we talk to her immediately," German continues. "There's been a few developments with her situation, so for her safety—"

"Her safety?" Eloise blurts out. "What do you mean, her safety? This is Oakley Island. It's the safest place on the planet."

"And what 'situation' are you talking about?" Merritt's voice is crisp and sharp as a blade.

While I feel every bit as concerned as they both look, I don't speak up or step in. I actually take a step back, sliding my hands into my pockets with forced casualness. If I slip away now, I could get to Sadie and give her a heads-up before these guys figure out where she is.

At the very least, I owe her a warning.

"Respectfully, ma'am," German says dryly, "this is official SUCS business and I'm not at liberty to provide the details. But I can assure you Sadie's safety is our only concern. If you don't cooperate fully, it could put your sister at risk."

Somehow, I know that if Sadie were here, even knowing her safety was in jeopardy, she would still laugh at *official SUCS business*, and I feel a sharp longing to have her beside me.

The joke is lost on her sisters, though. Understandable considering the information they're trying to process. Eloise's face blanches at Agent German's words, and she reaches for Jake. Hunter wraps an arm around Merritt's waist, and I can see the way she's clenching her jaw.

"Does anyone know where Sadie is right now?" the agent asks.

Eloise and Merritt both glance my way. Of course, they

do. Sadie was with me most of the night. And they both know she's staying on my boat.

"Do you know?" German says, his focus shifting to me. His partner takes a step closer, his arms folding tightly across his chest.

So much for slipping away.

I try to school my features, but I feel every bit as concerned as Merritt and Eloise now look.

"If you know where she is, it's best that you tell us," Agent German says. Then, clearly reading my hesitation, he adds, "She's expecting us."

I step forward, swallowing against the lump in my throat. "She's not here," I say. "But she was. Left about twenty minutes ago. She said she needed a break from the crowd, so I let her take my car."

"She was *here*?" German says. "At a party?"

His tone is chastising, like we all should have somehow known better than to let Sadie be here. As though this isn't a party on the back lawn of a house her family has owned for generations but some kind of dangerous area known for drug deals or shootouts. As though Sadie actually *mentioned* whatever trouble she's in, and we disregarded it just for fun.

"Of course, she was here," Merritt says. "Why shouldn't she be?"

"Because we told her to keep a low profile." German pulls out his phone, grumbling under his breath, but I'm standing close enough to make out his words. "Does that woman ever do what she's told?"

Ha. Not likely. For the first time since we started talking to these guys, I want to smile. I also have an irrational thought, one that would make Sadie roll her eyes and probably take a swing at me: *That's my girl.*

The truth is, Sadie might very well have thought she *was*

keeping a low profile. This is Oakley Island. It's a tiny, sleepy beach town, and this party was mostly for residents, for people I've known my entire life. Yes, tonight is a big event as far as the island goes, and there are some out-of-towners who arrived early for the Flower Festival.

But I can't see a world in which anyone here could or would harm her.

"To be fair, Agent German," I say, "most of the people here tonight have known Sadie since she was a little girl. They're all friends. People she can trust."

"Sounds charming," he says, his words thick with sarcasm. "Like a scene right out of a movie. But I'm less concerned about the people here and more concerned about the people who are looking for her. The fewer who know she's in town, the better."

Behind us, a booming laugh echoes across the lawn. I turn and see Frank filming a video of a very tipsy Harriett doing a very bad rendition of the chicken dance. It will almost certainly be on TikTok the second she finishes. Frank's been filming and posting videos all night.

Which means … *Sadie* is probably on TikTok.

Frank is usually harmless. He's had a few videos go viral, but mostly he only gets traction with a small but loyal following of current and former Oakley residents.

Still, his account is public. And it's almost a guarantee that as much as Sadie and I were together tonight, he's already posted something about the two of us.

"Frank's TikTok," Eloise says slowly, clearly reaching the same conclusion I did. "He's already told the whole internet Sadie is here. And I might have posted a few things too. Just in my stories but …"

Before Merritt finishes saying, "Delete them," Lo already has her phone out.

And Hunter makes his way toward Frank.

Agent German swears, shaking his head as he starts typing into his phone. "We'll have to move her," he says.

My phone buzzes with a text, and I reach for it, thinking it might be Sadie, but that's a stupid thought. I don't have her number and she doesn't have mine. It is a message *about* Sadie though.

John: Just wanted you to know Ms. Markham has arrived and retired for the night, and the yacht is secure.

"Move her to where?" Merritt says, her voice rising. "And why? You still haven't told us what's going on."

"Like I said. The why is confidential," Agent German says. He looks at the other guy. Daniels. "Can we get a track on Sadie's phone?"

Maybe it's the hint of possessiveness in the guy's tone, or the thought of them tracking her down using the pings coming from her cell phone, but government agents or not, the idea of these guys whisking Sadie off to some unknown location sends a jolt of panic straight through me.

Also, I may not be a trained agent, but I'm no slouch. I could hold my own in a fight if it came to that. A surge of protectiveness has me wanting to locate Sadie and not let her out of my sight.

Which I'm sure she'd hate. Then again, I can't imagine her liking these guys following her around either. Which is the only explanation for what I say next. "Actually, I have an idea about where she could go. Safe. Secure. Off the radar completely."

"I'm listening," German says.

I might have a death wish, honestly. Sadie would never go for this if she were part of the discussion. But it only takes a tiny bit of mental gymnastics to convince myself the plan is brilliant instead of full-on crazy. She'll forgive me later.

Probably.

"How about the middle of the Atlantic?" I say. "I have a yacht."

Normally, I downplay it. But if there's ever a time to be crystal clear about *The Oakley*, it's now.

"Conveniently," I add, "Sadie is already aboard."

This earns a more probing look from Agent German, one that seems to be assessing *me* more than the idea of my boat. I suddenly wonder if he has some kind of relationship with Sadie. Or maybe he just wants to have one? Surely there's some kind of rule against that.

Then again, I have no idea how well Sadie knows these guys. Is she an official part of the agency they work for? Or are they only here because she's in danger?

"What's your relationship to the Markham family?" German asks. Definitely sounding territorial.

Which makes me *feel* territorial. Before I can say or do anything stupid, Merritt steps forward.

"He's a close family friend," she says.

"And one we trust completely," Eloise adds.

The praise from Sadie's sisters impacts me in an unexpected way. Their words—their praise—came quickly, without any qualification or justification. I haven't felt that kind of open acceptance in a long time—not since Mom died. Warmth floods me, and I glance down at my phone to hide my smile.

I text John to see how fast he can pull together a crew. And if it can possibly be done tonight.

Too bad he can't also tell me how long it will take Sadie to forgive me.

"It would probably be best to stay off the grid for five,

maybe seven days," Agent German says. "And we'd need background checks on your crew."

An entire week at sea with Sadie? I'm all in—which means I need to make sure these agents understand I'll be aboard too.

I also really need to know more about Sadie's line of work, because I don't like how serious this seems.

"I've already had background checks done," I say. "Though you could certainly do your own if you've got time to waste." I take a step forward, shooting a sideways glance at Eloise and Merritt. "But my boat isn't going anywhere without me. And neither is Sadie."

German isn't the only one who raises his eyebrows. So do Eloise, Merritt, Jake, and Hunter. I do not meet any of their gazes. I can't. Because I don't know where this sudden protectiveness is coming from, and I can't seem to stop the flow of words from my mouth.

"And why is that?" German asks.

"Because *The Oakley* is *my* yacht," I reiterate. "And Sadie is my girlfriend."

SIX

Sadie

I JOLT AWAKE WITH AN IMMEDIATE, startled, panic-inducing rush of realization.

I don't know where I am.

For a few solid seconds, I lie in bed, gasping as I frantically catalog details, head throbbing.

The light in the room isn't right—darker than my bedroom. And the crack of sunlight is on the wrong side of the room. I don't hear cars honking or the sound of my upstairs roommate's bass vibrating through my ceiling the way it does every morning.

The sheets are too soft. The pillow is too firm.

And the underwire of my bra is digging into my ribcage, which tells me I must have collapsed into bed without doing my nightly routine. At the *very* least, if I'm tired, I'll usually unhook my bra, wiggle it off through my sleeve, then toss it across the room. I'm wearing one of my sleep shirts, though, so I at least got that far. From the taste in my mouth, I did NOT brush my teeth.

I must have been exhausted when I got back. What was I—

Memories slam into me like too-fast frames of a movie being rewound but in jumbled order.

The party, Lo and Merritt's speech, German on the phone telling me to leave town, dancing with Benedict King for most of the night—I refuse to let myself slow down to linger on this—and stealing his keys to get to … his *yacht*.

I sit up, my eyes adjusting well enough to take in the room, which I remember from his tour yesterday.

Okay. This is okay. I'm on Ben's yacht in Oakley's harbor.

I drop my head in my hands and breathe deeply for a few seconds, trying to regulate my system, still high on adrenaline. But as my heart settles down, I notice a few other things. My head is pounding, and my stomach is roiling.

Maybe I drank too much? But I don't remember that—just one drink with Naomi and then I switched to water. Plus, I drove Ben's car, which I wouldn't have done had I been drinking. Ben never would have let me steal his keys.

It's probably just emotional exhaustion. Finding out scary men might be coming after me will do that to a girl.

I stand up, needing to locate coffee and NOW before this headache graduates into a migraine. They don't come often, but when they do, they knock me out for a day or two. Which means any old headache has to be treated like a precursor to the headache of doom and treated accordingly.

Caffeine. Water. Medicine, which I hopefully packed in my makeup bag.

Before I can take two steps toward the bathroom, I pitch sideways, landing back on the bed with an *oomph*. Okay, if I'm this unsteady, maybe I'm already dwelling in migraine land.

It's not unusual for them to impact my vision and my balance.

But then a horn blares, the room shifts, and I realize I didn't fall over because of my head.

The yacht is *moving*.

I make my way to the heavy curtains covering the balcony door and the floor-to-ceiling windows that line my stateroom. Jerking the fabric back, I gasp.

Yesterday, I stood on this balcony and saw the ocean and sky and then, off to the right, the jut of land that holds the black and white lighthouse I used to climb with my sisters every summer.

Now, all I can see is the endless blue of the Atlantic.

"No," I whisper, then squint against the too-bright sun before I pull the curtains closed again.

I channel my rage as I stomp out of my room and throw open Ben's door across the hall. Empty. He said he wouldn't stay here, but I wouldn't put it past the man to do it anyway. He also said the yacht would stay in the marina, and that clearly didn't happen.

Even with the advance warning, I'm still unprepared when I step outside, blinking and squinting in the blinding sun. I spin a full three hundred and sixty degrees. Not only can I not see the harbor, I cannot see *land* in any direction. We haven't just left the marina; we've gone out to freaking sea.

"*Benedict King.*" I say his name like a curse. Somehow, it's more satisfying than an *actual* curse.

I grip the railing with one hand and shade my eyes with the other. My head gives a very serious and heavy throb. *Right.* I still need to procure coffee and take meds. But first I need to find whoever is piloting—captaining? driving?—this yacht and have them turn it right back around.

If only I could remember where things are. It was only yesterday when I toured the boat, but I feel completely turned around.

Ben's yacht is more of a mini cruise ship, I decide, as I walk past the pool and through a door I thought might lead into a main living area. Instead, I only find a set of narrow stairs. Was the galley down a level?

Five minutes later, I've been on three different levels and peeked into more rooms than I can count. All empty. Though I do find a second living room, this one with an enormous fish tank full of what look like miniature sharks. Which—I cannot wrap my head around that right now.

I push my way out yet another door onto yet another deck, this one covered in shaded canopies. It still takes my eyes a moment to adjust. This isn't a ghost ship, so I just need to find where the people are and—

"Morning, sunshine!" Ben's voice is far too cheerful for a man on my most wanted list.

Scratch that. He's on my newly formed hit list.

Especially considering the scene in front of me. Ben is lounging on a teal deck chair, sunglasses on, shirt off, the breeze ruffling his blond hair like he's a supermodel with a perfectly adjusted wind machine. Meanwhile, a gust of wind sends a whole hank of hair right into my wide-open mouth.

"You!" I sputter, pulling the hair from my mouth. "Why are you here? Where are we? Why can't I see land?"

His grin widens, and he hops to his bare feet, ambling over to me. Because he's a smart man, he stops just out of reach. He's still close, though.

Too close.

Especially when he's showing off a broad chest full of tanned skin stretched over muscles that look like they were hand-forged by some kind of master craftsman. Or just a lot of hours in the gym. There's just the faintest dusting of blond hair across the center of his chest, stopping at his abs, then starting up again around his belly button and disappearing into the waistband of his bathing suit.

I jerk my eyes back upward when I realize where my eyes have wandered. But the sudden movement makes both my stomach and my head remind me how bad off I really am. Much worse than when I woke up not fifteen minutes ago.

Now that I know we're on a moving boat, how terrible I feel makes more sense. I've never been good at boats. It's most likely seasickness causing the nausea and the headache.

"I'm sorry I absconded with you," Ben says, lifting his sunglasses to the top of his head. I'm surprised to see his blue eyes actually look concerned, at odds with his smile.

"It's too early for SAT prep words," I tell him. "In as few syllables as possible, tell me where we are and why we are here."

His gaze flicks to the side, and it's only then I notice two men I've never seen before. They're tall and burly and look as though they just jumped to their feet from their own lounge chairs. They're both wearing dark suits, at odds with Ben's casual beachwear, though their jackets are draped over the backs of their chairs.

On a railing nearby, a massive pelican stares, watching like we're his favorite television show. I glare, and the bird fluffs his feathers, nonplussed.

"I'll let Agent German explain," Ben says.

"German?" I squint at the taller of the two men, who's now making his way over.

Of course, it's German. The deep frown is exactly as I imagined it would be through our many phone calls. As for the rest of him ...

I try to reconcile the giant in front of me with the man

I've spoken to at least once a week over the past two years. His skin is the color of skim milk—so pale I'd believe it if someone told me he spent most of his life in a cave. He's as big and broad as his deep voice would suggest, but with an oddly thin neck. It makes his bald head look like a volleyball balanced on top of a PVC pipe.

"Agent German," he corrects, holding out a meaty hand.

When I take it, his fingers stay limp in mine. It's as though he has no muscles in his hand, like I'm squeezing a dead squid. It's oddly unnerving.

"Hello," I say, dropping his hand and then shooting another glance at Ben. "You're here. And we're ... at sea?"

"Yes. Ben offered his yacht and said you were already on board," German says. "We thought you wouldn't mind a few days at sea with your boyfriend."

I choke. "My ... boyfriend?"

Ben won't look at me. Instead, he's frowning at the pelican perched on the rail. I glare anyway, then press my fingers to my aching temple.

"This is actually a uniquely perfect solution while things are being handled," German says. "It's pretty much a vacation for you."

I'm hardly concerned at all about the "things being handled," aka, the powerful men I've ticked off, because my brain is still processing the word *boyfriend*.

Ben.

My *boyfriend*. Ha!

Ben shifts on his feet, finally meeting my gaze, his expression sheepish. *Oh, boy.* I can't wait to hear *how* and *why* he came up with this lie.

But first: coffee. And medicine.

I'm reminded of my need for both when what feels like a tiny elf with a not-so-tiny hammer smashes right into the center of my forehead. I lean on the railing and groan, squeezing my eyes closed.

A hand clasps my arm. I know it's Ben's because it's not limp and boneless but warm and solid, holding me with just the right mix of strength and gentleness.

"Sadie? Are you okay?"

I wish his voice weren't so tender. It would be far easier to stay angry with the man. I hazard a glance at him, then immediately wish I hadn't. It would also be easier if his concerned blue eyes weren't so dang attractive.

"I don't feel great," I admit, closing my eyes again. But I think that's making it worse, so I force them open a crack and swallow, my mouth too full of saliva. "I need coffee and my headache meds and maybe some seasickness meds if you have any of those?"

"Of course," Ben says. "Let's get you downstairs. And, um, maybe find you some pants?"

I glance down, only just now realizing I'm still in my sleep shirt. And *only* my sleep shirt. I left the room without changing first, fueled by my anger and my headache. Which means now I'm standing on deck in front of Ben and two men I've only just met, wearing a loose shirt that barely skims the tops of my thighs.

How is it that I can wear a bathing suit at a pool or beach and feel totally normal, but swap the bikini for a loose sleep shirt, even one that covers a lot more skin, and suddenly, I feel completely naked? I'm about to make this argument to Ben—why should I need pants if he can walk around without a shirt—but I don't get the chance.

Instead, the boat rocks, my stomach rolls, and I barely manage to lean my head over the railing, throwing up into the ocean instead of all over Ben's bare feet.

"I HATE THE SEA," I grumble through the darkness. A warm and heavy weight presses against my back, something that should bother me, since I normally hate being touched when I have a migraine.

When they hit, I want darkness.

I want quiet.

And I don't want to be fussed over.

Yet, when fingertips drag a slow, rough path through my hair, the groan I make sounds more like a purr. I shamelessly whine when the fingers disappear for a moment, then sigh again when they return, rubbing softly and with the perfect amount of pressure.

Does it ease the sharp yet crushing ache at the top of my skull, between my eyes, and at my temples? No. But it adds a layer of pleasure, something to stave off the very worst of the pain.

I did not, as it turns out, get coffee or medicine in time to hold off the migraine, which hit me at full force just after I threw up overboard.

"I hate the sea, and I hate all sea creatures."

"Even dolphins?" Ben asks in a voice barely above a whisper. I can feel his breath on my neck, and surprisingly, I don't hate it. "They always look so happy."

"Right now, yes—even dolphins. And I hate your yacht," I say. "It's too big."

"Mmm," Ben murmurs. Then, "That's what she said."

A bark of laughter escapes me, but then I gasp, sucking air through my teeth because laughter is *not* the best medicine when you have a migraine. I whimper, feeling my stomach pitch.

"Shhh," Ben whispers, and somehow, it doesn't sound

irritating the way it should to be shushed. "I'm sorry. It's hard not to be funny."

"You're not funny," I tell him, my words coming out slow and thick like syrup as his magical fingers begin rubbing my head again. "But if you stop doing that, I'll throw you off the boat as soon as I can stand up."

"I thought you said I should call it a yacht, not a boat," Ben says.

"I hate you," I say through another whimper.

"I know, baby," he says, and it shows how horrible my headache mixed with seasickness is that I don't immediately tell him not to call me baby.

I also don't question the fact that I'm in Ben's bed with the lights off, or that one of his arms is wrapped around my waist, holding me to his chest while the other rubs my head.

Apparently, desperate times call for desperate willingness to let a man I don't want to like hold me and rub my head.

"I look forward to it," Ben says.

"You *want* me to throw you off your yacht?"

"Boat," he teases. "And no. I don't want you to throw me off." His fingers squeeze the base of my skull, and I let out a soft moan. "I just want you to feel well enough to try."

There is so much tenderness in his voice, it should surprise me. And yet, somehow, even through the fog of my pain and discomfort, I'm intensely aware that what I'm getting here, in the hazy darkness, is the *real* Benedict King. This shouldn't make me so happy, but in my current state, I don't have the fortitude to argue with myself so I give up and give in, relaxing into Ben's warm, firm body and somehow managing to fall asleep through the pain.

SEVEN

Ben

I TELL myself it's not creepy to watch Sadie sleeping. It's not.

Not when I've been taking care of her basically nonstop for the last twenty-four hours. I'm only paying such close attention to make sure she's well. Like a doctor would. Or someone conducting a clinical trial.

Yep—that's why I'm letting my gaze rove over her cheekbones and the pale lashes resting there. It's why I'm watching the curve of her shoulder as it rises and falls with each breath. Why I let my eyes linger on her lips, lightly parted as she makes soft breathing sounds.

It's what any doctor would do.

Okay—maybe a doctor on one of those TV dramas where they fall for their patient even though they shouldn't.

But I can't help it. I have to drink my fill of her because, at some point, probably very soon, Sadie is going to wake up and feel better enough to remember that I basically kidnapped her and lied about being her boyfriend.

I wonder if she'll also remember that every ounce of food or water she's put in her body since she got sick has come from me. Or that I've been the one to walk her to the bathroom, hovering outside the cracked door, eyes averted but close enough to hear her if she gets too wobbly on her feet. I wonder if she'll recall how I spent the night spooning her, running my fingers through her hair and massaging her scalp. How she told me she hated me but also whimpered with raw need any time I stopped touching her.

Though, knowing Sadie, remembering these things might infuriate her more than my lie about being her boyfriend. Once she's fully cognizant, she'll hate that she needed me, that I saw her in such a vulnerable state. Knowing Sadie like I do—which I'd argue is pretty well after this—I bet she won't just back off to settle into our previous status quo of precarious friendship mixed with disdain.

No—this brief intimacy is going to have her bolting for the hills. As much as she can, anyway. Since there are no hills and, despite the size of my boat, very few places to run.

Regardless, I don't have any regrets. I still don't know anything about why Sadie is in trouble or who might be looking for her. But as soon as we were out of sight of Oakley Harbor, Agent German visibly relaxed, as much as he *can* relax, so I feel certain I made the right call. And pretending to be her boyfriend was probably the only reason the agents agreed to take my yacht—and me—in the first place. Even if my current status as Sadie's definitely-not-a-boyfriend doesn't entitle me to feel so protective, there's no arguing that she's safer out here than she would be back on land. Her ire is worth that alone.

"What did you get yourself into, Sadie girl?" I murmur as she shifts in her sleep.

Before we left the marina, a little before dawn yesterday, Agent German tasked a second pair of agents to stay on Oakley to watch over Sadie's sisters and their families. The thought sends another wave of uneasiness washing over me. I'm sure they'll be fine, but I'd feel better if I could check in with Jake just to make sure.

Acting on instinct, I reach for my phone, but draw my hand back, abandoning the effort. *The Oakley* has a satellite internet connection that my phone is usually connected to, but as a matter of safety, we've cut off all communication with the mainland. Agent German insisted I disable the internet, so even though I still have my phone, it's basically useless.

Which is more than Sadie can say. Her sim card is in Agent German's pocket, but her actual cell phone is sitting at the bottom of Oakley Harbor, where he tossed it with a grumbled, "Better safe than sorry."

Yet another reason Sadie is going to be furious. Hopefully, no one will tell her it was *me* who showed German to her room and let him inside. I had no idea he'd go through her things and take her phone. I definitely didn't expect him to destroy it.

Sadie shifts, lifting a hand to her face. I lean forward in the armchair I moved close to the bed yesterday. The room is mostly dark, heavy shades blocking out the sunlight, but there's enough light for me to have spent hours watching her and to notice now, as her eyes slowly crack open.

Licking her lips, Sadie glances toward the nightstand where I've set a bottle of water. "What time is it?" she asks, her voice rough with sleep.

I reach for the water bottle and uncap it, then move to the

edge of the bed so I can offer it to her. "A little after two p.m.," I say.

Sadie takes the water, propping herself up on her elbow while she takes a long drink. It's the most I've seen her manage in the last thirty-six hours. I hope this means she's feeling better.

"Good girl," I say gently as she hands the water back and drops onto her pillow.

"Two p.m.," she says, eyes glassy. "Does that mean—?" She frowns. "How long has it been?"

"Since we left Oakley?" I ask. "Or since you christened the side of my boat?"

She closes her eyes again, but there's a small smile playing on her lips. "I did not get any vomit on your yacht. I had good aim. It all went in the water."

"Boat," I correct, "and yes you did. At least according to the guy who rigged himself up in a harness and dangled over the water to scrub it off."

"Please tell me you're joking," she says.

"Okay. I'm joking," I say easily. Too easily, because Sadie lifts one eye open, shooting me a doubtful look. I say nothing to confirm or deny it, but *yes*—Danny absolutely had to clean the side of the boat.

"How are you feeling?" I ask. "You look a little less like death reheated."

She snorts softly and shakes her head, her hand moving back to her forehead. "Be careful with your flattery, Mr. King, or I just might start to think you *like* me."

I say nothing to this, my heart quickens the slightest bit at her words.

"I feel better," she says. "Slightly. The throbbing has lessened, but the thought of light still makes me want to cry."

"Any more aura?" I ask. I've never experienced the

dancing lights that streak across your vision during a migraine, but my mother had migraines when I was a kid, and I remember her mentioning the symptom. Sadie experienced a few different episodes yesterday. "Or nausea?"

I hope the seasickness patch and bracelet I gave her along with the medicine helped that, at least.

"My stomach feels better." She yawns and rolls onto her side, curling into a ball, and I move a hand to her neck, massaging the back of her skull like I have so many times over the past twenty-four hours. She doesn't flinch at my touch, instead leaning into it with a soft sound that makes my pulse quicken even further.

"Ben, this might be impossible, but I think I want to take a shower."

For a split second, my hand stills, my throat going dry at the thought of Sadie in my shower. But I quickly push the thought away and resume the massage.

"It's not impossible at all," I say. "There's a bathroom less than ten feet from here. My shower has a very comfortable bench inside."

"Of course, your yacht shower has a bench."

"Dang straight it does. What self-respecting yacht owner doesn't have one?"

She smiles, the spark in her eyes making me unreasonably happy. "I knew it was a yacht," she says. She pushes up on her hands, but then stills, wincing like the movement brought her pain.

"I don't know if I can walk," she says. "Or get to the bench."

"I can help."

She lets out a half-hearted scoff that makes me grin, despite how terrible she must feel. "You *would* volunteer for that job," she mutters.

"I can help get everything *ready*," I clarify. "I'll help you get to the shower, then leave you on your own like the Southern gentleman I am."

She barely arches one eyebrow. "You—a Southern gentleman? Don't forget, I googled you."

And I'd rather not know what she found. Actually, very little would come as a surprise, I'm sure. There are rumors about me dating a string of models and Savannah debutantes. Even a few from Charleston. And, I somewhat regret to say, most of those rumors are true. At least, in part.

Those relationships always felt cold and empty, but never more so than now—when I've felt the warmth of Sadie's back against my chest and the fire of her words aimed at me.

I clear my throat. "My shower is fully stocked but tell me what else you need. Your suitcase from your room? Clothes to change into? Just say the word."

I must have asked too many questions because Sadie doesn't respond, instead dropping back onto her pillow and shaking her head, pulling the blankets a little higher.

"Too hard," she says softly. But less than a minute later, she must feel a new burst of energy because she pushes herself all the way up so she's sitting on the edge of the bed.

"I don't need help," she says, looking toward the bathroom through narrowed eyes. "I can just—" She tries to stand, but her words cut off when she immediately wobbles and drops back onto the bed.

"Hey," I say gently, steadying her with a hand on either shoulder. "Slow down. No shame in needing help every so often. Even if you are a capable, brilliant, independent woman."

Too far, Ben. Too freaking far.

"Let me just get you started, all right? I'll turn on the water and get out some towels and find you something to put on after. I'll leave it all in the bathroom for you. Then, I'll help you walk in and let you do your thing. Okay?"

She rolls her head forward like she's stretching her neck, wincing with the motion. "No funny business?" she finally asks.

I let out a low chuckle. "No funny business. I promise."

Not unless you want it, I think, watching her. Because if she did, I'd be the funniest guy in town.

It only takes a handful of minutes to get everything ready. I'm not thrilled about leaving Sadie alone in the bathroom with its granite counter and hard tile floor—I'd never forgive myself if she got hurt—but she's on her feet, her arms wrapped around her middle, so maybe she'll be okay?

"You're sure this is a good idea?" I dim the lights to almost nothing, steam billowing out of the waiting shower beside her.

Sadie nods. "I'll be okay."

I spend the next ten minutes pacing outside the bathroom door, debating whether I should call Leandra and have her on standby in case Sadie really does need help, but then I hear the water cut off and the shower door opens and closes.

Nervous energy pushes through me as I listen for any sound indicating that Sadie needs me, bracing for the sound of her falling, or worse, hitting her head, but nothing goes wrong and eventually, she opens the door.

It's so stupid to feel so much pleasure at the sight of Sadie wearing a pair of my pajama bottoms, the waist cinched up, paired with one of my old t-shirts falling off one of her shoulders.

It's not like I planned this. She needed something to change into. Giving her something of mine felt simpler than going and rummaging through her suitcase. Or expecting *her* to rummage through her suitcase. In her current state, my goal was to make things as easy as possible. My clothes were accessible and comfortable and *right here*. It's a bonus that they look incredibly sexy skimming over Sadie's curves. But that wasn't the point at all.

It's more of a … bonus.

As though reading something in my expression—hopefully *not* reading my mind—Sadie says, "I'm only wearing your clothes because my suitcase feels very far away right now."

"Noted," I say. "I won't let it go to my head."

"And I'm only getting into your bed," she says as she climbs in, as slow and bumbling as a child, "because it's right here."

"Of course."

But I don't miss the way she buries her nose in my pillow and takes a brief inhale.

"Yale," Sadie says, tugging at the hem of the t-shirt left over from my college rowing days. "Is that where you went?"

"I thought you googled me." When she glares, I grin.

"I didn't spend *that* much time on you."

I clutch my chest. "Ouch."

"This shirt is really soft," Sadie says.

I pull the covers over her shoulders, tucking them below her chin. "I picked it for that reason."

She hums in appreciation, then reaches out from under the covers, snaking a hand behind my thigh to tug me onto the bed. I don't bother to hide my grin, but I don't need to since Sadie already has her eyes closed. She wiggles toward the center of the bed, taking my pillow with her, and makes room for me.

I climb in, staying on top of the covers as I scoot toward the headboard. She follows, nudging her head into my lap.

We've done this enough times now that we don't need

words. I know exactly where to sit, and she knows exactly where to lay so I can hit the pressure points in her head and neck for maximum impact.

She really must be feeling terrible to be this desperate. Because desperation is the only thing that would make Sadie rely on *me*, of all people.

But not *just* because it's me. I don't know Sadie as well as I'd like to—at least not yet. But I sense she's a woman who likes to do things on her own terms, with her own strength. She wouldn't like needing *anyone* like this.

But that doesn't mean I won't soak this up as long as I can. That I won't commit to memory the feel of her skin or the way her breath catches when I hit a pressure point just right.

It definitely won't stop me from hoping that eventually, Sadie will stop fighting and recognize whatever this thing is between us. Because there's definitely something here.

At least, there's the potential for something. If she'll just stop telling herself she doesn't like me. Or believing everything she reads.

Sadie lets out a low moan and sinks further into my lap, her damp hair soaking through the fabric of my shorts. Not that I care. Even if Sadie isn't willing to admit it, something is definitely shifting inside of me.

I've been perfectly content to let the world think I'm a privileged screw-up without a purpose. An aimless millennial with too much money and not enough sense. It's been a nice disguise—an excellent way to hide in plain sight.

This act started when I was younger and needed some protection from my father. Any of my successes drew his attention—and increased his attempts at getting me to involve him in my business dealings. I quickly learned if he thought I was a good-for-nothing screw-up, sure to blow through my inheritance, he had less use for me.

As I got older and found it easier to stand up to him, the need to keep up the act faded. But by then, it was comfortable, like a perfectly worn-in pair of shoes. Showing people—even those I trust—how much I do care is ... scary. Sticking to my script feels safer.

But for the first time in ... maybe ever, I don't really want to be that man anymore. At least not in front of Sadie.

Sadie relaxes against me as she drifts back into sleep. I lift my hand from her neck, running it over her hair. It's wavy when it's wet, and I find myself wondering if she straightens it every day or what it would look like if she let it dry in the breeze up on deck. My own hair gains a certain unruliness when I'm on the water, a reaction to the humidity and salt in the air.

I vastly prefer that look for myself—barefoot, casual, hair doing whatever it wants to do.

I trail my fingers through Sadie's hair again, and she sighs in her sleep, then lightly snores. I hold back a laugh.

I should get up. Leave her to rest and check in with German and the rest of the crew. See if there's any news from Oakley or any new intelligence about the threat that sent us out here in the first place.

I *should* get up. But I don't. And maybe that's the scariest thing of all. I'm not even going to pretend that I want to.

EIGHT

Sadie

WAKING up for the third time on Benedict King's yacht is a wholly different experience from the first two. For one—I am nausea and headache free. Hallelujah!

I'm currently in what I like to call post-migraine euphoria. I don't know if this is typical for other people with migraines, but for me, once they pass, it's like I have a sort of high. Everything is better than normal—I feel happy and floaty and peaceful.

Even more significant: now that I'm feeling better, I'm more keenly aware that I am *not* alone in bed.

I should definitely *not* be snuggling with Benedict King. Aka, the man who convinced an agent of the United States government to kidnap me and take me out on the high seas. Apparently, the pirate flag hanging on the yacht was less of a joke than I thought.

Okay, *fine*. Maybe I'm being a tiny bit dramatic. But in

technical terms, it's true. I had no say in the matter, which makes it kidnapping. As to what makes the seas *high* versus *regular* ... that, I don't know. Maybe I should consult *Moby Dick*. I bet Melville can tell me. I just need to find my phone, then I can google and learn for myself.

Ben shifts, and his hand tightens on my hip, bunching up my shirt. *His* shirt, actually, as I'm wearing his clothes. Wearing his clothes. Sleeping in his bed. Snuggling.

Yeah, I need to get up.

I don't.

The thing is—I *am* upset about the situation. More like, I *should* be, just on principle. Someone could have at least woken me up to fill me in on the situation before we left Oakley.

But if I'm being honest, hiding out on the yacht is actually a smart idea. If we forget about the two days of crippling discomfort and seasickness, there are definitely worse places I could be. German hadn't given me details about what we'd do when he reached me. But I'm pretty sure it would have included being sequestered in some janky hotel somewhere with him watching the door while I ate bad room service and climbed the walls.

Instead, I have a pool and a hot tub and a gorgeous view and a private chef who is undoubtedly fantastic. It's like a forced vacation. I'm not sure I realized how much I needed one until now, when I don't have a choice. Rather than scratchy hotel sheets you *hope* were washed before you checked in, I'm lying on sheets with a thread count higher than anything I've known before. I could live in these sheets.

Which brings me full circle, back to the man in bed beside me.

Based on the steady rise and fall of his chest underneath my cheek, Ben is still dead asleep. Even if his fingers are flexing on my hip in a most distracting manner. His light, occasional snores are another indication.

How can snores be cute? Somehow, they are, and I find myself biting back a grin.

The poor man is probably exhausted after playing my nanny and nurse—two roles I'd never imagined Ben playing. But oh, did he ever play them.

Honestly, I've never had a guy do this kind of thing for me. Not that I've had many boyfriends. Just the one—and Justin *never* would have done anything like this. Five minutes with me groaning—or even just the one vomiting incident—and he would have been gone.

I can't remember a time I felt so well cared for. Ever. Ben made me feel … treasured.

A hot flush rises in my cheeks when I parse through my fuzzy memories of the last day. Day and a half? Two days? I'm not even sure how long it's been.

I remember Ben carrying me to bed after I barfed over the side of his boat.

I remember him tucking me into his bed, making sure I got medicine and drank water—even as I protested.

I remember him rubbing my head for what must have been hours.

And me: needy, desperate for his touch. Actually *whining* when he stopped massaging my aching head. Pretty sure the only thing that interrupted his ministrations was me giving him trouble, telling him I hated him or scolding him for calling his yacht a boat.

I am pretty much the worst.

I can almost hear Merritt and Eloise scolding me for treating Ben—whom they both seem to love like they're BFFs—this way. They'd tell me I should be grateful and thankful. Eloise would be aghast at the words that came out of my mouth.

For once, I totally agree with my imaginary sisters.

But ... it's *Ben*.

Benedict King. I'm not even typecasting when I say he's the richest of the rich playboys. The fact that he owns the whole of Oakley Island is a testament to the first. Proof of the second was in the many, many gossip articles I saw linking him with various hot and, in many cases, famous women.

I also might have searched the price of yachts this size, and the number was staggering. Like, it made me want to vomit. Again. It also made me want to be super careful not to break anything because I for sure can't afford to fix it.

Even aside from my moratorium on serious relationships post-Justin, Ben is a hard pass on principle. Which is why I need to get out of bed right this instant before I catch feelings like a virus.

Ben shifts, smacking his lips and muttering something about pineapples. I barely manage to stifle a giggle.

He might be my nemesis when he's awake, but I can admit he's adorable when he's asleep.

He's also pretty great in a crisis. Tender and thoughtful and willing to sit beside me while—

NOPE. That's feelings talk. And we will have no feelings aside from a healthy disdain.

Very slowly, I inch my way out of bed, pulling a move Indiana Jones would be proud of as I replace my body with a pillow for Ben to cuddle with. I'd snap a photo, but I don't have my phone.

Goodbye, Ben, I think as I watch him breathe. *Time to reset this relationship.*

Back in my room, I take a shower and change into my

own clothes. Though I should return Ben's shirt and pants ... I don't. Because he's asleep, I tell myself. But it might also be because they're soft. And still smell like him. And I may or may not want to crawl back into them the next time I go to sleep.

It's dark out but I still can't find my phone, which is concerning, so I'm not sure if it's ten o'clock or three in the morning. Whatever the hour, a need for coffee drives me to locate the galley.

I'm no better off now than I was the first time I sought a caffeine fix on what I'm quickly determining is just a giant, floating maze. This time, it takes almost ten minutes and several wrong turns, but I finally make it. When the door finally swings open, revealing the gleaming, modern kitchen space, I can't stop myself from muttering an exasperated, "Finally!"

Four sets of eyes blink at me. They're all sitting on stools, playing cards on the marble prep counter. Pretty sure I met three of them the other day, though the details feel a little fuzzy.

Leandra is the grandmotherly stewardess who's known Ben forever and calls him Benedict. The man with the closely cropped gray hair is John—the chief something-or-other? I remember the chef, who has a line of silver hoops on one ear, but his name escapes me. There's another, younger man with a blond ponytail I don't remember meeting. He jumps up when he sees me, like I've interrupted something insidious rather than a card game.

"Hello!" I pause inside the doorway, waving awkwardly. "Sorry to startle you. It took me a minute to find the galley."

Leandra stands, walking over to give me a smile and a brief hug. "Ms. Markham! So glad to see you up and about. Feeling better?"

"Yes, thankfully. I hope I'm not interrupting. I just needed to find coffee." My stomach chooses that moment to let out a Godzilla-like roar.

"And maybe food?" Leandra says with a chuckle.

"I don't want to be any trouble," I say.

Leandra waves away my concern. "It's no trouble. Coffee can be ready in a few minutes, and Tao can whip something up to eat, I'm sure. I don't think you met Danny"—the man with the ponytail grins—"but he'll get you a stool so you can join us. That is, if you'd like to. We're just playing a little friendly poker."

"Not so friendly," the chef—Tao—says, as he gets up. "I fold. Take my money, you thieves. Sadie—what sounds good? Are you craving anything in particular?"

I'm about to say something else about not wanting to be trouble, but Leandra levels me with a look and then pats the stool Danny brought over. I sit.

"I don't actually know what time it is, but breakfast sounds amazing."

Tao grins, revealing a tiny gap between his top teeth. "Breakfast at midnight is one of my favorites."

"It's midnight? Oh, then definitely don't—"

Leandra touches my arm. "If you're about to say another word about us going to any trouble, I'll have John put you in the brig."

John snorts, staring intently at his cards. "Don't listen to her. We don't even have a brig."

"Do you have a plank?" I ask, which makes Danny laugh.

"There's a retractable diving board," he says. "Which, I guess could work just as well."

Of course, there's a retractable diving board. What kind of yacht would this be without one?

"Let's finish this hand so we can deal Sadie in," John

says, tossing a blue chip in the center. "I raise. It's to you, Danny." John glances at me. "Do you know how to play poker?"

"A little," I say.

Danny grins again. The man reminds me of an oversized golden retriever. "I bet that means she's good. Decent players always undersell themselves. I fold. This one's yours, John. Were you bluffing? You were, weren't you?"

John's smile is smug as he gathers chips from the center and deftly shuffles his hand into the rest of the deck. "I'll never tell. Are you in, Sadie?"

"What's the buy-in?" I ask. "I have zero cash, but I'm good for it."

"Don't worry about it for now," Leandra says, counting out a stack of chips from a silver case. She slides them in front of me, and John begins to deal.

Ten minutes later, the whole room smells like bacon, I've got a cup of coffee in hand, and I've taken almost all of Danny's money. I'm having a blast.

"I knew you were good," Danny says, looking as unperturbed as if he'd been the one to clean *me* out.

"I had good hands," I say, which is partly true. The other part is that I've been playing for years with a group of guys I met through a mutual friend. The mutual friend moved, but I kept the poker group. Also, I learned from the best, and the best was Gran. "What's your job, Danny? I didn't get to meet you the other day."

"I'm a deckhand. I do pretty much all the grunt work, especially with such a small crew."

"It's a very important job," Leandra says, giving his forearm a squeeze.

I notice a tattoo peeking out from Danny's sleeve. Hard to tell without seeing the whole thing, but it looks like it could be Mickey Mouse. I barely know the guy, and still, a Mickey Mouse tattoo absolutely fits.

"I'm not complaining," Danny says. "Ben pays better than anyone else. Plus, he offered me time and a half for this trip, since I basically had less than an hour to pack and get myself on board."

This reminds me of the whole kidnapping thing. And the fact that I didn't run into German or the other agent while searching for the galley. I wonder if one of them has to stay awake and on duty even when we're out at sea. Shouldn't they be keeping track of me?

By my count, they're doing a pretty poor job.

"What, exactly, did Ben say about this sudden trip?" I ask, trying to sound casual as I shuffle the deck and start to deal.

Tao grins. "What he *said* was he wanted to show his girlfriend a good time."

I stiffen, having forgotten that little tidbit of information. *Girlfriend*—right. I remember German saying something similar—right before I threw up over the side of the boat.

Yet another reason to be angry with Ben. Lying about me being his girlfriend is definitely *not* okay. If I had to guess, I'd say it was probably how he convinced German to do this whole Take-Sadie-to-Sea plan. Which, *fine*. I understand they were all operating from a place of concern. But not a single one of them consulted with *me*. Told me what was happening. Asked if I had an opinion on the subject.

My frustration rises, which is good considering how much it softened through Ben's excellent caretaking skills.

You don't like him, I remind myself. *You* can't *like him*.

"But since we know Ben doesn't *have* girlfriends," John starts.

"And since you're clearly out of his league," Leandra adds with a smile.

Danny holds up a finger. "And because there are government agents on board, we can only conclude that Ben's covering for you because you're some kind of spy."

I snort, then take a sip of coffee.

"Or in the witness protection program and had your identity compromised," Tao says, plating a stack of small, strange-looking pancakes.

"Which can't be true as I knew Genevieve Markham for years," Leandra says. "Sadie's grandmother," she explains to the men.

I start to deal, hoping my hands don't shake. "You knew my gran?"

"I did. Firecracker of a woman," Leandra says with a soft smile that makes my chest feel tight. "I see where you get your spark. And why Ben likes you so much—even if you *aren't* actually his girlfriend."

"He should be so lucky," Tao says. "Food's ready, everyone. Grab it and growl."

The poker game goes on hiatus while we plate up our food, which looks amazing. I'd be happy with plain crackers at this point, but Tao made bacon, fried eggs, and what he says are his easy version of Chinese scallion pancakes.

"Not usually a breakfast food," Tao says. "But then, it is midnight, not morning. And I had a craving."

We all dig in, and for a few minutes, the only sounds are forks on plates and happy moans of happy eaters. Not that I'm surprised, but Tao can cook. Even this simple meal is impeccably good. Somehow both homey and refined.

"So," I say, taking a bite of perfectly crisp bacon. "Leandra was supposed to give me embarrassing stories about Ben, but I'm still waiting."

The more embarrassing, the better. Especially if they're

not *cute* embarrassing, but the kind of story that will help solidify my defenses against the man.

Danny laughs. "Where should we start?"

"How long have you worked on the yacht?"

"I've been his first officer for five years now," John says before taking a bite of eggs.

"And it's a full-time job? I hope that didn't sound rude," I add quickly. "I'm not sure how yacht life works."

"The three of us are full time," Tao says.

"He needs a chef full time?" I ask.

Tao nods. "He does when he's living on the yacht full time."

Living on the yacht full time, huh? I *knew* Ben's room looked well lived-in when he gave me the tour. And he was willing to give that up … so I would feel safe.

Do not let this change your opinion of Ben! Do NOT.

But it's getting harder and harder to listen to the voice of caution in my head.

"Danny and a few other deckhands come and go as needed, and there are some other part-time staff who might work if Ben has an event," Leandra says.

"Who drives the yacht?" I ask.

"Ben doesn't always hire the same crew," John says. "Right now, it's Art."

I tilt my head. "Is *driving* even the correct term?"

"Driving, piloting, captaining, helming," Danny lists off. "Just don't call the captain *skipper*. Which is technically correct. But Art doesn't like it, and he has *no* sense of humor."

"Or you're just not funny," Tao says.

"Ha ha," Danny says. "Maybe you should stick to cooking." Then he takes a bite of a scallion pancake, and his eyes roll back in his head. "No, really, you should. Definitely stick to cooking."

"It's delicious," I agree. "Thank you, Tao."

He grins. "Clearly, you weren't the only hungry one. Will Ben be joining us?"

I suddenly feel like I'm shrinking under their interested gazes. "Um, no? He's asleep. I think."

No need to mention I was just asleep with him. In his bed.

But from the knowing looks I see when I glance around the table, they all know exactly where I've been for the last two days. Gah! I am not usually a blusher. But I can feel my skin growing hot as I look down, focusing on my food.

"He's probably worn out," Leandra says, with a bit of a smirk. "I've never seen him go to such lengths for anyone."

"It's strange," John says in an even voice. "We all knew Ben was lying about you being his girlfriend, but you'd never know from the way he's been behaving."

Tao's grin widens. "He's a smitten kitten."

I laugh. I can't help it. "No, he's just a flirt."

And a kidnapper, but I don't say that part out loud. Leandra hums but doesn't otherwise respond. Neither does anyone else, which speaks volumes.

Volumes I don't want to interpret.

Danny clears the plates as we finish, and Tao deals the next hand, cleaning out Danny completely and taking a good bit of what I won earlier. A few hands later and I'm out too, having lost it all on a bluff from Leandra.

I yawn and catch John looking over. Danny catches my yawn and yawns too.

"Shall we settle up and call it a night?" John asks.

"More like a morning," Tao says. "It's one-thirty."

Danny groans. "Tomorrow is already kicking my butt."

"How much do I owe?" I ask, reaching for a phone that isn't in my pocket. Did I leave it back on Oakley? I have a distinct memory of plugging it in beside my bed, but it wasn't in my room when I showered and dressed. "My wallet is somewhere. But I might have to do Zelle or Venmo whenever I find my phone ..."

I trail off, watching as Danny pulls out a stack of bills. Hundred-dollar bills. My mouth falls open as he counts out a stack and settles up with Leandra, who's acting as banker.

"Don't worry about it, hon," she says with a wink. "I'll spot you."

I sputter. "But ... those are hundreds. How much was each chip worth?"

In my poker games, the chips are usually worth ten dollars, five dollars, one dollar, and a quarter. I'm trying and failing to do math in my head. I think the sight of so much money broke my brain.

Leandra pats my hand. "Please don't worry. Ben pays us all very well."

"Very, *very* well," Danny says, leaning back on his stool with a big smile.

Tao stands up, moving to clean up the dishes, and kicks Danny's stool, sending him crashing to the ground in a heap. Which leads to the two men chasing each other around the room, Danny swatting at Tao with a dish towel and Tao deflecting the strikes with a cookie sheet shield.

"Can't you do something?" Leandra asks John.

"Boys," John says in a completely flat tone, clearly not interested in getting involved. "Stop. Don't. No."

Danny corners Tao near the sink, swatting him over and over on the thighs. It must hurt because Tao howls. And then he grabs the hose from the sink, extending it toward Danny. Tao's hand clutches the faucet, clearly itching to turn it on.

Danny drops the towel and holds up both hands. "I surrender. Drop the hose, Tao."

"Surrender isn't enough," Tao says. "Apologize."

Danny drops his hands to his hips. "You first. You're the one who started it."

Three things happen at once. Tao turns on the sink, releasing a stream of water. Danny ducks, dropping to the floor.

And Ben walks through the swinging door just in time to feel the full effects of Tao's very damp attack.

NINE

Ben

IT TAKES a minute for me to process the scene in front of me. At first, because I literally cannot *see* through the water streaming down my face. Then, because I can't make sense of what I *do* see.

An overturned stool. Towels and a cookie sheet on the floor next to ... wait—*Danny*? Sadie stands next to Leandra, near the opposite door, her hands pressed to her mouth like she's trying to stifle her laughter.

And then there's Tao, eyes wide, the spray nozzle from the sink still in his hand.

Leandra moves first, crouching down to pick up one of the discarded dish towels. She slowly hands it to me while Danny pushes himself up to his feet. It's not lost on me that the entire room is holding its collective breath, clearly waiting to see how I'm going to react.

I take the towel and wipe off my face, then toss it onto

the counter. "Next time, y'all better not play poker without me."

Danny chuckles. "You didn't miss much. Just Leandra taking most of our money. Even Sadie got schooled, though she held her own."

My eyes settle on Sadie, really taking her in. I endured a brief moment of panic when I woke up and she wasn't beside me. The feeling only worsened when I didn't find her in her own room either. I'm not saying I jogged through the ship in a mild panic to find her. I also wouldn't deny it.

I'm relieved to see her. Especially because she looks good. *Better.* The sparkle is back in her eyes, and she looks more like herself in leggings and an oversized sweatshirt, though I can't say I don't have a moment of missing her wearing my clothes.

"Also, food," Sadie says. "You missed really good food."

"You ate," I say, not even trying to hide how happy this makes me. "I'm glad you feel good enough to eat."

Sadie nods, a flush spreading across her cheeks. "Yeah. I..." Her eyes dart around the room, like she's suddenly aware of our audience and doesn't want to say more.

Leandra must pick up on the vibe because she motions to John. "We're done here, right? I think it's time for us to say goodnight."

"Sounds good to me," John says. He claps Danny on the back, bodily ushering him toward the door.

"I just need to clean up," Tao says, but I stop him with a shake of my head.

"I'll do the dishes. It's late. You can head to bed too."

His eyebrows go up. "If you're sure," he says. When I nod, his lips twitch. "Do you know how to wash dishes?"

"Shut up."

He laughs, then strips off his apron and follows behind

the others, murmuring a quiet goodnight to Sadie on his way.

"You're doing the dishes?" Sadie says as soon as we're alone. "With those soft, billionaire hands?"

I snort, moving to the sink. "Let me guess. You're also surprised I know how?"

She rolls her eyes. "We're on a yacht worth a gazillion dollars. I'm not surprised you know how. But I'm a little surprised you're choosing to do them."

"Not quite a gazillion," I say as I carry the plates on the counter over to the sink and turn on the hot water. "But I understand your point."

To my surprise, Sadie moves in beside me, dish towel in hand. I was planning on just loading these into the dishwasher, but if Sadie's willing to help, I'd rather this process take as long as possible, so I'm happy to wash them by hand. Slowly. Very, very thoroughly. The best, most meticulous dishwashing of my life.

I pick up a scrub brush and start with the first plate. "It was actually your grandmother who taught me how to wash dishes," I finally say.

I hand the plate to Sadie, and she holds it for a second, frozen before she seems to remember why she's holding it and starts to dry it off. In that brief moment, I glimpse a rare vulnerability in her face, like she's not only dropped her guard but lost it altogether.

"Really?" she asks softly. "Gran? When?"

"You know she sort of took Jake under her wing after his mom left," I say, and Sadie nods. "I was Jake's best friend, which meant I got to be around her by default. Not nearly as much as Jake, but she always had a few words of wisdom for me." I chuckle. "Well, wisdom or rebuke."

"Sounds like Gran."

"She said she didn't want me to get too big for my britches just because I had a little spending money in my pockets."

Sadie scoffs. "A little spending money. That's funny."

"It *was* just spending money," I say. "Definitely more than I needed, but I was still a kid. It's not like I owned my own yacht *then*."

"Right, right, you didn't start making exorbitant purchases until you were an adult. That makes sense."

She gives my elbow a playful nudge, which takes the bite out of her words, but I get the sense there's truth in them anyway. Most women are impressed by my wealth, but Sadie couldn't be more *unimpressed*. Which would ordinarily be a good thing—I've definitely had my fair share of women interested in me only for what I own.

But for Sadie, it's more than being unimpressed. She's almost antagonistic.

And I get it. I deserve it, even. Sort of. I've gone out of my way to cultivate the very image she disdains, so I can't be annoyed that it bothers her. But I don't want Sadie to think that image is the real me—that I'm lazy and good for nothing but throwing fancy parties and wearing expensive clothes. I can't argue about having inherited a lot of money. I did. But what I inherited is only a pittance of what I've turned it into through my own hard work.

I could just show her. Explain that I really *do* work and not just on Oakley. I've made some very smart investments in technology and real estate, and those investments have served me well. The yacht was my mother's, so I've kept it for sentimental reasons, despite the cost it is to maintain it and keep it nice. But for every dollar I spend on myself, I match it in charitable giving. Fifty thousand in updates to the yacht means fifty thousand to a Savannah shelter for at-risk youth. A new car means a whole lot of meals for the food bank.

But something keeps me from saying all that to Sadie. Maybe it's my pride. Maybe it's because she's judging me without truly getting to know me. Maybe because I want her to decide to like me on her own, for the things below the surface rather than what's sitting right on top.

"I'm glad you're feeling better," I say, because changing the subject is a lot easier than thinking about how much I want Sadie to like me for *me*. "It's good to see you up and about. With your sharp wit and utter disdain for me firmly back in place."

"Oh, I didn't lose my disdain for you even while I was sick."

She grins, but it falls fast. Her attention turns to the dish in her hand, and she rubs it over and over again, long past the point where it's dry. I wonder what's going on behind those blue eyes of hers. And I wish we had the kind of friendship where I could ask, and she'd answer honestly rather than with some kind of sarcastic deflection.

Finally, Sadie breathes out a sigh and puts the plate down. "Thank you for taking care of me, Ben. I appreciate it. Even if I did tell you I hated you a time or two."

"More like ten or twenty. But who's counting?" I ask, flashing her my best smile before I lean closer and lower my voice. "It was twenty-three times. I *was* counting."

Sadie bumps my shoulder with hers. "Should I make it an even twenty-four?"

"I don't know. You might want to bide your time, ration them out. Not use up all your hatred in one fell swoop."

"Good point. Especially when I don't know how long I'll be stuck here with you."

Stuck here with you. I try not to let the words sting. They do anyway.

Setting down the towel, Sadie turns, propping a hip against the counter to face me. "For real, though, thank you. Leandra made it sound like—" She hesitates, then shakes her head.

"Like what?"

"Nothing, really. Just … thanks."

For once, her voice is free from any teasing or sarcasm, so I answer with equal sincerity, even while making a mental note to ask Leandra what she said.

"You're welcome, Sadie. I was happy to help." I pause. "My mom used to get migraines."

She meets my gaze, her big, blue eyes holding mine. All the Markham women have ocean eyes. It's the first thing you notice when you're looking at any of them. As I've gotten to know them better, I've seen the slight differences in color. Eloise's are light blue—a tropical shade, like the sea lit by the sun. Merritt's are stormier, pale blue laced with gray. Sadie's eyes are darker than either of her sisters—almost navy. Only hers arrest me like this, but that could just be because they're *hers*.

The moment stretches between us and again, I wonder what's going on behind those gorgeous navy eyes.

Then she blinks and shifts her gaze to the sink.

"Ben, the water," Sadie says quickly, taking a step back.

I look down, realizing that the way I'm holding the plate, I'm tipping water out of the sink—and right down the front of my shorts. When Tao sprayed me a few minutes earlier, he made me look like someone dumped a bucket of water on my head. Now I look like I also wet my pants.

Perfect.

"At least now my shorts match my shirt," I joke.

Sadie grins. "It's a good look on you. I should take a picture. It would go nicely on your Instagram feed." She takes the plate and dries it before adding it to the stack. "Speaking of, do you have any idea what happened to my phone? I haven't seen it since I went to bed after the party. I thought I left it next to my bed, but I couldn't find it when I showered earlier."

I wince and look away, but not so fast that Sadie misses my expression.

"What's that look?" she demands, a fierce look in her eyes. "Where is my phone?"

"Maybe you should ask German—"

"I'm asking you, Ben. What happened to my phone?"

I sigh as I hand Sadie the last plate. "Don't shoot the messenger."

"Depends on the message. I make no promises."

"Your government pal German threw it in the harbor before we left."

She freezes. "He—what? He just … threw it into the freaking ocean? Rather than, oh, I don't know—something sane and reasonable like turning off my location?"

"He said something about an IMEI?" I'm still not sure what that is, but at the time, I was more concerned that Sadie was in enough trouble to need her phone destroyed in the first place. "He still has your sim card," I say, as if this lessens the damage somehow.

"Oh great." She rolls her eyes. "Does my SIM card hold all my photos? Or all of my contacts or my calendar or, I don't know—all of my entire life?"

"You don't have your phone backed up?" I ask. As someone who works in tech, it seems like a stretch that she wouldn't.

She huffs and folds her arms across her chest. "I mean,

yes. Of course, it's backed up. But *he* didn't know that. And it doesn't make it any less of a violation."

She reaches to the stove and grabs the pans Tao used to cook whatever it is he cooked, thrusting them toward me with much more force than necessary.

Not that I blame her. I'd be livid if someone threw my phone into the ocean.

"Speaking of violations—you do realize this is technically kidnapping." She's on a roll now. Like the phone issue unlocked all her frustration and it's spilling out all at once. "I went to sleep with Oakley Island in sight and with promises of being left alone by a certain billionaire, and I woke up in the middle of the Atlantic. Not alone. I don't have the first clue where we are right now. Do you know how weird that feels? I barely talked to my sisters the other night, and now I can't even text them and tell them I'm okay. I can't explain. I'm just ..."

She presses her lips together. But I can tell she's not done, so I stay quiet, scrubbing the pan a bit harder than necessary.

"I feel like an actual prisoner."

She grabs the towel she used to dry dishes and starts rubbing it across the already clean counter, like she just needs something to do with her hands. I want to reassure her, but it's hard when I can't argue with anything she's said. When I suggested this plan to German, all I could think about was Sadie's safety and wanting to be with her. I know German and Daniels have training and are probably very good at their jobs, but they aren't me.

And there's no way they care about Sadie's well-being the way I do.

Was it selfish? Absolutely.

Do I regret it? Nope.

But I do wish I could have made this choice in a way that didn't leave Sadie like a prisoner. I also wish I'd hidden her phone away or something. By the time I realized what German was going to do, it was too late. Still—I shouldn't have even let him go in her room. Just because he's some kind of agent doesn't mean he can overstep human decency.

Says the guy who lied about being Sadie's boyfriend and ... I guess *technically* kidnapped her.

"Don't even get me started about the whole dating thing," Sadie continues. "What was that about? Why did you tell German I was your girlfriend?"

Because I want you to be. The words pop into my head so quickly, I know they must be true. Not that I'll ever say them out loud. Especially not now.

I finish washing the last pot and set it on the counter, then turn off the water and slowly turn to face her, crossing my arms over my chest. "I didn't think they would let me come if I didn't claim some personal connection to you."

She shakes her head, like my answer doesn't make any sense. "Let you come where? Onto your boat that we're all living on at *your* expense?"

"I didn't think they would want to take the yacht at all," I explain. "As soon as German realized that Frank and Lo both had already posted videos of you on social media, he talked about needing to move you, and I just ... I don't know. I panicked at the thought of you leaving. At the idea of you being out there somewhere with only German and Daniels to protect you. It was a knee-jerk reaction."

Her expression softens the slightest bit, and her lips twitch. "You didn't think that two armed agents were capable of protecting me without your help?"

I run a hand over my hair as I meet her gaze. "When you say it like that, it sounds foolish. But I was acting on instinct.

And I …" I pause, clearing my throat. "I guess I just didn't want you to leave. Especially not if you're in some kind of trouble. And for the record, you don't need to worry about your sisters. They know where you are. They were there."

Sadie's eyes narrow. "And they didn't say anything about you not being my boyfriend?"

Whoops. Sorry, ladies. I accidentally just threw you under the Sadie bus.

"They probably just felt relieved that someone they could vouch for personally would be with you."

Sadie drops onto one of the barstools that line the prep counter in the middle of the galley, then lowers her head onto her hands. She has to be feeling so incredibly overwhelmed. I resist the urge to rub the back of her neck, massaging her the way I did so often over the last two days. She wouldn't let me now—I know this without even trying my luck.

Instead of touching her, I take a seat across the counter, absently shuffling the deck of cards.

"I am sorry about your phone, Sadie."

"And about the kidnapping?" she asks, arching a brow.

"That, too."

Sort of. I feel more than a little guilty over how much I loved having Sadie all to myself for a while.

"And telling everyone I'm your girlfriend?"

I don't answer right away. Because I'm just not sorry, and I don't want to lie. I'd do it again in a heartbeat. "Can I plead the fifth?"

Sadie laughs, and the sound makes me feel buoyant. "No. We are not in a court of law."

"Or maybe we are. A court of maritime law?"

She laughs again, and it's like I've won the lottery. Shaking her head, she swipes the deck of cards and shuffles them absently. I like watching her long fingers move deftly over the cards. She keeps her nails short—not bitten but neatly trimmed. They're painted a matte gunmetal gray that I find stupidly sexy. And so *very* Sadie.

"You're ridiculous," she says.

"I won't disagree with you there. I know it doesn't change anything, and I really *am* sorry that all this happened without you knowing, but I'm still glad you're here. I like knowing you're safe."

Her smile falters as she cuts the deck. "I didn't even think about Frank or Lo taking videos at the party. Or that anyone would possibly care enough to search the internet at large for any trace of me."

I wait for a moment, then when she doesn't offer up anything else, I say, "German hasn't told me anything. Just that everything is *classified*."

She makes a face. "Sounds about right. And sounds very *German*."

"Is it too classified to share with the man offering you sanctuary aboard his yacht?"

"You mean the man who kidnapped me?" she asks, pinning me with a look.

"Even if I say please?"

She rolls her eyes at this, but I don't miss the way her lips quirk up the slightest bit. Seems like those smiles are getting easier.

"I can tell you I'm what the government calls a white hat hacker," Sadie continues. "Mostly, my job is to find the holes in security systems. Figure out how to break into stuff to prevent other real hackers from doing the same thing. But sometimes, they use me for other things too. To look for stuff. This time … I went a little too deep. I kicked the wrong anthill, so to speak."

"And now, what—someone's coming after you?" I'm not sure why, but this all sounds a lot more serious than when German talked about it. Maybe because I can see the worry etched into Sadie's features—the worry she's trying to hide.

She shrugs. "I guess they were able to track what I did back to me, and that was enough for German to think I'm in danger."

I so badly want to ask what, exactly, she did. What anthill did she kick over? My heart rate has kicked up, and I have to tell myself to breathe and make an intentional effort to tamp down the uneasiness swirling in my gut. But the idea of someone being after Sadie—I don't know how to get over that.

I at least plan to have my own conversation with German. He may not have clearance to tell me too much, but I feel like he at least owes me a little more, considering the circumstances. I also want to talk to John and let him know that things might be a little more serious than I thought. He may not look like it, but the man has serious training. I'd trust him over German any day.

I stand and hold out my hand. "Hey. Come with me? I want to show you something."

Sadie stifles a yawn. "Right now? Really? Isn't it the middle of the night?"

"Technically, but you slept all day, and your grabby little hands wouldn't let me get out of the bed, so I did too." I shake my hand. "Come on. Just trust me. I think this might make you feel better."

She purses her lips. "I did *not* have grabby hands," she says, but she stands and slips her fingers into mine as she says it.

I take a risk and entwine our fingers, giving her hand a

playful squeeze as I tug her out of the galley. "You *definitely* had grabby hands."

"I was *ill*, Benedict. If I needed head massages and the warmth of your furnace-like body, it didn't have anything to do with you, specifically."

I smirk at her over my shoulder. "Furnace, huh? So, you think I'm hot?"

"Temperature-wise," Sadie says.

"Sure," I say easily. "I'll bet that's what you meant. Only that."

She gives an exasperated laugh but doesn't pull away. We take the hallway out of the galley and step out onto the deck. The salty breeze is cool, not quite cold, and the stars are gleaming in the inky night sky. The deck skirts around the front of the yacht, and we walk hand in hand until we reach a narrow stairwell that leads up to the wheelhouse. We're anchored for the night, so I doubt we'll find Art at the helm, but I'm used to handling his grumpy demeanor if we do.

I tug Sadie up the stairs, tossing a glance over my shoulder. "It's good that it wasn't about me specifically, because I had John swap in for me whenever I got really tired."

Sadie stops, jerking my hand as she does. I don't let go.

"You did not."

I smirk. "You don't remember?"

I actually *do* wonder how much she remembers. If she knows how easily her body curled into mine, or how many times she ran her palms across my chest or slid them over my shoulders and down to my biceps, her fingers lingering on the curve of the muscle.

Her eyes flash, and she licks her lips, and I get the sense that she *does* remember. Even if she won't admit it. Or doesn't want to.

"Pretty sure I would remember *John*," she says.

I tug her up the last of the stairs, her hand still cocooned in mine. I can't help but notice that our hands fit the same way our bodies do. Perfectly.

The landing outside the wheelhouse door isn't particularly spacious, so she's standing close to me, her body near enough for me to feel the warmth of her radiating off her skin.

She tilts her head up, looking at me almost shyly. "Did you actually trade out with John?"

I lean closer. Just a little. I'm still nervous about scaring her off. "No one saw you wearing my clothes but me, Sadie," I say, voice low. "No one put hands on you but me."

And if I have my way, no one else ever will.

It could be wishful thinking, but as Sadie stares up at my face, it almost looks like she's looking at my lips. Like her eyes are darkening. Like she's thinking the same kinds of thoughts I am.

The idea sends a bolt of longing coursing through my veins. I could kiss her. Right here, with her hand in mine, her body close enough that it would only take one tiny tug to press her against me.

But I won't do it. Not yet. Not until I know she really wants it. And not just because there's an attraction here, not while she's feeling vulnerable.

She probably thinks I'm the kind of man who would kiss her just because I can. Just because she's here.

Sadly, I've kissed enough women for that exact reason that Sadie is justified in thinking so. But I won't do it with her. When I kiss Sadie, it will be because it means something.

For both of us.

I reach behind me and open the door to the wheelhouse,

stepping inside and taking a deep, steadying breath as I finally let go of her hand.

"Where are we?" she asks, following me inside.

"The wheelhouse," I answer. "This is where Art steers the yacht."

She looks over the array of controls and blinking lights, clearly not understanding why I brought her here, of all places. "And where is Art?"

"Sleeping, probably. Since we're anchored for the night. This is what I wanted to show you." I step forward and touch the largest screen in the center of the control panel. I press a few buttons, pulling up a map of our location, then zoom out enough for Sadie to recognize the land masses directly west of us.

I point at the screen. "This is where we are," I say simply. I slide my finger to the right. "This is—"

"Florida," she says, finishing my sentence. "And what's this one? Directly in front of us?"

"That's the Bahamas," I say, though it's still hundreds of miles away.

"Is that where we're going?" she asks.

"We aren't really *going* anywhere," I say. "We're cruising slowly, doing our best to avoid the most popular cruise ship routes. But if you're ever curious, you're always welcome to come up and look. You're entitled to know where you are."

It isn't much. It isn't her phone or a way to communicate with her sisters or any of the answers I can't give her because I don't have them. But it's something.

She nods and gives me a small smile. "Thanks. That actually helps."

"I'm glad. And Sadie?" I pause until her gaze is fixed on mine. "If you want to clear up the whole girlfriend thing with

German, or if you want me to, that's fine. Just let me know. The last thing I want is for you to feel uncomfortable."

A smirk I'm beginning to recognize returns to Sadie's face. "Why, Mr. King, are you fake breaking up with me?"

"I would never."

She hums. I wait for her to say more about it, perhaps to clarify where we stand, but instead, she asks, "Then are you saying you're sorry for kidnapping me?"

I grin. "Do you *want* me to be sorry?"

She doesn't answer, turning to the control panels and running careful fingers over the gleaming controls. Crossing my arms over my chest, I watch Sadie explore the wheelhouse, her face open with curiosity. And all I can think is that I'd do it all over again tomorrow if it meant we ended up right here.

TEN

Sadie

THERE'S something hypnotic about staring at the sea. All the tiny waves, shifting constantly, white peaks appearing and disappearing, the water broken up by the occasional leaping fish or diving bird. It's almost enough to make me forget the twitch in my hand whenever I reach for my nonexistent phone. Or forget the ridiculousness of my current situation.

The breeze lifts my hair, and I squeeze my eyes closed, inhaling the salty air. There really is something magical about the vastness of the ocean—not to mention enjoying it from my own private balcony.

But I can only hide out here so long.

And I'm not just talking about the scary guys who have German all concerned and hovering. At least in this moment, I'm hiding from a lot more than that.

Namely—the pesky and unwelcome loneliness that's been chasing me since I woke up alone. Without Ben.

It *should not be a thing*. But one day and night spent with his warm body near mine is apparently all it took to break me. *Ugh.*

I startle as a huge pelican lands on the railing nearby, settling in like this is exactly where he belongs.

"Dude! Where did you come from?" I demand, as though I expect the bird to answer me.

He tilts his head like he actually *wants* to answer. Or, at least, like he understands the question. Land is still nowhere in sight, so where is this guy sleeping? Or … roosting—is that the right term?

I vaguely remember seeing another pelican my first morning here. Could it be the same one? Are there a lot of pelicans this far out at sea? I study him, as though I'd ever be able to tell him apart from any other. His feathers are the weathered brown-gray of some of Oakley's oldest clapboard homes. Around one leg, he's sporting a pink tag. I lean closer, trying to see if there's any kind of identifying information, but the pelican skitters away, wings half-raised like he's ready to take off.

"Sorry, dude. The balcony's all yours."

Trying to avoid scaring him—though I'm not sure why I care about his feelings—I inch back inside, carefully closing the balcony door. The last thing I need is a bird inside my stateroom. When Lo first started renovating Gran's house, she found a pelican roosting inside the screened-in porch. I'd love to not make that particular adventure a repeated family experience.

Although … I grin at the idea of Ben finding a pelican inside his pristine yacht. Then again—he might surprise me and find it amusing. It's not like he doesn't have the money to pay for any damages.

Is it bad that thinking of Ben immediately reminds me of

how it felt to wake up with him curled around my back, his hand on my hip?

Yes—it is very, *very* bad.

We are not going to fall for the playboy billionaire, I tell myself, knowing just HOW bad off I must be if I'm talking to myself with the royal we. *We are going to remember how he dates and dumps models*—okay, the dumping part I just assumed from the articles, but it's probably true—*and that we learned the hard way that we don't like rich, preppy men.*

Think of Justin, I tell myself, a last-ditch effort to compare Ben to my awful ex.

The problem is, the more I get to know Ben, the less like Justin he seems. Every hour I'm here, I'm learning more and more about Ben that contradicts my original assumptions.

Turns out, I very much like a man spending a day tending to me while I'm out of commission with a migraine. Not to mention the way he treats—and pays—his staff. He also washes dishes. And lets his employees give him a hard time.

Justin couldn't walk across a room without seeming pretentious, and Ben seems to go out of his way to make sure that he doesn't talk down to anyone. He treats everyone as his equal, from Harriett the deli-owner to Danny the deckhand to German the SUCS agent.

Ha. I'll never not laugh over the unfortunate acronym of the government agency that so frequently hires me. I wonder if Ben has heard the acronym. I have a feeling he'd definitely joke about it. One more thing to add to the list of Ben's impressive qualities. His wit and sense of humor.

I think about his hands, gently massaging my head, the way he readied the shower for me, the concern in his eyes as he left me standing on shaking legs. Then there's his protectiveness. I mean, *yes.* Technically, it led to him kidnapping me and lying about our relationship status. But hearing him explain his reasoning, how he just couldn't imagine me hiding out in a hotel somewhere with German and Daniels hovering nearby—I can't be anything but grateful he had the forethought to make a different suggestion. That he cared about my comfort and wellbeing enough to intervene.

Still. Even with that very long list of qualifications, I can't trust myself in a relationship with Ben. I can't trust that once the shiny new *feelings* wear off, I won't grow frustrated with all the same things that drove me crazy when I was dating Justin. Not to mention the fact that I don't live in Oakley. I've always been a city girl at heart, which means my presence here is temporary. As soon as all this madness is cleared up, I'll go back to Atlanta and Ben will stay on his island, and I won't have to worry about the possibility of *feelings* ever again.

Which means the first order of business today: clear up our relationship status. With Ben and everyone else. We are not and never will be dating.

I repeat this to myself a few times just to make sure my brain gets the memo.

Sighing, I reach for my phone, only to pat my empty back pocket and remember I no longer have one. I let out an audible grumble. This is getting old fast. It's also revealing how addicted I am to my device, but that's not the point. The point is that feeling stranded *and* isolated is a really terrible feeling.

My second order of business today is to give German a piece of my mind. I hope the government is ready to fork over the cash to replace my very expensive iPhone. And then some. Maybe I can guilt—or no, *threaten*—them into getting me an upgrade. A new iPad too. Hell, a whole new system. Paid for by Uncle Sam by way of German.

After brushing my teeth, I throw open my stateroom

door. Ben's door, directly across the hall, opens immediately after.

"Oh, hello," he says, with far too much casual innocence in his voice and a flirty gleam in his eye.

He's wearing dark swim trunks with a faded white t-shirt that somehow looks ultra-casual and ultra-expensive at the same time. It also looks *way* too good on him. He's barefoot, which should make him look young or immature, like a frat boy spotted in the wild, but instead, to my clearly broken brain, it's somehow endearing.

He has nice feet, I find myself thinking.

I need to drag myself into the corner and repeat my earlier line a hundred times: *We will not fall for the playboy billionaire.*

"Were you listening for me to come out?" I ask, narrowing my eyes.

"Of course not," he says. "I just happen to have impeccable timing."

I don't believe this for a second, but also, I'm not in the mood to argue. Not with anyone but German, who should have had the decency to tell me before feeding my phone to the sharks.

Ben leans against the door jamb, folding his arms across his chest and making his biceps pop. My eyes linger there, tracing the curve of the muscle, my brain immediately reminding me that I know what it feels like to have that arm wrapped around my waist.

Maybe I'll clarify my fake relationship status ... *after* I talk to German. It can be my *second* order of business.

"Where are you headed?" Ben asks. "Breakfast? Coffee?"

"To locate German," I say grimly. "So we can discuss matters such as my phone's burial at sea."

"Ah," Ben says, shoving his hands in his pockets and

rocking back on his heels. "How about coffee first? Might help things go a little more smoothly."

"Maybe I don't want things to go smoothly," I say. "Maybe I want to unleash all of my pre-caffeinated wrath on German."

"I won't stop you," he says. "I'd rather like to watch. But after coffee."

When Ben smiles and starts off down the hall toward the galley, I follow. Because, as it turns out, I really *should* have coffee before doing other human things.

Tao is in the galley bustling about, and he looks up to offer us a quick smile. There are three cutting boards, all with various ingredients in states of being chopped or diced or *whatevered*. I don't know my culinary terms. Nor do I recognize all the vegetables he's working on. But I'm already excited about whatever we'll be eating today.

"There's a fresh pot of coffee," Tao says. "But if you want to be fancy, you can make yourself a latte or cappuccino."

"There's an espresso machine?" I ask, feeling a sense of wonder. Then I spot it.

How did I not notice it sitting on the counter when I was here last night? I recognize the brand because while I may not know my culinary things, I do know my coffee. This is a La Spaziale—the kind of machine I'd never even dream about because it's *so* expensive.

"You were holding out on me last night, Tao," I accuse.

He only laughs, and I practically float toward the machine, then run my hands along the gleaming chrome face. "Hello, gorgeous."

Ben snorts, coming up beside me and turning it on. "I have a whole yacht, and the thing you're most impressed with is the espresso machine?"

"Yes."

Tao laughs. "Knock yourself out. You know how to use it, yeah, boss?"

"I'm passable," Ben says, eyeing the machine.

"Can I?" I ask.

Ben waves a hand, then takes a seat at the counter, popping something from one of the cutting boards into his mouth. "Knock yourself out."

Tao slaps at Ben's hand. "Hey! Stay out of my way."

"What would you like?" I ask Ben.

"Can you make a cortado?"

I give him a dirty look because I know from his mischievous grin that he's testing me. "Yes. Tao?"

The chef blinks in surprise, then smiles. "Double espresso. Thanks."

I locate the milk and the beans and grinder, getting right to work. Using the machine is like second nature, despite the fact that it's been years since I've used a real espresso machine. The cheaper kind I have at home is not hardlined into the plumbing to have the right amount of pressure, so it doesn't really count. This machine, on the other hand, has nine bars, the optimal pressure for the optimal shot of espresso.

There's something so comforting about the whole process. Before I landed my current gig, I worked mornings at a local coffee shop. I love the smell and even the hissing roar of the machine. It feels like home.

"Mugs?" I ask Ben, who gets up to retrieve them, standing far too close as he does.

"Are these okay?" he asks in a low rumble near my ear.

The smell of him mixed with the smell of espresso is *killing me*. I'm human and only have so much resistance I can employ.

I give him a shove. "They'll do."

The three white mugs are all the same size—definitely not what you'd use for these specific drinks—but who cares. Tao laughs when I hand him a mug with the double espresso barely filling it a fourth of the way.

"Blame your boss," I tell him, but he downs the espresso in a few quick swallows.

"She's all yours," Tao says, tipping his mug toward the machine. "Any time you want to fire her up."

"Thank you. I suspect you'll be seeing a lot of me." I hand Ben his mug. "And here's your cortado."

Ben smiles down at his drink, where I've made a leaf pattern in the foam. "Someone's had some experience," he says.

"A little."

I finish making my flat white, creating three hearts in the foam before I clean off the machine, wiping down the milk wand and rinsing the espresso from the group heads. Satisfied the machine is as good as I found her, I lean back against the counter and take a sip, my eyes closing at the rich, creamy taste.

This is how all mornings should be.

My eyes fly open at the thought. Only to see Ben, with a small smirk on his face, staring right at my lips.

Nope—this is NOT how all mornings should be. Not on a boat. Not with Ben looking like he wants to devour me. Not even with this quality espresso.

Okay, maybe the espresso is the only part that can stay.

"Where might I find German?" I ask, and Ben hops to his feet.

"Let's go find him."

The ship is moving as we wander the decks, faster than it has been, which makes me both nervous and hopeful. If we're going somewhere with purpose instead of idling out at sea, could it mean we're going home?

Maybe all the big baddies have been rounded up and I can return to my regularly scheduled programming. Which would be amazing. *Of course*, it would be amazing. But there's a teeny tiny part of me that feels disappointed at the thought.

Because of the espresso machine, I tell myself, full-well knowing that's a lie.

After ten minutes of searching, we find German in the wheelhouse with Art.

"Morning," Ben calls out as we enter.

Art barely acknowledged the greeting, giving a curt nod before returning his attention to the controls. I'm not sure what I imagined a boat captain to look like, but Art is probably in his mid-fifties, with close-cropped dark hair and tattoos creeping up his neck from out of his crisp, white collared shirt. The beard combined with his strong expression gives me strong Captain Ahab vibes, and I can see why Danny would warn that he has no sense of humor, and I shouldn't call him *skipper*.

I, of course, am immediately tempted to do just that.

German turns, awarding us his full attention. "Feeling better?" He gives me a clinical once-over, his expression pinched.

"Yep."

This is only the second time I've been face to face with my government contact, and now that I'm functioning at full capacity, I want to laugh at myself for *ever* imagining there might be something between us. A Hemsworth he is not. Don't get me wrong—the man is big and muscular (other than his strangely scrawny neck), but there's just something about the way he carries himself and the flat expression in his eyes that makes him an immediate hard pass.

Not to mention the whole destroying-my-phone thing.

"Is it true you threw my phone into the ocean?"

"I did," he says with zero apology in his voice. "I'll return your SIM card when this is all over."

"And replace my phone?"

He only grunts at this. "We'll have to fill out paperwork, but I'm sure that can be arranged."

I can only imagine the red tape that will be involved. This is the government, after all. Nothing is ever fast.

"You had no right," I seethe.

"Just doing my job. Which is to keep you alive."

Beside me, Ben stiffens, and I even notice the way Art shoots a look back our way.

"That's a little dramatic," I say, hoping I'm right. But German doesn't respond.

My skin prickles with unease, goose bumps appearing on my arms. Ben shifts slightly closer to me, and I appreciate the warmth of his body right now.

"Isn't it?" I ask, hoping I don't sound as desperate as I feel. "A little dramatic?"

German runs a hand across his face. "We're monitoring the situation," he replies simply.

Awesome. Very helpful to my mental well-being and sense of security. "Is there anything else you can tell me?" I ask. "About *whom* you're monitoring or whether you have any more intel about them looking for me? I deserve to know, German."

He purses his lips. "The only thing that you need to know is that right now, you're safe. Just try to relax. Enjoy yourself. This will all blow over soon enough."

"What, exactly, will blow over?" Ben asks.

"And what about my sisters?" I ask, my voice tight.

"We have people keeping an eye on things in Oakley,"

German says. "But it's just a precaution. You don't need to worry."

That news sinks in a little bit. I've been so preoccupied, distracted by feeling so terrible, but if German is concerned enough to have agents watching over Eloise and Merritt—that sounds a lot more like a *real* threat and not just a precautionary one.

And German says I don't need to worry? He might as well tell me I don't need to breathe.

Art suddenly swivels away from the main panel and pulls on a headset. He mutters something, then turns to catch Ben's eye. "We have a bit of a situation, and I'm not sure what you want to do. Given our current circumstances."

Ben takes the headset from Art, and I turn my attention back to German. "So, what's the plan? How long will we be out here?"

He lets out one of his trademark longsuffering sighs. "Sadie, I don't have answers for you."

"But when will you feel like it's safe again? What, exactly, are you waiting for?"

German just stares with his cool blue eyes. I'm not typically a fan of violence, but I sure would like to wrap my hands around his tiny, little neck and squeeze more answers out of the man. Overall, this whole conversation has left me so unsettled that my lost phone is the least of my concerns.

Ben clears his throat, and I realize he's now standing with his hand on the door. "Slight change of plans," he says. "There's a stranded boat nearby who radioed for help. We're going to see what we can do."

"What boat?" German frowns. "This is not a good idea."

"I didn't ask your permission." Ben frowns right back.

"Given the circumstances, interacting with strangers, no

matter how dire their situation, is not prudent. I won't allow it."

Ben's gaze moves to me, then quickly away. "That's just it. They aren't strangers," he says.

"Friends?" I ask, wondering if there's some secret society of yacht owners who all hang out together, offering assistance as needed.

"More like ... acquaintances," Ben says. Again, he looks at me, and my gut tightens. Exactly what kind of acquaintances are we talking about?

If I had to guess? Women. THAT kind of "acquaintance."

I don't feel any particular way about it. Nope.

Not when we walk out of the wheelhouse, German and Ben arguing the whole way about safety and background checks. Not when we get on deck and see a white boat in the near distance, growing closer as the yacht picks up speed.

But I'd be lying if I said I didn't feel anything about it when we slow, the yacht coasting as we pull close, and I see three women in string bikinis on deck, jumping up and down like they're in some kind of music video.

And I definitely feel a whole *lot* of ways as the women, still jumping up and down and testing the limits of their bikini tops, squeal, "Benjy! You came!"

Ben—sorry, *Benjy*—rubs the back of his neck, which is growing alarmingly red, and shoots me a sheepish look.

Jealousy claws at my throat and I suddenly, probably irrationally, decide that maybe setting the record straight about him being my fake boyfriend doesn't need to be on the agenda today at all.

ELEVEN

Sadie

"WHO EVEN *ARE* THEY?" I ask, not even trying to hide my annoyance. Or the whiny pitch to my voice.

"No one of consequence," Leandra says with a sigh.

I'm sitting at the outdoor bar next to the yacht's small pool, while opposite me, Leandra dries off a tray of glasses with practiced precision. I'm fully in the shade, but I slip my sunglasses off my head and put them on anyway, if only to make it easier to stare at the women fluttering around Ben like a gaggle of hyped-up groupie butterflies. Gaggle is the term for geese, not butterflies. I think kaleidoscope is technically correct, but I don't think these women deserve the term kaleidoscope.

Gaggle is more fitting. Because watching them is making me gag.

They've been on the boat for less than an hour, and the fluttering *still* hasn't stopped. If I see one more manicured hand reach out to touch Ben's forearm, I might throw someone into the ocean.

Possibly I'll just throw *myself* into the ocean.

I at least find some satisfaction in the fact that German confiscated all three ladies' phones the moment they boarded.

They were probably hoping to connect to *The Oakley's* wifi, which I'm told has been disabled anyway, but German made quick work of gathering their phones. I'm sure their devices are somewhere on board, probably stowed away in German's room and sadly *not* in the ocean like mine. Either way, the women's whining made me happier than it should have. Two of the three stomped around enough to give three-year-olds a run for their money.

The two guys who boarded with them, the boat's captain and a guy I think is a brother of one of the women, didn't broach nearly as much of an argument. The captain disappeared up to our wheelhouse, probably to get a good look at the fancy instrument panel. The brother dude hasn't left German's side and looks to be pumping him for info about government agent stuff, only getting glares and deep sighs in return.

One of the gaggle laughs at something Ben says, and the way she throws her head back thrusts her chest directly toward him.

"If those things were spears, he'd be a dead man," I mutter, and Leandra laughs.

Rather than looking down at the weaponized cleavage aimed his way, Ben meets my gaze from across the deck. Something passes between us. Trouble is, I don't know him well enough to know *what*. The look just feels intense and electric. Meaningful in a way I wish I could read.

I look away first, glancing down to adjust my bikini top

not for the first time. I'm usually pretty comfortable in my body and hate that I'm feeling self-conscious now. I'm far from flawless, but I'm too pragmatic to get too caught up in worrying about it most of the time. This body is mine, and it's functional and healthy and whole. There's a lot more I'd rather do with my time than sit around wishing for longer legs or visible abdominal muscles.

Still. In my current situation, some degree of comparison seems inevitable. Honestly, it's ridiculous. All three of the women who boarded the yacht are insanely beautiful in that perfectly polished kind of way. Smooth skin. Shiny hair, which I have no idea how they're managing with all the salty humidity. By comparison, all this sea air has electrified my hair into a poof ball of riotous frizz.

The woman with the dark hair and sun-bronzed skin looks vaguely familiar—enough that I think she might be an *actual* model. It's hard not to feel ... I don't know, *shabby*.

"Really, though—who are they?" I ask Leandra. "Because I'm pretty sure I recognize at least one of them. Is she famous? The one on the end?"

"The one in the pink is Jasmine Wainwright," Leandra says. "Her family is in the hotel business. The redhead—hm. I can't remember her name, but her mother is in fashion. Some big designer up in New York."

I'm less irritated by the nameless redhead. She isn't pawing at Ben like he's her personal scratching post. In fact, she's standing at a more respectful distance, looking slightly uncomfortable by all the giggling and attempts to ensnare Ben by way of cleavage.

Leandra's face pinches slightly. "And the other is the one you probably recognize—Ana Olivera."

It clicks into place the moment Leandra says her name. That's why the woman looked familiar. The big sunglasses and the unexpectedness of her being here kept me from recognizing her at first.

"The actual supermodel," I say. The woman is famous enough that she only goes by one name: Ana.

Something feels so incredibly pretentious about not just being known by one name, but by a name with only three letters. Two of which are the same. Or maybe I'm just being petty.

Fine. There's no maybe about it: I am being petty.

What's even worse? I know why. And I refuse to even *think* the word.

Hint: it starts with the letter J and loves the color green.

"They're not so bad," Leandra says, sounding like she's trying to convince herself. "But they're not so good either. At least, not for Benedict."

I press a hand to my stomach, suddenly feeling queasy. Leandra *knows* these women. She recognizes them, can name them. That has to mean they've spent a good deal of time on Ben's yacht. With Ben. He called them acquaintances, but they're clearly more. And, by the looks of things, if they had their way, they would be *even* more.

The thought makes me irrationally possessive (and that other word I still won't admit), which makes me even more irrationally irritated.

I'm not supposed to be any of these things. I'm not supposed to *care*.

I have zero claim on Ben. And I shouldn't be surprised about a supermodel appearing out of thin air, because I *knew* this is the kind of life Ben leads. I've seen the pictures. Read the articles attaching him to dozens of women exactly like these three.

There's just a difference in knowing it and seeing it close-up. There's also a difference in how I felt about Ben when I googled him and how I feel about him now. Which is wild, as it hasn't been that long. I guess being trapped on a yacht will do that, especially when a significant number of those hours were spent having him take care of me.

Leandra's eyes shift to me, and her smile is sly. "For what it's worth, I've never seen Benedict look at any of those women, or *anyone* else for that matter, like he looks at you."

Heat gathers in my chest, and I take a deep, steadying breath. I know the look Leandra is talking about because the way Ben looks at me has practically been my undoing.

I don't know how he does it, but somehow, Ben makes me feel *seen*. Which is quite the accomplishment because I am very good at hiding.

"Are you honestly going to sit here and let those women think they might have a chance with him?" Leandra asks, tilting her head toward where it looks like Ben is trying—and *failing*—to extricate himself from the clutches of the two women and their gel-tipped nails.

"Are you telling me to stake my claim?" I shake my head. "Because you already know we're not really dating."

Leandra hums. Which only makes me want to protest more. Of course, if I do, then I'll be the lady who protests too much, and anyone who's ever studied Shakespeare knows what a mistake *that* is.

I don't admit to Leandra that when I was downstairs changing into my swimsuit, I had every intention of marching back up here and leaning into the girlfriend role—HARD. If anyone on this boat needs to believe Ben and I are together, these women definitely do.

But then I came up here and saw the women up close, my willpower immediately evaporated, and I detoured over to Leandra. Sweet, safe Leandra.

Who, right now, is still being sweet but feels a lot less

safe. Not when she's challenging me to stake a claim over a man I definitely don't have the right to.

But it isn't that easy. I've never been in competition with a supermodel—a woman who has walked on runways in Milan and New York and Paris, whose breasts defy gravity, whose genetic code probably rejected cellulite in utero. I'm all about body positivity, and on any normal Tuesday, I will feel nothing but positive about all the bodies. But the longer I sit here watching these women, the less positive I feel about *mine*.

I don't like this reality, but it *is* reality.

"If not for you, consider Benedict. He sure looks like he could use a rescue," Leandra says, tipping her chin toward Ben. "Is that the look of a man who's happy being pawed at by supermodels?"

Ben *does* look uncomfortable. In fact, his eyes meet mine, and I swear he tries to blink out some kind of message. Too bad I don't know Morse code. Good effort, though!

"Sadie, they've got nothing on you," Leandra says, her voice low. "*Go get him.*"

"Fine," I say. "But it's for Ben. Not because I need to or because I feel … or because I'm—whatever. It's for *him*."

"Keep telling yourself that," Leandra murmurs.

Buoyed by her encouragement, I stand up, adjusting the cut-offs I put on over my suit, and walk toward Ben, channeling Merritt's confidence and Eloise's charm.

As soon as I reach him, I stop thinking and let momentum carry me forward.

Ben wanted to kiss me last night—I'm almost sure of it—so I have to believe he won't be mad about this.

"Hey," I say in my softest, sultriest voice.

Ben startles a little as I slip my arm around his waist, my free hand pressing against his bare chest—a definite *claiming*. I might as well have tattooed my name on his neck.

Ben is just starting to smile as I push onto my tiptoes and kiss him right on the mouth. After all, Leandra said *go get him,* and I have never been a woman who does things by halves.

It isn't much as far as first kisses go, but that's completely intentional. I want it to look like a hello kiss. The kind of kiss you give someone when you've already kissed them a million times.

Ben's lips are warm and soft and yielding, and he kisses me back with an easy comfort that belies the fact that we've never actually done this before. There is a brief moment when it almost tips the scales past hello and more into *HEL-lo* territory, but I break away, forcing a smile I hope looks natural. On the outside, I think I pull it off.

On the inside, I am a riot of emotions. Because something sparked when our lips touched. A fuse lit. Desire ignited. And now all I can think about is kissing him again.

Not here, obviously, with three women watching us, their perfectly arched eyebrows lifted in surprise. Not for show. Not to make a point.

But just because I want to. Somewhere private though. Where we can be unhurried, where we can explore whatever it is we felt when we kissed. Because the look in Ben's eyes says he absolutely felt it too.

The voice in my head starts to protest, ringing all kinds of annoying alarm bells and shouting loud, royal-we warnings. *No! That is* not *what we want. We do not want to be alone with Ben, exploring and unhurrying anything at all.* But I've been pretty good at ignoring warnings lately, so I silence the voice and lean into Ben's embrace, smiling wide.

"Sorry it took me so long to change," I say. "I couldn't

find my swimsuit top. Somehow it wound up under your bed."

I giggle, hating myself a little as I do, because I'm pretty sure I sound like I could be part of the gaggle.

Ben must be an incredible actor because he doesn't even flinch. His grin, however, stretches to match mine. I'm going to hate myself later for this lie.

"Ah. I think I remember when that happened." His hands tighten around my waist, humor lacing his expression. "That was when you were showing me—"

I stomp on his toes to stop him from saying whatever terrible thing he was about to say. He grunts, but it sounds a little like a laugh.

"Are you going to introduce me to your friends?" I say, walking my fingers up his chest and across his collarbone.

"Of course," Ben says smoothly.

We turn so we're standing side by side, facing them, his arm around my waist and mine around his. It feels so blatant—like if we were in high school, we'd have our hands slipped into each other's back pockets while all our friends rolled their eyes behind our backs.

It also feels strangely *right*. Like this is the most logical place in the world for me to be—plastered against Ben's side with his hand warm on my bare skin. The feeling is totally *ill*ogical, seeing as how I'm in the middle of the Atlantic, on a yacht with a man I didn't even think I liked a week ago.

"This is Jasmine, Ana, and Riley," Ben says, pointing to each woman in turn.

"Nice to meet you," I say, hoping it sounds like I mean it and not like I'd really love to put them back on their broken-down yacht and leave them for the Coast Guard.

Or the sharks.

"And this is my *girlfriend*, Sadie Markham," Ben says, making my breath catch.

I know this isn't the first time he's called me his girlfriend, but it's the first time I've heard him make the claim. And it has more of an impact than I want to admit. Even to myself. Mostly, it fills me with a sort of peaceful confidence. Like he's just given me permission to settle into my own skin and forget about comparing myself to any of these women, perfect though they may appear. I know I don't need his approval to be happy with myself. But the validation still feels good. Benedict King is choosing *me*.

I force my gaze toward the three women—I cannot keep staring into Ben's eyes without kissing him again—and try my hardest to give each of them a warm and sincere smile. I'm not a mean girl. I can't blame these women for being hot and wealthy or famous and, in two out of three, fascinated with Ben. Even if I only relate to the last one—despite my best efforts.

In return, I get two fake smiles and one that actually looks genuine. The latter is from Riley—the redhead who wasn't trying to hit on Ben.

Not surprising. But so long as Jasmine and Ana respect the boundary Ben just created with the word *girlfriend*, they can lounge by the pool in their tiny bikinis all they want. We don't have to be friends, but we can coexist on this yacht until we dump them back on land or whatever the plan is. Except ... I'm not actually sure what the plan *is*.

Ana of single-name fame is the first one to respond. "Wow. Someone actually managed to lock you down." She shakes her head. "That's hard to believe."

My grip on Ben's waist tightens, even as my uncertainty grows. Isn't this why I *didn't* want to consider a relationship with Ben in the first place? I don't want to think about him having hundreds of relationships, casual or otherwise, with other women. I especially don't want to think about him with *these* particular women.

Was he actually ever *with* Ana or Jasmine in a romantic sense?

Forget the bravado that made me kiss Ben moments ago. If my imagination starts playing out scenarios, I'm liable to scurry back to my stateroom and hide for the rest of the day. Or longer. Maybe I can hang out with the pelican on the balcony.

Ben saves me from my thought spiral when he leans down and presses a soft, lingering kiss against my temple. One I feel all the way down to my pinky toes.

"I'm smart enough to recognize something real when I find it," he says, his gaze warm and genuine as he looks me over. "And to hold onto it with everything I've got."

His voice is low, and I get the sense he said those last words just for me.

"I'm really happy for you guys," Riley says. "It seems like you make a really great couple."

I like Riley. Riley respects boundaries. Riley doesn't call Ben *Benjy*. Riley can stay on the boat.

Jasmine, on the other hand, doesn't even try to hide her sneer. "Sally, was it?" she says. "How is it that you came to meet Ben? I've never heard of you before."

I understand this to mean: *you clearly aren't in my society circles, so how did you snag a billionaire?*

So ... not mean girls, but mean *women*. Fabulous.

"It's *Sadie*," I correct, holding Jasmine's gaze until she flinches and looks away. "And yeah, I don't think our paths would cross. I stay pretty busy with my work."

"What kind of work do you do?" Riley asks. I can tell she's trying to steer the conversation and keep things positive, and I appreciate the effort, but I'm not sure it's doing much good.

"I work in tech," I say, sticking to the vague answer I always give, even if, right now, I'm tempted to toss around my credentials. Though I doubt Jasmine would be impressed even if I did.

Ben's fingers lightly squeeze my waist. "Sadie has a PhD in applied and computational mathematics," he says. "From MIT."

My eyes jump to Ben's face, but he's staring Jasmine down like he's Superman ready to fry her with his laser eyes. And I don't hate it.

I didn't even know Ben *knew* about my degree. I don't talk about it much—partly because I don't like it when people make it a big deal or treat me differently because of it. I mean, getting into MIT is kind of a big deal. So is receiving a PhD from there. I'm pretty dang proud of myself. But talking about it often feels braggy.

The other reason I don't like to talk about it is because my memories of MIT are tainted by Justin. I'll do whatever mental gymnastics are necessary to avoid thinking about that dumpster fire of a relationship. And most especially, the person I *became* in that relationship. I don't like thinking about her. MIT Sadie sucks. She was naive and stupid—despite being *so* smart—and embarrassingly codependent, drunk on the attention of an older (and off-limits) man.

So, my desire to avoid MIT talk sometimes means giving vague, textbook answers about what I do or what my qualifications are.

But the warmth spreading through me at Ben's praise—this feels *good*. I don't know how he knows—probably one of my sisters told him—but I *like* that he knows. And I like that he's bragging about me.

"My brother went to MIT," Riley says. She offers me a friendly smile. "When were you there?"

We spend a minute talking about graduation years—her brother is a few years older than I am so we didn't cross paths—then Riley mentions her own degree program. She's working on a master's in public health, and she clearly feels passionate about it. This makes me like her even more.

"Shall we eat?" Ben asks, then slides his hand away from my waist.

I'm about to be more disappointed than I want to admit, but then he links our fingers together and tugs me toward the food. Jasmine and Ana drop back, probably to talk behind my back *literally*, but Riley keeps pace.

"So, you two met through mutual friends?" she asks as we move to the bar, where Tao has set out an array of finger foods.

I'm not sure how the chef magically has enough to feed five extra people, but he seems to have adjusted things just fine. It's still a little early for lunch, but I'm only running on the espresso I had earlier, and my stomach rumbles at the sight of all the food. I look over the fancy cheeses, cuts of meat, tiny crackers, and an assortment of vegetables. There are even some little radish roses for garnish. Or for eating? Maybe both?

Ben gives my hand a squeeze before letting go and handing me a tiny plate with the kind of smile that makes me a whole different kind of hungry. *Focus on the food, Sadie*, I tell myself. *Not the snack of a man you really aren't dating.*

I start with some bruschetta—warm bites of toasted bread topped with diced tomatoes, cheese, herbs, and what looks to be a balsamic drizzle.

"How we met—that's kind of a long story," I answer, glad plating some food will give me time to think.

Ben and I "met" for the first time on a video call. I was on the phone with Eloise who was talking in person with Ben, who stole the phone. I poked fun at him about his rich boy looks and his ridiculously pretentious name, while he gave Eloise a hard time about not picking the paint colors approved by the historical preservation society.

The preservation society that, of course, Ben runs—being the owner of the island and all.

He and I exchange a glance, and it looks from his expression like he's remembering our first meeting too. Fondly.

"Sadie's sister is married to my best friend," Ben says, nudging me forward. I didn't realize I'd slowed down the line by stopping to sample the bruschetta. His hand on the small of my back sends goose bumps skittering up my bare skin, and I wonder if he notices. If he feels me reacting to his touch.

His pinkie dips just barely into the top of my cutoff shorts —still inches above my bikini bottoms, but that tiny movement has my knees wobbling. I take a big step forward, and his hand drops. Relief and disappointment arm wrestle somewhere inside me.

"We've known each other for a few years now," I add. Which is almost true if we're rounding up. Even if we've only been around each other in passing, and mostly were sniping at each other when we spent more than two minutes in the same room. "The chemistry was instant," I say, though I really mean the kind of chemistry that starts fires, "but this part is relatively new."

"New," Ben adds, "but very, *very* serious."

The look he gives me is a challenge, but right now—I'm not arguing. Ana gives a tiny frown, which makes me stand a little taller and feel slightly more secure. Maybe the romantic relationship between Ben and me isn't real, but there *is* something between us. Something warm and good.

Ben's eyes darken as his gaze drops to my lips. Warm and good and ... combustible.

The thing is, I have always given Ben a hard time. We've argued about everything from the way he dresses to his wealth to the way he's always just assumed that I would eventually want to date him. But no matter how much I *say* he irritates me, I always come back for more.

Because you like it, dummy. You like HIM.

This time, the voice in my head sounds a lot like Grandma Genevieve. I smile at the realization and concede her point. I do like him. And I do like the way we've always sparred with each other.

Ana and Jasmine retreat to the opposite side of the deck once they have their food—they are clearly done with the likes of me—but Riley sits down directly across from Ben, who is nestled in beside me, our thighs touching.

We fall into easy conversation. It's nice to have someone to talk to, someone to distract me from the way her friends are eyeing my (fake) boyfriend like they're ready to pounce and steal him away from me. But it's also nice to *not* think about the fact that I'm technically in hiding. That two armed government agents are in constant communication with the mainland, keeping tabs on what could be a fast-approaching threat. Or a whole lot of nothing.

"So, the government agents," Riley eventually asks. "Am I allowed to ask what that's about? Are they FBI?"

My gaze skirts to Ben, whose face remains calm and impassive. "Unfortunately, you aren't allowed to ask," he answers easily. "But I appreciate you being a good sport about your phone."

She shrugs. "It would have been useless anyway, since

your wifi is down. He certainly seems to be talking on *his* phone a lot though." She motions toward German, who is standing across the deck, and is, in fact, yammering into a phone. Not a cell phone, though. It's bigger. A little boxier.

"That's *The Oakley's* satellite phone," Ben says. "But don't ask him to use it. He'll get very grumpy if you do."

An uneasy silence settles over the table, but what else is there to say? We can't really pretend like there's nothing going on, but we can't really explain what *is* going on either.

"Right. Well, I hope everything works out okay." Riley's gaze settles on Ben. "And that you aren't in any real sort of trouble."

Of course, she would assume Ben is the reason the agents are on board. It's his boat, and he's the one with all the money. If spy movies have taught me anything, it's that billionaires with fancy yachts are much more prone to involvement with criminals than unassuming blond women who work in tech.

Ben doesn't correct Riley, something that adds a few more points on the *pro* side of my Dating Ben For Real pro/con list. He's already done so much to cover for me, to keep me safe, and now he's putting his own reputation on the line.

"Thanks for your concern," Ben says. "I appreciate it."

Eventually, Riley excuses herself to find her friends, who have already gone down to the staterooms Ben offered them —ones, I was happy to learn, that are on the opposite end of the yacht.

German and Daniels have disappeared too, and Leandra is nowhere to be found, so, at least for now, Ben and I are alone on the deck.

The cloudless sky is a brilliant blue overhead, and the water is a bright, sparkling turquoise. A breeze lifts the hair from my neck, and for a brief moment, I almost forget that this moment isn't actually real. I'm not *really* vacationing in the south Atlantic with my uber-rich boyfriend, eating fancy food and lounging on the deck of his superyacht.

This is all nothing more than a mirage. A sound stage in a movie studio. A silly hoax to cover up my not-so-silly actions.

"Hey." Ben nudges my knee, then scoots his chair a little closer, leaning forward onto his knees in an effort to catch my gaze. "What's going on in that big, beautiful brain of yours?"

I give my head a little shake, partly to keep Ben's sweet words from burrowing too deeply. "Nothing, just … thinking, I guess." I look out at the view one more time. "It's beautiful out here."

"You give the scenery a run for the money," he says, his smile flirtatious.

I roll my eyes. "Stop it."

"Stop what? You're the one who kissed *me*, Sadie. If I'm your boyfriend, I'm allowed to call you beautiful as often as I want."

"*Fake* boyfriend," I say. "And there's no one here you need to convince."

"Beautiful," he says again, this time giving me an appraising look. His tone is playful, but there's an undercurrent that feels wholly serious.

"Ben, come on." My protest is half-hearted.

Because I like the way Ben's words sound the opposite of half-hearted. They sound like he means them. Like if I asked him to take away the *fake* and make this thing between us real, he would agree in an instant.

"Speaking of kisses," Ben continues, his voice dropping low. "That wasn't exactly the first kiss I imagined for us."

"You've *imagined* our first kiss?" I say through a huff of laughter.

"Since the first time I met you," he says without breaking my gaze.

"That's an awfully long time." My voice catches as heat pools in my belly. Does he have to look at me so intensely? It feels like his gaze alone could singe the clothes right off my body.

He stands up, slowly, moving with intention and giving me more than enough time to tell him to stop. I don't.

Leaning forward, he puts his hands on the arms of my chair and drops close, his body hovering over mine.

"A very long time," he says. "Feels like forever."

The air crackles between us, electricity zipping through my body, making me feel flushed and jittery. If I don't kiss him—a *real* kiss this time—and soon, it's possible I might spontaneously combust.

Either that, or I really *will* need to throw myself into the ocean if only to cool off.

I lick my lips and look up at him. "Well, do it, then. Show me how you imagined it, Ben."

His eyes darken, and his gaze drops to my lips. My own lips part in anticipation, and I have to fight the very real urge to grab the man and pull him these last few inches. I may not have spent much time imagining a kiss with Ben, but I sure am now.

Just when I'm sure he's going to close the gap between our mouths, Ben scrapes his teeth over his bottom lip and gives his head the tiniest shake. The heat in his eyes turns to something a whole lot more ... rational.

I don't like *rational*. I kicked my own rational to the curb a while ago and was ready to go full-tilt *irrational* with this man.

Now, I'm ready to melt out of embarrassment instead of attraction, but then Ben leans forward and presses a lingering kiss to my cheek, just by the curve of my jaw.

"Not here," he whispers. "And not yet."

He stays close, his mouth brushing across my skin, and I arch my neck, giving him access, willing him to kiss me again.

Definitely here, I silently beg. *Absolutely yet.*

Ben obliges—though still not on the mouth—kissing once, twice, three times over the curve of my jaw and grazing his lips down the side of my neck in a slow slide. It's the most blissful kind of torture, and when he pulls away, standing to his full height, I immediately miss his nearness. And his lips.

When I kissed him, it was for show. To warn the other women off. To stake some sort of claim—if even a fake one—and save Ben.

But now I've opened Pandora's box, and there's no way I can shove all these feelings back inside. Forget my concerns about Ben being too similar to Justin. Forget my job and the stupid bad guys who may or may not be hunting me down. Forget German and Daniels and all of it.

I'm tired of denying that I *like* Ben. I do. I like him. And owning that emotion is the most terrifying thing I've done in a very long time.

Ben's eyes are fixed on my mouth as he backs away. I want to call him out, to tell him he's a tease or a coward—anything to get him back over here and kissing me.

As though he can hear all these unspoken words, he grins and says, "Soon, Sadie girl. But not yet."

And then he leaves me alone on the deck, simmering with equal parts pent-up desire and rage.

TWELVE

Ben

WAS what I just did to Sadie cruel? I mean ... not comparatively. If we're talking about actual, legitimate cruelty.

But maybe it wasn't the *wisest* or *kindest* thing ever to confess how long I've thought about kissing her and then NOT kiss her. Especially when she clearly wanted me to.

Here's the thing, though: I can't say with certainty that if I kissed Sadie for real, she wouldn't immediately regret it.

She isn't sure about me yet, even if she felt *physically* sure in the moment. I don't doubt she wanted the kiss, wanted *me*. Which felt really, really good.

But I suspect if I'd kissed her then—*poof!* Her wanting would be done and then gone. Over. The end. While I'm not opposed to a little instant gratification sometimes, with Sadie, I want *more*.

I don't just want *a* kiss. A *fake* relationship. A fling on a yacht when she's hiding out from what sounds more and more like legitimate trouble.

I am a patient man. And I can wait for our kiss to be more.

And if the waiting makes Sadie want me more, well, that's okay too. There's something to be said for anticipation and delayed gratification.

It's anticipation I'm thinking of while getting dressed for dinner. My hair is still shower-damp as I adjust the collar of my shirt. I chose a simple blue button-down, tucked into khaki shorts with a belt. It's a little nicer than what I typically wear around the boat. But then, with all the added guests, tonight will be something of a dinner party.

Am I also dressing to impress Sadie? I'd be a fool to deny it when literally everything I've done the past few days has been geared to impress her. Or more—to just make her like me.

As to whether it's working or not ... ask me in a few days.

I knock on Sadie's door but there's no answer. "Sadie?" I call, but after a moment, I decide she must have already gone to dinner.

I head to the dining room alone, hearing laughter and music before I even enter. I'm the last to arrive. Even Danny is here, though he probably shouldn't be. At times, I treat my staff so much like friends that they—or I—forget their roles.

Danny clearly got wind of which guests we happened to pick up earlier and wanted to meet Ana. He's currently staring at her like she's a fantasy come to life, which only makes her preening more insufferable.

I should probably cut the guy some slack. It's not every day you have the chance to hang out with an actual Brazilian supermodel. Danny wasn't working for me the last time Ana spent time aboard, so I get it. She's beautiful—in a purely aesthetic sense. But she doesn't do anything for me. She didn't back when she wanted to hook up either. Despite what the tabloids report, I do have some standards. And they include not getting involved with people who have the personality of a honey badger.

Danny doesn't seem to care about personality, and I watch him practically bend over backward to bring Ana a glass of wine and a bottle of water.

"Is this room temperature?" I hear her ask.

I resist the urge to roll my eyes as Danny nods with all the eagerness of a puppy. He must feel the weight of my gaze because he glances my way, startles, then throws Ana one more look before heading off to do whatever he's actually supposed to be doing. Which does *not* include hitting on my unexpected (and unwanted) guests.

Sadie is standing by the doors to the walk-out patio, talking to Leandra and Riley, laughing at something one of them says. She is pure beauty when she laughs, her eyes sparkling and her hair dancing around her face in soft waves. I like Sadie best when she's lit up with that spark—the one that comes from somewhere deep within. The same one that makes her unafraid to give me a hard time, even from the moment we met. Somehow, she seems more alive, more vibrant than normal people, and it's this extra alive-ness that colors her beauty in such rich hues.

Okay, I'm starting to sound a little too besotted. But then, who cares? I've never gone all-in on a woman. Never had a woman who even made me consider it. Now ... I don't want to consider what will happen if I can't win Sadie over for real.

When she sees me, the laughter dies, and another look takes its place. Determination. Maybe mixed with a little irritation as her eyes narrow.

Good. She's right where I want her to be. I wink, which

makes her jaw clench and her eyes flash. As I see her break away and head toward me, I move in the opposite direction, turning my back on her as I move to the bar. I start to pour myself a bourbon.

Three ... two ...

"Well, someone's looking pleased with himself tonight," Sadie says from behind me.

I turn, glass in hand, blinking as though I'm surprised she's there. Not like I was hoping she'd come after me.

"Evening, Sadie," I say, ignoring her words and the challenge in her eyes. "You look ... stunning."

"Stop it with the flattery," she says, but she can't hide the way the corners of her mouth lift.

I take a sip of my bourbon, feeling the burn move steadily down my chest. "Is it still considered flattery if it's true?"

"How can I know if *anything* you say is true, Mr. King?"

"I've never lied to you, Sadie," I tell her. "And I never will."

Then, casually, I give her a slow once-over. She's wearing a light blue sleeveless sundress that deepens the blue in her eyes. The neckline is not quite deep enough to be scandalous, just enough to be intriguing, and I find my gaze snagging on her collar bones.

Are clavicles supposed to be sexy? I've never thought so—but right now, I'm thinking of tracing her delicate collar bones with a finger, then following with my lips. And it's possibly the hottest thought I've ever had.

I tear my gaze away, moving it to Sadie's shoulders. They are the most delicate pink from our time outside today, matching the rosy tint in her cheeks. Which could be from the sun or just a blush. As I suspected after seeing her shower-damp hair the other day, her waves are wilder and more pronounced, barely skimming those alluring collarbones.

I finally allow my gaze to lazily travel from her lips to her blue, blue eyes, darkened with anger or maybe a mix of anger and desire.

"Like I said—*stunning*."

"You are an infuriating man," she says through clenched teeth.

"Isn't he though?"

Seizing an opportunity the way a jungle cat might spot a gazelle separated from the herd, Jasmine steps up beside me and flutters her eyelash extensions at me. I immediately shift toward Sadie, but Jasmine follows, setting a possessive hand on my arm.

"I think that's part of his charm," she says. Her voice drops to something throatier. "It's a special talent he has—to make women want him and want to kill him at the same time."

I half expect Sadie to show a feral display the way she did earlier when she claimed me with a kiss. I *hope* she does.

Instead, she laughs. Fake, but I bet Jasmine can't tell.

"He does excel at that special skill," Sadie says with a smirk. "Did they teach you that at billionaire school, *Benjy?*"

"It was a prerequisite for graduation," I say, downing the last of the bourbon and setting my empty glass on the bar. Jasmine's hand tightens on my arm, and she steps closer, brushing her body against mine.

"Always *so* funny," Jasmine says, and her laugh grates on my eardrums.

"Billionaire humor—another requirement for graduation. Excuse me," I say, intending to slip away.

But Sadie links her arm through mine as I step out of

Jasmine's clutches. "Not so fast, Mr. King," Sadie murmurs. "You're not leaving me alone to deal with the wolves."

I chuckle as we move toward the table. "Wolves, huh?"

"What would you call them? Oh, right—*acquaintances.*"

"Wolves might be better. Is Riley at least being nice? You two seemed to hit it off. She's not so ... you know."

"Oh, she's great. I'm not including Riley when I talk about the wolves. Just the other two."

Tao will be serving dinner any minute now, and I want to choose our seats. I pull out a chair for Sadie, then push it in as she sits, letting my fingertips trail over her shoulder. I don't miss the little shiver Sadie gives at my touch, or the way the pink in her cheeks darkens to more of a red.

I seat myself to Sadie's right, at the head of the table. Not because I think I'm so important, but because it will be easier at the head to keep my distance in case Jasmine or Ana try to move close again.

Sadie watches me as I sit down, her gaze tracking my every move. Is she thinking of my promise to kiss her later? I know I am.

Patience, I tell myself.

I don't want to be demeaning with animal comparisons, but my strategy in this situation feels a little like fishing. I'm dangling the bait in front of Sadie, every so often moving the line to catch and keep her attention. But it isn't about teasing her or tricking her into taking the bait. I'm waiting for her to figure out she wants to be caught in the first place.

Because I'm not interested in throwing her back.

Philip, Jasmine's brother, takes the seat on my other side, earning a scowl from Jasmine and a pout from Ana. But once everyone is seated, the distance and number of people at the table make it easy to ignore them both.

Tao and Leandra serve the meal—a beautifully cooked red

snapper with saffron rice, a vegetable souffle, and a crab bisque. As we all start to eat, I nudge Sadie's foot, surprised when she slips off her shoe and rests her bare foot on top of mine. I expected her to kick me away. Her touch under the table is enough to distract me, and I end up dropping my spoon in the soup and splattering my shirt.

Sadie's smirk tells me she knows exactly what distracted me, and she's more than a little pleased.

It feels like we've settled back into what we know—a deliciously addicting game of give-and-take, push-and-pull. I can only hope that this kind of game will end with two winners.

Things could be so good between us.

Does Sadie see this? Does she know that I'm not just playing around?

Okay, I'm playing a *little*. But only because this is a long game, and I think with Sadie, giving her time is the best thing. Well—giving her time while also making her wait. And pushing her buttons.

I only hope she understands that in the grand scheme of things, I'm taking this—taking *her*—very, very seriously.

Sadie's toe runs across my ankle, and my fork clatters against my plate.

Okay. I might have to shorten the timeline on the long game I'm playing. This woman is going to be the end of me. Maybe we just need to have a conversation before we kiss again, before we kiss for *real*. I could just lay it on the line and tell her how I really feel, what I really want. At least then, she'll know where I stand.

On the flip side, knowing where I stand might scare her all the way back to Atlanta. But that's a risk I'm going to have to take.

Still, the thought of that kind of a conversation—it would

be the first of its kind for me which makes it more than a little terrifying.

But what's the saying—do it scared? And then there's the other one about nothing worth doing ever being easy. Put them both together, and ... I guess I should do this while scared and because it's not easy? Or something like that.

In keeping with my plan to tantalize Sadie into a state of complete abandon, or maybe because I just can't help myself, I don't stop touching her through dinner. I lean close enough to drape my arm over her shoulders, then let my fingertips drag over her skin as I pull back. I brush my knuckles over the back of her hand when she reaches for her spoon. I tuck a strand of hair behind her ear. I lean close enough that my lips graze her cheek when I murmur something to her.

I can see the resulting flush in her cheeks, the dilated pupils, the quick intakes of breath. And it's doing just as much for me, making the ache for her as real and palpable as a bruise, if a little more pleasant.

As Danny clears our plates and serves up coffee before dessert, Ana taps her glass with her knife. So hard I'm relieved the glass doesn't break.

"I'd like to offer up a toast to Benjy for saving us," she says.

"Here, here," Philip says, not waiting for her to finish before taking a swig of his vodka tonic.

I keep forgetting he's here. Partly because I'm focused on Sadie, and partly because he's barely spoken a word at dinner. So long as he doesn't cause issues or hit on Sadie, I don't mind him being here. *Or mind him getting drunk*, I think as he drains his glass.

"To Benjy!" Jasmine adds. "Always up for a good time"—I don't miss the way Sadie tenses at this—"and helping a damsel in distress."

"Sometimes two damsels at once," Ana says, shooting me a decidedly evil smile.

Sheesh. Really laying the lies and implications on thick there, ladies.

But Sadie may actually believe their very untrue insinuations, which are clearly intended to upset her. Based on the way she pulls her foot from mine and won't look at me, it's working.

I stand, raising my own glass. "No need to thank me for coming to your assistance," I start. "It's what any decent man would do for anyone in need of help." Placing a hand on Sadie's shoulder despite the way she stiffens, I gently brush her bare skin with my thumb, silently begging her to hear me. "And definitely no need to give me credit for things I have absolutely *never* done nor *want* to do."

Sadie looks up at me then, eyes searching, and I give her a slight nod. Relief is palpable in the way her shoulders drop.

I raise my glass to my lips, eyes still on Sadie's. "Here's to old acquaintances, leaving the past behind, and fresh beginnings," I say.

We all lift our glasses then, even Philip with his empty one, and I don't miss Sadie's soft smile, just for me.

AN HOUR LATER, dinner has ended and everyone has gone their separate ways. Including Sadie, who, after giving me a wink, linked arms and left with Riley to go look at the stars.

Okay, then. Guess I am not as alluring as I thought. Or maybe Sadie's just giving me a taste of my own medicine.

Should I be surprised? Nope. I can't say I'm even that disappointed. I mean, yes—I'd like Sadie to be out here on my balcony with me, preferably in my arms, but I appreciate that she is a woman who will never make things easy.

And as a man who's had a lot of easy things, I appreciate this quality more than I can perhaps articulate.

Just in case, I left my door cracked and the balcony slider open as well. Call me an optimist, though I'm really, *really* hoping Ana or Jasmine don't take advantage of my open doors.

I've always loved this balcony, which is private and spacious and has its own small hot tub. Really, I love this whole boat, something I'm loath to admit considering how over-the-top it is. Beyond the money and the expense to maintain and keep up, it guzzles gas and requires a full crew to run it.

Oakley is home, and I don't see that ever changing, but I don't like feeling constrained. Trapped. Static. The boat gives me the sense of movement my inner restlessness sometimes needs. And out here, with the stars pin-pricking the deep velvet sky, I'm always filled with a sense of calm. A surety of my place in this world, of my purpose, that I don't feel anywhere else.

Would Sadie ever want to live on Oakley? I know she relocated from DC to Atlanta this year—is she a city girl at heart? Would life on the island be too small, too static for her? Would the yacht be enough to give her what Oakley lacks?

"There you are."

Sadie's voice startles me. I may have left all the doors open as an invitation, but I wasn't sure she'd really take it. I stand, my chair making an inglorious screech across the decking as I turn to face her.

With her arms crossed over her chest, feet bare and eyes

flashing, she looks furious and beautiful. *My* kind of beauty—the kind with a wild edge.

"Hey." I slide my hands in my pockets, feigning a cool I don't feel as my heart hammers in my chest. "Are you—"

I don't get to finish because Sadie steps forward, places both hands on my chest, and shoves me.

She's surprisingly strong, sending me back against the rails. I'm grateful they're sturdy. Going overboard at night has never been on my bucket list. I laugh, stretching my arms wide on the balcony rail, as though I meant to be here, leaning casually as I watch to see what she'll do next.

"You are the absolute worst," Sadie says, stepping closer. We're toe to toe, her face tilted up toward mine and her spicy vanilla scent invading my space.

"You'll have to be specific," I say, smiling lazily, the opposite of how my heart feels. It's gone from hammering to sprinting. "The worst at what?"

She leans closer. "Everything."

"Hm. Would you mind giving me an example? Whenever I receive feedback about my performance or character, I like to have tangible things I can improve on."

Sadie's eyes narrow. "You know exactly what you've been doing."

I shrug. "Enlighten me."

"First of all, you—"

This time, I interrupt her *without* words.

In a move too swift for her to see coming, I cup her face in my hands and fuse my mouth to hers. There is not even a millisecond of resistance from her. Instead, it's more like we instantly elevate this faux fight with words into a different battle with mouths.

It's urgent and passionate, full of fire and fight. She tastes like wine and salt and summer days. Her lips are soft and pliant, but there is no surrender in this kiss. It's all the challenge I've come to crave, wrapped up in the most delicious package.

Sadie lets me lead for a moment before she places her hands on my hips, turning me and pretty much shoving me into a chair. She topples into my lap right after, landing heavily and with a sharp exhalation of breath.

"I don't actually think you're the worst," she says against my mouth, barely breaking the kiss to speak.

"No?" I slide my hands from her cheeks to her jaw, then around to her hair.

"You might actually be the best," she murmurs, nipping at my bottom lip. "But don't get a big head about it."

"I won't," I promise. "Hearing you compliment me only makes me want to live up to your words."

This must be the right thing to say, because Sadie groans and kisses me with renewed vigor, angling her head to kiss me deeper, pressing her chest more firmly to mine.

While one of my hands plays with her hair like I did the other day, I let my other trail down her spine. She shivers under my touch and moves closer still, the warmth of her body like a fiery furnace against me.

Her waist is tiny, especially next to the curve of her hips, and I flatten my palm against her lower back. She kisses me softly, teasingly, pulling back before coming back in hungrily. Sadie kisses the way she does everything—unabashed and fierce.

It's so very Sadie, which makes it all the better.

"I should have asked permission before kissing you," I tell her, trailing open-mouthed kisses across her jaw and down her neck.

"Consent is sexy," she says. "But you had mine earlier. I never took it back."

"Are you sure? Because I seem to remember you telling me I'm the worst," I say, blowing lightly on a spot I just kissed on her neck. Sadie shivers in my arms.

"And then I said you're the best." She turns my head so she can kiss a spot just below my jaw. Now I'm the one shivering. "Don't make me take it back."

"Never," I promise.

Time stretches slow and warm as our kisses move from passionate to teasing and lazily indulgent, then back again. I am a firm believer in the idea that not enough people give kissing its due these days, too much in a hurry to move past it to something else. But I'm happy camped right here. I could hold her like this—kiss her like this—all night. It's only when I catch Sadie yawning that I hoist her into my arms and say, "Time for bed, Sadie girl."

When I walk past my bed, still cradling her to my chest, Sadie makes a grumble of protest. But I don't stop until we're right in front of her door. I slowly lower her to the ground, smiling as her confused eyes meet mine. I'm sure she's thinking about the night she spent in my bed.

Believe me, I'm thinking about it too.

With gentle fingers, I trace the slope of her nose and then the bow of her top lip. Then I follow the same path with my mouth.

"Despite what you might think about me based on my reputation—much of which was incorrectly inferred—I would very much like to take things slowly." I pause. "With you."

"How slowly?" Sadie asks, biting her lip.

Not slowly at *all* when she's looking at me like that. But I force myself to stay firmly planted where I am, drawing my hands up her arms until they rest lightly on her shoulders.

"Slow enough that I won't scare you away." I lift my

hands and push them into my pockets, because if I don't, I'll keep touching her, and then I'll never be able to walk away. "This isn't about the chase for me, Sadie. I want you for real." It isn't the whole conversation I had planned. But it's a start.

I give her one more lingering kiss right next to her mouth and then, using every bit of discipline I possess, I walk across the hall to my own room. Alone.

THIRTEEN

Sadie

FUN FACT: There are a lot of places to hide on a yacht.

The walk-in pantry just off the galley is fairly large and smells like garlic. The chances of someone walking in on you are slim. But not zero—as I learned when Tao opened the door and screamed like a teen girl in a horror movie when he saw me. At least by that time, Ben had left the galley, so it was safe to come out.

Next to the wheelhouse, there's a room full of life vests and life buoy rings. Counting them took a whole twenty minutes. And I would have started over and counted them again if German hadn't walked in, looking suspicious and demanding to know what I was doing. He seemed to be under the impression I was plotting an escape, I think, because the grumpy giant lumbered around behind me for a while, making it impossible to hide in any more small, unused spaces.

At the end of a very long hallway one level below my stateroom, I find an empty theater room with very comfortable recliners next to what looks like some sort of meditation room. These rooms were left off my original tour, which must have only hit the highlights, but they're lovely and comfortable and both unoccupied. They're also entirely too obvious if my purpose is to *not* be found by the one man who knows about every single room on this enormous boat.

Is there a crow's nest on this thing? If so, I'd happily climb up there if I didn't think German would follow and drag me back down.

Eventually, I shake the gloomy agent trailing me and wind up on the far back end of the yacht, the end without the pool and the huge wraparound deck where, based on the splashing and laughter I heard while sneaking around, everyone else is hanging out. I'm sure there are official nautical terms to describe where I am, but I have no idea what they are. I'd look them up if I could, but that would require my phone.

Or the man I'm presently trying so hard to avoid.

There's a smaller deck back here, but it doesn't look like it's used nearly as frequently. It's closer to the water though and has the retractable diving board Danny mentioned. *Aka the plank.*

The only downside to the solitude I've finally managed to find is that now, I'm alone *with my thoughts*. And honestly, I'd like to avoid those as much as I want to avoid Ben.

Why, exactly, am I avoiding the man I kissed last night?

Desperate times call for desperate measures—that's why. And I am *beyond* desperate to take a minute to figure out how I'm feeling. Without having to face Ben.

Which, fine. Call me a coward.

But it's more than just the kissing. Last night when he

walked me to my door, Ben said he wants this—*us*—for real. And that triggered some capital F feelings and some capital F fears that I'm not sure how to handle.

Up until this week, faux fighting with Ben whenever I'm on Oakley has only ever been a game. A harmless way to flirt. I've never given the idea of dating him any *real* consideration. Because aside from how fun our verbal sparring is, he has always been everything I'm not interested in. Polished. Monied. Handsome and confident and just arrogant enough.

In short, Ben always shared way too much in common with Justin. The wealth, the preppy dress, the smug charm was all so familiar. The deeply instilled sense of entitlement that comes standard with this kind of upbringing. Entitled to things, entitled to people. Even having a boat—though Justin and his upper-crust, old-money Boston family were into sailing, not yachts.

Had this been a sailboat, I never would have boarded.

These similarities made Ben my personal version of a walking red flag. But something started to shift when I danced with Ben at Eloise and Merritt's party. I wrote it off as a purely physical thing. I always found Ben attractive. So, dancing with him, cutting loose in that way, letting him touch me in ways that felt safe—it turned out to be a little more dangerous than I thought.

But I could write off simple physical attraction.

What I can't write off are all the things I've learned about who Ben really is. The way he took care of me when I had my migraine. Not leaving my side, snuggling close and rubbing my head, making sure I had water and medicine. Even making sure I could shower—with*out* making a single move or flirty remark.

Justin *never* would have taken care of me like that. Not if it would have so much as wrinkled one of his perfectly tailored shirts. Demand that his housekeeping staff take care of me? All day long. But he wouldn't have *stayed*. Not in a million years. Ten minutes into me groaning—or maybe even when I threw up over the side of the boat—Justin would have been setting up a tee time.

I dangle my legs over the end of the diving board and stare out at the sparkling turquoise sea. A few minutes ago, a pelican nearly collided with my head, but flew on too quickly for me to check if it had a pink band. I'm wondering if we should make this one the yacht mascot. Just after, a pod of dolphins swam right by. Like a scene right out of a movie.

Had it been a Disney movie, they might have stopped and offered a few words of wisdom. Sadly, I'm no wiser, and there is no happy soundtrack to escort me to my happily-ever-after.

If I even *want* a happily-ever-after. I never really have before. But now?

"There you are."

I turn to see Riley standing on the small deck behind me. "Oh, hey."

"What are you doing way back here?" She grins. "Tired of Jasmine and Ana complaining about their lack of cell phones and trying to hit on your man?"

No, but now that she mentions it ...

"I just needed a minute." I stand up and walk back to join her. It's more than a little awkward trying to carry on a conversation while sitting on a diving board, and I find that I actually *do* want to talk to Riley. Even if I'm underdressed in leggings and a t-shirt.

Riley's wearing an emerald green swimsuit that makes her eyes pop and a gauzy white cover-up. It probably cost a thousand dollars even though it's clearly supposed to look effortless and easy. I notice again how perfectly smooth her red hair is and *almost* ask her how she pulls it off.

Justin always wanted me to straighten my naturally wavy hair, and I spent my years in grad school in constant search for the perfect product. I never found one—at least not one good enough to keep Justin from frowning at my perpetually untamed locks. The thought leaves a bad taste in my mouth, and I push it away, ignoring Riley's perfectly smooth waves.

Ugh. I don't know when I decided to let Justin on this boat or back in my head, but he absolutely needs to be drop-kicked off the plank.

"A pod of dolphins just swam by," I say, dropping into one of the deck chairs.

"Really?" she asks. She leans forward and scans the water.

"At least half a dozen. I bet if you keep watching, you'll see them again."

We slip into an easy silence, something that makes me think, in different circumstances, I could be good friends with Riley. She's the right level of chill for me, and I always appreciate someone who's confident enough to be comfortable with silence.

"You must hate having your romantic vacation being crashed by a bunch of strangers," she says, turning to lean her back on the railing as she studies me.

I scoff before I can stop myself, and Riley's eyebrows shoot up.

"Sorry," I quickly say. "That reaction was based much more on you calling this a vacation than about you guys coming aboard."

"Right. True," Riley says. "I guess FBI agents do put a damper on the whole *vacation* vibe."

"Hopefully it'll all blow over soon," I say, a response that I hope is vague enough for her not to dig for more details.

"I think Jasmine and Ana might lose their minds," Riley

says. "Or try to commandeer the ship and head back to shore. I don't think they've spent a day without their phones since ... well, maybe ever. Add in the fact that Ben's taken, and there's not much on board to keep them entertained."

"Don't take this the wrong way, but you don't seem to have all that much in common with them."

She laughs and shakes her head. "I do and I don't. Our families know each other, and we run in the same circles. They'd both be loyal to me—so far as it didn't come down to me versus them. But they are definitely not my closest friends. We hang out once or twice a year, maybe. That's about as much as I can take."

"Did you ever find out what was wrong with your boat?" I ask.

She shrugs. "Something about blown gaskets and a flooded engine? I have no idea. Philip said he's got someone coming out to tow it back to Charleston for us."

"Charleston? Is that where you were headed?"

"That's home, so yeah. I've got all summer before my program starts back in the fall, so I could stay out here for months, but Ana has a modeling event coming up and has to be in Brazil next week."

Next week. I really, *really* hope that doesn't mean they'll all be on this boat with us until then. Other than Riley—she could stay.

But also ... will I still be on the boat next week? When will it be safe to go home? I think of my sisters, running the inn on opening week. Though I hadn't planned to come for it, I really am sad to miss it.

Or maybe this whole trip is making me homesick. Or just ... peoplesick? I really do want to make more effort to visit my sisters. That's why I moved to Atlanta, after all, and I've barely seen them more than when I was in DC. Which is sad.

As for seeing Ben more ... I'm not ready to think about anything even in the near future with him. Not if I can't even think about him in the present.

"So, you and Ben," Riley says with impeccable timing. She stretches out on the chair next to mine. "Y'all are cute together. And that's saying something big because I could never have pictured Benedict King in a real relationship. The way he looks at you!" She clucks her tongue.

I swallow my protests. I'm not about to talk to Riley about the inner workings of my relationship—can I even *call* it a relationship?—with Ben, especially when I have no idea what to think about it myself.

"Yeah, he's pretty great," I say instead. Because he is.

I'm at least willing to admit that. That whatever screw-up, womanizing billionaire bad boy I thought he was before, he's clearly more than that. Or ... something else entirely.

"Hey, are you interested in watching a movie?" I ask.

It's either that or stand out here and talk about my fake-*ish* relationship, and since I'm declaring myself the queen of avoidance today, I might as well keep it up.

Riley lifts her eyebrows. "A movie? Like, a *movie* movie?"

I assumed Riley had been on the yacht before, given all three of the women's familiarity with Ben, but maybe they only stayed up on deck for pool parties. I grin.

"Have you not seen the state-of-the-art theater room? With reclining, heated leather seats?"

"I do love a good heated seat," Riley says with a smile.

"Then let's get going and raid Benjy's incredibly extensive old-school DVD collection and watch something ridiculous and distracting." I stand up and start toward the narrow stairs that will take us inside.

Riley is mercifully game, and we start with *Dirty Dancing*. When the credits roll and we switch to *Return to Me*, I start to get slightly restless, unable to stop thinking about a certain blond man with a penchant for boat shoes. I'm both shocked and ever-so-slightly disappointed Ben doesn't come looking for me. But then, this *is* what I wanted, isn't it?

Leandra appears with a tray of snacks ten minutes into the second movie. "Someone thought you ladies might need refreshments," she says with a wink aimed my way, and I realize Ben didn't quite leave me *all* the way alone.

Once again, he's giving me space while also taking care of me. The tray holds two kinds of popcorn—regular butter and a sweet kettle corn drizzled with chocolate and caramel—and boxes of candy, just like a real movie theater. Danny follows a moment later with a wide smile, an appreciative glance for Riley, and a bucket of drinks on ice.

The moment they're gone, Riley clinks her glass bottle of soda to mine. "Here's to catching your own white whale."

I want to protest but instead smile before downing a handful of the chocolate and caramel drizzled popcorn. Which is, of course, delicious. I owe both Tao and Ben a round of thank yous.

The credits on the second movie are rolling, and Riley and I are finishing up a box of Junior Mints when Ben barrels into the room, clearly done giving me time. But he still gives me space, standing just inside the door with his hands shoved into the pockets of his khaki shorts.

My heart catches at the sight of him. The memory of last night comes flooding back, the way he held me, touched me as he kissed me over and over again, the way he whispered promises against my lips.

My face flushes, and I bite my lip, forgetting every reason I had for avoiding him. He looks good. *So good*. It's all I can do not to stand up and fold myself into his embrace.

"Are you avoiding me?" he says, without preamble. "It

feels like you're avoiding me."

"Um …"

My eyes dart to Riley. She's smart enough to read the room and immediately jumps up. "I'm gonna go see how Ana and Jasmine are doing," she says. She gives me a little wave, then slips out of the theater room, closing the door softly behind her.

"Hi, Ben," I say, feigning a nonchalance I definitely don't feel. "How are you?"

He lifts an eyebrow, slipping his hands from his pockets to cross his arms over his chest. "You still haven't answered my question."

"I was just watching a movie," I say. "You know—hanging out with Riley."

Ben studies me for a moment, then crosses the room, tugging me up so I'm standing in front of him. He waits one more beat, eyes locked intensely on mine, and then wraps his arms around me, pulling me into the hard planes of his chest.

Despite my doubts and questions and propensity toward avoidance, I offer up exactly zero resistance.

"I missed you," he says, lips ghosting over my cheek. "I'm not good at waiting."

"You did pretty well," I say through a smile.

"Until now."

"Until now," I agree.

Cradling the back of my head, Ben presses his lips to mine. The greediness in his kiss makes me weak-kneed and limp. I can tell he's been out on the deck because he smells like sunshine and tastes like salty sea air. I lean into the kiss, tilting my head for a better angle. I run my hands up his strong arms and over his shoulders until my fingers thread through his hair.

"That's what I think about you avoiding me," he says when he finally pulls away, his low voice sending shivers up my spine.

I don't often see the commanding, bossy version of Ben, but it suits him. I am not mad about it at all.

"Tell me what's going on," he demands.

He spins and drops into the chair, tugging me down so I'm sitting on his lap.

"There's nothing going on," I lie, but I don't resist when he wraps his strong arms around my waist. It's completely disconcerting to want to resist and also melt into him at the same time.

"Sadie, you stood in the pantry for fifteen minutes while I was getting my coffee this morning."

Busted. "You knew I was in there?"

He's quiet for a beat before he asks, "Did I overwhelm you last night? Is that what this is about? I said too much, moved too fast? I'm really out of my depth here."

"No!" I quickly say, but the word feels wrong as it comes out of my mouth. He *did* overwhelm me, and something makes me want to be honest about that. "I mean, *yes*," I amend. "But not in a bad way. You didn't do or say anything wrong."

"Then what is it?"

I lift my hands to Ben's face, cradling his cheeks as I press a quick kiss to his lips. Then I stand up and move off his lap because if I'm going to be honest, I need to be honest from across the room where he won't be able to distract me with his strong arms and soft lips and tantalizing scent. He leans forward, his elbows propped on his knees, his gaze never wavering.

"I'm not good at being vulnerable, Ben," I say. "I'm not good at this."

Ben just listens, not trying to downplay my feelings or give false assurances. Which is so *not* like Justin. I don't want to keep comparing the two in my head—that's not exactly fair.

And yet, in some ways, it's exactly what I need to do in order to reassure myself that maybe this could work.

I take a few more steadying breaths, appreciating that he isn't pushing me. That he somehow knows that with me, time and patience will go a lot further than pressure. And suddenly, I don't want to be across the room. Space is the last thing I need or want.

Without giving myself time to rethink, I plant myself back in Ben's lap, wrapping my arms around his neck.

I lean up and kiss the side of his jaw. "Just be patient with me," I say, my lips close to his skin. "And if I freak out, try not to let it freak *you* out."

He chuckles, the vibration rumbling through his chest. "Duly noted." He lifts a hand, sliding it over my back, rubbing circles across my shoulder blades. "But just to clarify. Does being patient mean there will be or there will *not* be kissing?"

I meet his gaze head-on. His eyes are bright blue and full of mischief and there is nothing I've ever wanted more than hours of kissing this man.

There is only one way to answer his question. It will be much easier to *show* Ben what the answer is rather than *tell* him.

Well, that's not *entirely* true. Telling him would only require a couple of words. A few seconds, tops.

But *showing* him will be much more fun, so I lean down, lifting my hands to his face, and show him *exactly* how I feel about whether kissing should remain on the agenda.

FOURTEEN

Ben

"WOULD you believe I've never been to Charleston?" Sadie says as we walk down the wide planks of the Charleston Harbor Marina.

"Not ever?" Charleston is only a few hours up the coast from Savannah, but then, if Sadie's family only went to Oakley to see Genevieve, that's maybe not so hard to believe.

"Nope. But I've always wanted to, so this is quite an impressive first date, Mr. King." Sadie loops her arm through mine, not even trying to hide the flattery, the excitement in her words. It's so different from the way we used to spar, tossing insults back and forth. Now, she's openly admitting she wants to spend time with me. That she's *impressed*.

"But don't get cocky," she adds. "The night is young, and I'm not promising you a second date until the very end."

And … there she is.

I grin, not minding this new mix of genuine and sass. "Good to know."

After we (finally!) said goodbye to our guests when we docked late this afternoon, it took my strongest powers of persuasion to convince German that it would be safe to take Sadie into Charleston for the night. My reasoning was sound—why would anyone tracking Sadie suspect she's in downtown Charleston? She has no ties here the way she does to Oakley, and we've had no outside communication since we left the island.

Even Daniels agreed—silently with just a nod, of course—but German looked uneasy. It makes me wonder if there's something he knows—or at least suspects—that he's not sharing with the rest of us. Or if he's just that much of a stick in the mud. Maybe both.

Once again, I find myself really wishing someone would share more about the situation Sadie's in. It was easy to be lulled into simply enjoying time on the water, forgetting why the two agents were there, why we left Oakley in the first place.

In the end, after I promised we'd keep a low profile, and had German approve all my plans, made by using his cell phone once we had reception in the harbor, he finally relented. The fact that he'll be shadowing us all night makes me feel like a teenager on a date chaperoned by a parent, but I'll take what I can get.

It's worth it. To be on a *real* date with Sadie. To eat dinner in a real restaurant and feel, even just for one night, like we've outrun all the madness that's been chasing her the past few days and feel some sense of normalcy.

Almost normalcy, anyway. If we could only remove the grumpy, tiny-necked agent standing a few feet away.

When we reach the parking lot, a sleek Mercedes SUV is waiting for us. The driver hops out as soon as he sees us and opens the back door.

"Seriously?" Sadie says as I help her inside. "Is this what it means to be rich? You just have cars and drivers sitting around in every city in case you decide to show up?"

"It's just a car service," I say, sliding in next to her as German gets in the front. "John called and made the arrangements while we were getting ready."

She runs her hands over the smooth leather seats. "Not exactly your standard Uber," she says.

"Definitely not. It's safer. Requires more thorough background checks for drivers and gives us the assurance of knowing Dean will be available for us all evening long, no matter how long we take or where we ask to go."

Dean nods from the front seat, and I give him the address of Magnolia's, my favorite restaurant in the city.

"Why not a regular Uber though?" she asks. "Is all this really necessary?"

"I know it probably seems excessive when you aren't used to it," I say. "But the extra security and precaution is important."

Sadie's quiet as she buckles her seatbelt, then leans forward to fiddle with the hem of her dress. The dress is amazing—made of a white, flowy material. It comes up high in the front and hooks around her neck, but the back is open to her waist, revealing a whole canvas of skin I'd like to explore. When she first came out of her room and we were walking up the stairs, I had to resist the urge to trace my finger up her spine. I definitely plan to do so later. More than once, if possible.

"So, you wanted the extra security because of me?"

It was one of German's stipulations, but I often use a car service anyway. "Today, it's all about you. But generally, it's …"

My words trail off because I'm not sure how to explain without seeming self-important, or worse, without freaking Sadie out. There are a lot of things that wealthy people do that are undoubtedly ridiculous and over the top. But sometimes, it's simply a matter of keeping ourselves safe.

"On Oakley, I can just exist. People know about my wealth. But most of them also watched me grow up. I'm just Ben to them. Off the island, though, it's not the same." I reach over and clasp her hand, reveling in the way even this simple touch feels like *more*. "It's not like I'm a household name or that my face is recognizable to everyone."

Sadie grins. "You mean, you're not Taylor Swift-level famous?"

"Not quite." I grin back at her. "That said, my wealth is public knowledge. I'm not paying for the luxury as much as I'm paying for peace of mind."

Her lips lift into a small smile even as she shakes her head. "It makes sense when you explain it that way, but I'm still not sure I'll ever get used to this."

The fact that we're even talking about her *needing* to get used to this sends a pulse of anticipation racing through me. We're actually doing this. I'm on a *date*—a real one—with Sadie Markham.

I stretch my arm across the back seat, brushing my fingers across her bare shoulder. "I hope you will. Now, tell me how you feel about fried green tomatoes."

I'VE HAD dinner with a lot of women. Wined and dined them. Enjoyed the attention it earned me in return. But I've never done this. I've never sat across from someone and been so wholly invested in impressing her. But not because of my wealth or my possessions or even my fancy Yale education. I just want her to like *me*. I want her to think I'm the kind of man who can make her happy.

Unfortunately, all this *wanting* is making me stumbling and awkward. I've dropped my butter knife three times, and I just knocked my water glass over onto our very patient server when she took our order. My hands are trembling, I keep making very bad jokes involving very bad puns, and my upper lip won't stop sweating.

"Hey," Sadie says when the waiter leaves with a pile of sopping wet napkins and a good chunk of my dignity. She reaches over and picks up my hand, slipping her fingers into mine. "What's going on with you? You seem all flustered."

There's a hint of laughter in her eyes, but also a measure of legitimate concern.

"You know there's no one watching," she says. "Mostly because you rented out this whole room. I don't want to know how much that set you back, by the way."

She definitely doesn't want to know. The Wine Room upstairs at Magnolia's normally seats twenty-four. Tonight, after making a phone call, it's just Sadie and me at a table in front of the bay window overlooking historic Charleston.

And German, hulking at a table toward the back. But we'll ignore the agent lucky enough to get a delicious meal out of this.

I squeeze Sadie's hand gently and lift my shoulders in an easy shrug. I'm determined to be completely transparent with this woman, even if that means owning feelings I'd never admit to anyone else. Or even feel with anyone else.

"I'm nervous," I admit, and her expression softens.

"Ben, why?"

Because I want this.

Because I want YOU.

"Because I want you to have a good time," I say. Still truthful, but not quite as bold as my initial thoughts.

Before Sadie can respond, our server returns to top off our wine glasses and drop off our appetizer—a serving of arguably the best fried green tomatoes in the entire South. And I know. I consider finding the best fried green tomatoes something of my own personal quest.

"I don't know, Ben," Sadie says, eyeing the dish. "I don't have the same Southern roots that you do."

"You do too have Southern roots. You might not have been born on Oakley, but your dad was. Your grandmother was, and that counts."

"And don't take this the wrong way, but isn't this kind of a cliché dish?"

I mock gasp. "Blasphemy. Just sit tight. Let me feed you and show you why fried green tomatoes could never be a cliché."

I slice through the tomato, working to assemble the perfect bite for Sadie. They're served here over white cheddar grits with creamy tomato butter, country ham, and a sweet tomato chutney, and you really need a little taste of all of it at once.

"I haven't had grits since the last time I was at Gran's *before* she died. She was the only one who ever made them for me."

"And I'm sure they were good. Gran knew how to make a good pot of grits." I hold out my fork. "Trust me," I say. "It's the perfect bite."

Sadie leans forward, closing her lips around the bite and making me forget what's actually happening right now.

Are we in a restaurant? Is there food? All *I* can think about is her lips and how soon I can kiss her again.

"Oh my gosh," Sadie says with a soft moan. "That's incredible. I take back everything I said. You can totally say *I told you so*."

"I absolutely told you so." I take my own bite, closing my eyes as the flavors hit my tongue. "My mom used to bring me here when I was a kid."

"You haven't told me much about your mom," Sadie says. "How old were you when she died?"

I cut off another piece of tomato, using the time it takes to chew and swallow to remind myself that I *want* to share these things with Sadie. I never talk about my mom, so it doesn't come easily. But I owe it to her to try. I can't hope for vulnerability from Sadie without giving the same in return.

"You don't have to talk about this," Sadie says quickly. "Sorry if I'm being nosy."

"I want you to be nosy," I tell her. But it still takes me another piece of tomato and another few moments to gather my thoughts and my courage to be so open.

"I was sixteen when she died," I say. "Well, almost sixteen. My birthday was two weeks after."

"So young," Sadie says. "I'm so sorry. That's a tough age to have to lose a parent."

"It was. Not that there's ever a good age to lose someone you love."

"True." The smile she gives me is small, and I think of Genevieve.

I remember Sadie's drawn, closed-off face at her funeral a year and a half ago. I hadn't seen Sadie in years, and even then, when I knew I should be thinking of sadness and grief,

I couldn't help being drawn to her. Wishing we'd run into each other again under different circumstances.

I never would have dreamed we'd be here now.

"How old were you when your parents divorced?" I chuckle, then shake my head. "Man, this is hardly happy date conversation. Maybe we should go back to talking about food?"

Sadie touches my hand. "No—this is good. I mean, okay—it's not typical first-date conversation. But then, what about any of this has been typical?"

Absolutely *nothing*. So, I guess we're sticking with that.

"Maybe that's just not our style," she says, and I love the way she says *our*.

I slide the last piece of tomato toward her and Sadie takes it without hesitation, something I immediately appreciate. Not just that she eats like a normal human, but that she isn't insisting *I* eat it. There's none of the forced, mannered politeness, or pretending like she's never hungry for more than lettuce and lemon water.

"My parents split up when I was twelve," Sadie says. "Which was just old enough to be full of rage instead of sadness."

"I think I was angry about everything when I was twelve," I say. "Puberty was brutal."

Sadie smiles and points to the mass of blond waves that just barely reach her shoulders. "You should have seen this hair when I was twelve. It was out of control."

"I *did* see your hair when you were twelve. I remember it. I remember all three of you."

She blinks at me. "Oh my gosh. I keep forgetting. It's weird I don't have more memories of you."

"Maybe not. I'm a bit older than you, Sadie."

"You aren't *that* much older. Wait—how old are you now?"

"Thirty-four," I answer.

"You're right. Practically a grandpa," she teases. "Seven years really isn't much."

"Not now. But seven years when you were twelve and I was nineteen feels a lot more significant."

"Oh wow. Yeah, good point." She leans back in her chair. "And I was too busy playing spy, watching to see if I could catch Merritt and Hunter kissing so I could tattle."

I laugh. "Did you ever catch them?"

"I did. But then I was too embarrassed to tell Gran. Or anyone else."

Our server quietly takes our empty plate and leaves our second appetizer. We waste no time digging into the pan-seared scallops, which make Sadie groan.

"So, spying," I say. "You never outgrew that, huh? Just turned it into a lucrative—and sometimes dangerous—job?"

Sadie devours another scallop before answering, clearly mulling over what she wants to say. "It's not exactly spying," she hedges.

"Hacking?"

Her slight wince tells me I've hit the nail pretty darn close on the head. "It's really whatever is needed. Getting into servers, accessing data and information. Not the kind of cool stuff people typically think of or what's in the movies. Usually."

"And this time?"

She sighs and sets down her fork. "This time, I couldn't help crossing some lines. I don't always know what I'm looking into, or *who* I'm looking into. The information isn't always clear or in a context I can grasp. But this assignment, I saw more."

Her pause stretches on, and her gaze moves to the window. I take her hand. "And you couldn't let it go."

She meets my gaze and shakes her head. "No. I couldn't. Not when it's human trafficking."

Now, I'm the one wincing. Not just because trafficking—whether labor or sex trafficking—is despicable, but because I know exactly how ruthless those involved can be. I'm equal parts proud and terrified this is what Sadie got into. It's honestly no wonder she has agents assigned to her.

I wish there were more.

Giving her hand a squeeze, I say, "I think you're pretty amazing, Sadie girl. Fearless."

"Reckless?" she suggests, taking a sip of her water.

"Something tells me you weighed the cost before making your decision." I stroke my thumb over the back of her hand. "Which means it wasn't reckless but more of a calculated risk to yourself. Some might call it sacrificial. Or selfless."

I know I would. Even if this information makes me more than a little eager to get back to the yacht, back to our little bubble of safety until German gets whatever reassurance he needs that it's safe for her again. I'm not going to allow myself to worry more, though my mind could easily spin out with fears and worst-case scenarios. Especially considering the agency handling all this goes by the acronym SUCS.

I lift her hand to my mouth, leaving a lingering kiss on her knuckles. For a moment, I could swear I see her blinking back tears. Then, her sharp, beautiful smile is back.

"Is it weird I wasn't scared of this, but I'm scared of you, Benedict King?"

"That is a little … surprising. I don't usually inspire fear. Even if I do fly a pirate flag on my boat."

Sadie laughs. "Yacht."

After a beat, I catch her gaze, trying to read the expression there. "You know you don't need to be afraid of me."

"Don't even think about promising not to hurt me, Ben."

I frown. "But I won't."

"No one can promise that. Especially in real relationships." She sighs. "Not that I've seen great examples in the past. Certainly not my parents. Before Lo and Merritt, I had little hope for marriage and life-long love. But even with my sisters and their husbands, who are wonderful—there's always the eventuality of hurting people. Especially the ones you love."

I process her words, realizing the wisdom in them. "Hurt, sure. You're right. But heartbreak? You don't think your sisters' relationships will last? Even though my parents' marriage left me with no small amount of cynicism, I think Hunter and Jake are in this for the long haul."

"I agree," Sadie admits. "But even the best relationships can hurt us. Probably more deeply, because when we love big, the stakes are higher. That's why I'm so scared."

I squeeze her hand. "Because you know this will be good."

She squeezes back. "It's why you can't promise you won't ever hurt me."

Sadie pulls her hand out of mine and leans forward across the table, walking her fingers up my arm until she lightly grips the back of my neck. Her touch sends pinpricks of heat erupting across my skin.

"Which means you should be afraid of me too," she says.

"Believe me, I am."

Though we're talking very seriously, somehow this lightens the mood, and we both laugh before Sadie drops her hand, and our server brings out our main courses. Sadie went with buttermilk fried chicken, and I got braised short ribs.

Our conversation lulls as we eat and share and rave over the food.

Which is, as I knew it would be, amazing. It's rewarding to watch Sadie experience it for the first time, probably the same way I did when my mom brought me here. Though I was young enough I probably shoveled the food in my mouth rather than simply savoring.

I'm hit with the sudden realization that my mother would have loved Sadie. The knowledge is bittersweet.

Though we're both stuffed, it's a moral imperative to have dessert at Magnolia's, so we split the Caramel Apple Crisp with its signature bourbon caramel sauce.

"Do you remember the first time we met?" Sadie asks, distracting me as she licks caramel sauce from the tines of her fork.

I let out a strangled chuckle, trying to tear my gaze away from her mouth. "Actually met? Or the time I commandeered your sister's video chat with you?"

She laughs. "The video chat."

"How could I forget? I've never had such a riveting conversation about paint colors and roof shingles."

"From what I remember, you were incredibly obstinate," she says.

"How about we go with passionate?" I counter.

"We can go with that. But why *are* you so passionate about Oakley? I mean, I love that you are. I love Oakley, and I know you're the biggest reason why it's still a charming little beach town and not some campy touristy place like other beaches in the South. But I'm not going to lie—trying to fit Benedict King, island owner and historical preservation expert into the same box with playboy Benjy is breaking my brain a little."

My jaw tightens. Never have I wanted to get rid of the

ridiculous reputation I've cultivated more than I do right now. "Playboy *Benjy* doesn't need to be in the box at all."

"Then why, Ben?" she asks, the conversation suddenly taking a serious turn. "I read all the articles on Google. I know the tabloids don't always get it right, but I've seen the photos. And I heard the things Ana and Jasmine said about you with my own ears. If that isn't who you are, why does it seem like you worked really hard to make everyone think that it is?"

I play with my napkin, creasing it in half, then into fourths, then unfold it and start over. "It started with needing to make my *father* think that's who I am." I look up and meet Sadie's gaze. "The wealth in my family is largely from my mother's side. My father is successful, but not *superyacht* successful. Because of the stipulations of my mother's will, he isn't allowed to touch any of the money she left to me. But if I grow that money into something else, invest it somewhere and make a profit, there's nothing to keep my father from going after it. I mean, there's *me*. But I don't even want to deal with him asking. And I definitely don't want him lurking around Oakley, looking to freeload when he did so little for my mother when she was alive."

"So, the bad boy reputation is to make your father think you're sitting around, frittering away your mother's money? Does that mean that *isn't* what you're doing?"

My mouth twitches, and I rub a hand across my face and clear my throat to keep from laughing. "Did you just say the word *frittering?*"

"It's a good word," she says without missing a beat. "Don't criticize my language choices to keep from answering the question."

There's a fire in her eyes, but it's one that I like. Because she isn't afraid to challenge me on this—to challenge me on *anything*.

"You know I have Oakley," I say, "but there are other things, too. I've made investments in several tech start-ups that look really promising and in a biotech firm focusing on clean energy. I'm always looking for responsible places to invest or for causes that warrant support."

"And you don't tell anyone," Sadie says, holding my gaze.

"Some people know."

"And others just believe the image."

"The important people know the truth. It's just … a very small circle."

She stands and scoots around the table, leaning down to press a lingering kiss on my lips. "I'm saying there's more to you than meets the eye, Mr. King," she says. "I'll be right back. If our server returns, order me a coffee to go? That is, if a place this fancy has to-go cups."

They don't. But they do have stainless steel travel mugs for sale, so I have them add one to the bill. It's filled with fresh coffee and waiting for Sadie when she returns.

After dinner, we head over to Waterfront Park where Sadie forces a grumbling German to take a picture of us in front of the iconic pineapple fountain that Charleston is known for.

"If you didn't destroy my phone and take Ben's, you wouldn't have to do this," she tells him through a smile.

"This must be the part where being a SUCS agent really sucks," I murmur in Sadie's ear.

She groans, then giggles. "That's terrible."

"Terrible? No. We should really be making way more SUCS jokes," I tell her. "I mean, they're pretty much begging for it with that name."

"Are you done?" German demands.

"Just a few more," Sadie says, her voice dripping with sweetness. "If you don't mind."

He clearly *does* mind, and Sadie makes him take at least a few *dozen* more, likely *only* to annoy him. But I'll be glad when he sends them all to me later. I also don't mind posing with Sadie in my arms. Any excuse to touch her.

"Enough," German finally grumbles, and we wander a little further away from him, testing the limits of our government chaperone.

"I think it's kinda funny that our relationships with our fathers are so similar," Sadie says. She turns and leans her back against the railing at the edge of the short pier that extends over the Cooper River. If it were light out, we could look across the water and see where the Cooper merges with the Ashley River, then flows out to the open waters of the Atlantic. But it's late enough now that we can only see the flashing lights on Fort Sumter—the civil war era fort that sits in the middle of Charleston Harbor.

I nod, remembering the brief encounter I had with Sadie's father when he came for his mother's funeral. Our interaction was minimal, but I learned enough from Jake to trust that my first impression of the man was dead-on.

Genevieve was right to leave her inheritance to her granddaughters instead of her son—he would have sold and ducked out of town before the ink was dry on the deed transfer.

"Jake told me your dad called Eloise last week," I say. "Is he going to be a problem for y'all?"

Sadie shakes her head. "Not at all. Weirdly, he and his wife seem pretty happy, though I'm sure her very deep pockets help with that. Lo said he just seemed like he wanted to connect." She shrugs. "I'm not holding my breath, but we'll see how it goes."

"Do you *want* to connect?"

"About as much as I want a double root canal," she answers quickly. "But Lo will make it happen."

I nod. "That seems to be her way."

Sadie steps toward me, her hands lifting to the front of my shirt. "Your button came loose," she says as she fixes it.

When she finishes, she presses her palms flat against my chest, looking up like she's almost nervous to be touching me. She shouldn't be—I've been dying to touch her all night—but everything still feels so new between us. Like every touch, every moment is weighted double.

I move my hands to her waist, resting my palms on the swell of her hips, and lean down, brushing my nose against hers. "I'm having a really nice time," I say, my voice low.

"Best date ever," she says, her exhale fanning across my cheek. It's hands down the best date I've ever been on, but honestly, it doesn't even feel fair to make the comparison. Something tells me Sadie will always be the best everything. Best date. Best kiss. Best conversation.

Best *everything*.

"So, does that mean I get a second date?" I ask.

"The night's not over yet. You've still got time to screw it all up," she teases, booping me on the nose.

The problem is—I'm honestly afraid I will.

Behind us, lightning flashes, lighting up the harbor, and there's a low warning growl of thunder. I look up at the starless sky as a cool breeze picks up, tossing Sadie's hair across her face.

"We should get back to the boat if we don't want to get caught in the rain," I say, but my eyes drop to her lips.

"Probably yes," Sadie says, leaning a little closer. "But kiss me first?"

"Anytime." Cupping her jaw, I press my lips to hers in a

kiss that starts soft and quickly becomes more desperate. Hungrier.

After our lengthy dinner conversation, this somehow feels different. As though the intimacy of our words has now bled into our kiss, making it richer and deeper. I'm absolutely in new territory here.

We aren't alone on the pier, so I won't kiss her the way I'd really like to, but that doesn't mean I won't think about it. By the way she's bunching my shirt in her hands, Sadie's thinking about it too. I slide my hands over her shoulders, then cradle her face as I deepen the kiss one last time before pulling away.

Sadie bites her lip as I do, her gaze flicking to the side, and I'm overwhelmed by a sudden and hopefully unfounded fear that this might be the last time I kiss her, that I hold her like this. I remember her words at dinner, how it's inevitable that we'll hurt the ones we love.

Let's hope not. At least, let's hope not for a long, long time.

My fears are probably irrational. But I still don't know what's going to happen when we go back to Oakley. I don't know what comes next, and I think we've exhausted our deep emotional conversation for the evening. Talking about what comes next might be one step too far, making Sadie run again.

I know she's scared.

Hell, *I'm* scared.

But I'm more scared of losing whatever this is, more scared of losing her.

The rumble of thunder becomes a boom, just as the skies open over us. Sadie squeals, and we're both laughing as we start to run back to the waiting car. The sour look on German's face only makes us both laugh harder as we clasp hands.

"I hope this ending of our date doesn't reflect poorly on me." I have to shout to be heard over the rain, wind, and thunder. "I distinctly remember ordering clear skies and a warm night."

"I can't think of a more perfect ending," Sadie shouts back, grinning.

Or, I think as we reach the car, completely soaked and still laughing, *a more perfect beginning.*

FIFTEEN

Ben

"GO FISH," Sadie says with a laugh.

"How do you not have any sevens? You have like forty cards!" Danny groans and draws from the messy pile in the middle.

"I have thirty-seven," Sadie says loftily, just as thunder booms outside, rattling the cabinets.

She jolts, her shoulder hitting mine. I'm pleased when she doesn't move away but scoots even closer so we're pressed together side to side at the counter. Lifting her gaze to mine, she offers me a shy smile. The kind that seems almost surprised to find that it's me she's leaning into for comfort.

Me too, Sadie girl. Me too. Surprised—but not the least bit unhappy about it.

The other night, the game of choice was poker. But tonight, John, of all people, suggested we play this children's card game. Maybe to cut through the tension of the storm, which has worsened since we returned from our date, completely drenched through. To make it more interesting, we're using five decks of cards and requiring completed matches of twenty, not four. I'm honestly not sure there will ever be a winner at this point.

Though it's less about who wins the game and more about distraction. Personally, I could think of some other fun means of distraction—namely kissing Sadie—but when Leandra invited us to play cards in the galley, Sadie looked too excited for me to say no.

And though I imagined our date ending another way—as in, not with five other people playing a children's card game in the galley—I love watching Sadie with my crew. Not that I'm surprised. I think I'd love her just about anywhere. But it makes me feel warm and content to see the way she's folded herself right in with the staff members who have come to mean a whole lot more to me in the past few years. Sadie just *fits*. With this group, on my boat, in my life—with me.

I swallow, watching the curve of her cheek lift as she smiles. She fits so well that if she decides she doesn't want this when she returns to Atlanta, it's going to be like having a piece of my chest carved out and removed.

Which is a worry I'd rather shove away and save for another day. Or never.

John takes a queen from Tao and then sets down a group of twenty while everyone groans.

"Are you sure you're not cheating?" Tao asks.

"There's a real problem if I need to cheat at Go Fish to win," John says.

There's a sudden pitch to the left and everyone tightens their hold on drinks as a few cards slide right off the counter.

"You're sure we won't sink?" Sadie asks. "Or capsize? Or both?"

John chuckles, reaching across to pat her hand. "We'll be fine. It would take a tsunami to capsize us."

"And this isn't a tsunami, right?" Sadie asks.

I wrap my arm around her waist. "No tsunamis. Just a storm."

She nods but leans even closer with the next low roll of thunder.

Once we boarded *The Oakley*, Art maneuvered us out into the harbor so the yacht wouldn't be in danger of knocking into the dock or any other ships from the wind and swells. In all my time spent on the yacht, I've never fully weathered a storm—at least not one like this. John gave German and me a rundown of safety and precautions while Sadie was changing out of her soaked clothes. Danny handled tidying up the lines and closed all the hatches, while Leandra secured all of the interior rooms. It's rough, but right now, the mood is bright in our little galley.

Danny sets down his cards and rubs his palms on his jeans, pinning me with a look. "Tell me straight, bossman. Do I have *any* chance with Ana? Even like half a percent?"

John and Tao practically roar with laughter. I think we're about to have a repeat of the water fight until I clear my throat, and they manage to simmer down.

"You don't *want* a chance with Ana," I tell Danny. "Trust me."

Sadie tenses, and I press a quick kiss to the side of her head. My fingers tighten around her waist possessively.

I hated every minute the other women were on board—Ana and Jasmine, anyway. Between their attempts to flirt, demean Sadie, and their overall attitude, it was a miserable reminder of what now feels like a very distant past life.

And I'm not an idiot. Even though Sadie eclipses those women in every way, I'm sure it's not easy feeling like you're competing with a literal supermodel. The last thing I want is her thinking, even for a moment, that she needs to compare herself to them.

"Not that I'm speaking from any personal experience," I add. "I just know from being around her that she's too selfish and high maintenance for someone like you, Danny boy."

"She'd eat you alive and spit you out," Leandra says.

Danny grins. "That sounds fun."

"Give me all your kings," Sadie says, and Danny hands over three to complete Sadie's group of twenty. She grins proudly. "Now I only have seventeen cards."

"Good for you," Danny says, shooting her a glare followed by a smile. "How was Charleston, by the way?"

Sadie's eyes meet mine, and she smiles softly. "The fried green tomatoes were amazing."

John grins. "So, what you're saying is that the food, not the company, was the highlight of your date?"

Danny snorts, and I lightly tickle Sadie's ribs. She elbows me in return.

"Absolutely," Sadie says, the smallest of smiles curving her lips in a crooked grin. "The food was *very* memorable. No offense, Tao."

Tao glowers at us. "Where did you take her?"

"Magnolia's," I answer, and my chef throws his cards down and rubs his eyes. "And did you happen to bring back anything? Anything at all?"

I should have thought about it. Another night, when I wasn't distracted by Sadie, I would have thought about my crew, or at least my chef, and brought something back. Tonight, my whole focus was on the woman next to me.

"I'm sorry, chef," I tell him.

Danny elbows Tao. "He had other things on his mind."

"Like the fried green tomatoes," Sadie says with a laugh. "Or maybe the short ribs?"

"Stop!" Tao says with another groan. "You are absolutely *killing* me."

"The scallops *were* pretty distracting," I add, winking at Sadie. "But then, so was the company."

When Sadie places her hand on my jaw, then turns my head to kiss me, I'm so surprised, I simply freeze. I'm still just sitting here, staring like an idiot, when she pulls back with a pleased smile on her face. There's a collective *awwww*, followed by the scraping of stools as everyone but the two of us seems to have the same idea at once.

"That's it," Danny says, throwing down his cards. "I give up."

John starts to gather the cards together while Leandra and Tao clear the rest of the table. Sadie and I still haven't moved.

"HOW ARE YOU FEELING?" I ask, splaying my hand across Sadie's stomach.

An hour later, the storm is still raging. There's no hope for sleeping, and Sadie and I are sprawled on top of the covers in my bed with the lights down low. With all the talking we've already done, it's been nice to just ... exist.

One more thing I can say I've never done or wanted to do or even *thought* about doing with a woman—sitting in relative quiet together. Unsurprisingly, I love it. But only because of the company. Only because of Sadie.

"Is all this rocking upsetting your stomach?"

She giggles and swats at me. "I think I'm okay. But I

won't be for long if you don't watch it. I'm ticklish. And I'm not sure you doing *that* is going to help."

The boat pitches slightly, and Sadie squeals, grabbing onto me and hooking her feet around my legs. Thunder growls, and there are several flashes of lightning in a row. What sounds like a heavy sheet of rain batters against my balcony doors.

Things quiet outside for a moment, the boat's movements settling into more of a gentle dip and roll than the violent movements.

"Can I get you some seasickness medication?" I ask. "Just in case."

Sadie sighs. "I don't know that I need any. I've been fine since the first couple of days—is that normal?"

"Some people always struggle with it, especially if they get other kinds of motion sickness. But most of the time, it only takes a few days to get your sea legs."

Sadie lifts one leg straight up, sending her nightshirt fluttering down her thighs and making my heart pound. I'm well aware she has on shorts underneath, but *still*. There's a lot of leg on display.

"How are my sea legs?" She rotates her foot, turning her leg from side to side.

"I think they're pretty fantastic," I say, then start to sit up, reaching for her. "But I might need to do a closer examination …"

"I bet you'd like that." Laughing, Sadie gives me a hard shove, and I let the momentum carry me right off the bed, where I hop to my feet.

"Stay here," I order, then return a moment later with a bottle of water and two pills. I hand her one. "Just in case. I'm taking one too." I swallow the pill, chasing it with water before giving her the bottle.

I'm only taking it because I suspect Sadie won't if I don't. She's just stubborn enough to resist. It's amazing how quickly people can bounce back from being seasick and forget how terrible it was. The last thing I want is Sadie feeling that ill again.

And this storm is no small thing. I suspect it's a little bigger than anticipated, or else John might have suggested we stay in a hotel instead of boarding again.

As if to prove my point, in conjunction with a huge clap of thunder, lightning flashes repeatedly and the lights flicker and go out.

"Uh oh," she says. "Did your yacht just get fried?"

"Maybe," I say, tugging her closer in the dark.

"Does that mean we're stuck? How will Art drive the boat? Is everything up in the wheelhouse electrical?"

"We'll be fine," I say, hoping I sound more confident than I feel. "All of the steering equipment is on a separate system with a backup generator. Even if the rest of the boat stays without power, Art can still drive."

I *think*. I'm pretty sure. Honestly, I know more about the kinds of shingles used on homes in the 1800s than I do about how my own yacht runs. But I'm not going to worry about that now.

Instead, I pull Sadie closer until her back is pressed to my front and my nose is in her hair. I take a deep inhale. Is it possible to get addicted to a person's unique scent? Because I may need rehab whenever we finally get back to Oakley.

My gut twists at the thought, the fear from earlier tonight creeping back up and making my throat feel tight. I shove it away, determined to savor the *right now* instead of worrying over what comes next. Especially when we've had a great night. I can't even complain about the storm when it gives me a great excuse to curl up with Sadie in the dark.

She nestles into me, tugging my arm forward and wrapping it more tightly around her waist. "Why, Mr. King—did you orchestrate this situation to your advantage?"

I smile into her hair. Obviously not. But am I milking this situation? Little bit.

"You figured me out. I've got Percy Jackson on speed dial and called in a favor."

Sadie laughs. "Percy Jackson doesn't control lightning. That's Zeus."

"Then who's the lightning thief?"

"Oh, Ben. Clearly, we need to work on your young adult book literacy."

"Yeah, it's pretty low. I've never been much of a reader when it comes to fiction."

"What do you read instead?" she asks.

"Mostly history. Biographies. Deep dives into cultural anthropology. That's what I studied in school."

"Really?" Sadie says. "How did I not know that? That explains so much about your obsession with Oakley's history."

"People don't usually ask," I say.

"You're rich, so who cares what else you are," she says, her voice low. "Right?"

"Pretty much."

Turning in my arms, Sadie rests her forehead on my collar bone. I can only make her out when the lightning flashes, and even then, it's just a dim outline. It's kind of nice to rely on my other senses instead. The smell of her, like warm vanilla caramel with a bite. The feel of her in my arms, the softness of her hair under my fingertips.

"I'm sorry I judged you, Ben." Her breath fans across the skin at my throat. If I leaned forward, I could tilt her head up and taste her.

But as nice as that would be, I'm enjoying just this. I don't know that I've ever had such a quiet, intimate moment with a woman before, and I don't want to ruin it.

"Don't worry about it," I say instead. "I set myself up for it. I can't blame you for making assumptions."

Sadie's quiet for a moment, her fingers toying with the buttons on my shirt in a way that feels like nervousness. "Is this normal?" she asks.

"Cuddling in the dark, fully clothed, after a date?" I tease.

She finds my ribs, and though I never thought I was ticklish, her touch makes me squirm. I capture her hands, laughing as I tuck her tightly against me.

"I mean the storm," she says. "The lights going out. All of this."

"We haven't lost power before," I admit. "But you heard John—the storm should blow over in a few hours. This feels like a lot because we're out in it, but it's a pretty normal storm, not a hurricane or tropical depression. And we're still in view of the shore. Worst case, the coast guard isn't far."

I hope my words reassure her. I'm worried about the power too, but not more than a little. John would have come to find me if there were any significant issues. Still, if circumstances were different and I were alone, I'd probably be more concerned—concerned enough to be up in the wheelhouse, watching the weather and listening to Art talk through whatever decisions he's making to keep us all safe. But Sadie's nervousness somehow makes me feel the need to be steady—calm and confident where she's unsure.

Well. Calm and confident about *The Oakley* successfully weathering the storm. Not anything else.

Sadie has a life in Atlanta. A home. A job.

Would I ask her to move?

No—that feels like the kind of decision she'd need to

make for herself. I certainly don't plan to leave Oakley. Sure, I could handle things from afar—appoint someone else to run the historic preservation society, make decisions from another location. These days, so many jobs can be done from just about anywhere. Running an island is no different.

But I love Oakley. It's home. And I like handling the ins and outs while *on* the island. Maybe I don't want to live on this yacht forever, but I could figure out what to do about Mom's house.

I wonder what Sadie would want to do.

And if she'd want to do it with me ...

"You're thinking really hard over there," Sadie says.

"Mm."

"Care to share with the class?"

Mentally, I calculate my odds. Sadie already mentioned being freaked out once. Was that yesterday? This morning? The passage of time has been both fast and slow since we left Oakley.

And probably because of the nature of our situation—being trapped on this boat and around each other twenty-four-seven—things *are* moving quickly with us. Then again, I've had feelings for a while. A good, long while.

My interest was instantaneous—from that first video chat. Every time Sadie has been in Oakley, that interest has grown and grown. Maybe I didn't realize the depth of my feelings before now, or maybe they've been slowly inching into deeper water this whole time. Without much to compare this to, I'm at a little bit of a loss.

But we're too old for games, and the only kind I'm really interested in playing with Sadie are the fun kind, like our verbal sparring. When it comes to this, I'd rather lay it all out there and be honest.

"I'm just wondering what happens next," I say, taking the

leap. "Not tonight, in the storm. I mean, when we get the all-clear and head back to Oakley. Full disclosure: I've never wanted *this* before."

I realize I'm still being a coward, avoiding saying the actual terms. "A relationship," I clarify. "Something real, with the potential for a future."

There. I said it. And whether it's the seafood plus the storm or just my nerves, the rolling of my stomach matches the churning ocean outside.

"I've never wanted it either," Sadie says. "Well—sort of. I've had *a* long-term relationship before. But it was a while ago. Didn't end well or make me eager for another."

Why does this fill me with a hot and frenzied sense of jealousy? I swallow, trying to force it back down. The last thing Sadie needs right now is me getting all alpha male possessive over a guy from the past.

"And I haven't wanted or looked for anything serious since," she adds.

Those words—and the tone of finality in her voice—they hit me like the slap of an icy wave.

My instinct is to lighten the mood, make some kind of joke, but I think that's more of a coping mechanism. A way to escape talking about hard things. And while this conversation is making me super uncomfortable, I know it's important. It feels like some sort of test.

If I want to have a big boy, grownup relationship, I need to be able to talk about difficult subjects. I'm a thirty-four-year-old grown man who has often taken pride in my ability to talk about my emotions. This shouldn't even be a challenge. But then, talking to Jake about *his* relationship is very different than talking about things when my own heart is on the line.

"Do you ... want to talk about it?" I ask, torn between

wanting every detail and not wanting to have to imagine Sadie with someone—*anyone*—else. Ever.

"I just ... think I'm maybe a little bit broken."

Sadie is anything but broken. If anything, she's one of the strongest people I know. But I bite the inside of my cheek to avoid saying this out loud. The last thing I want is to dismiss or diminish her concerns. Even if I happen to disagree.

So, I listen. I wait. And though I can't see her face in the darkness, I offer what reassurance I can through touch, lightly sliding my hand up and down her back.

"Dr. Justin Treemont," she says, her tone acidic.

I already hate the guy.

"He taught in the mathematics department at MIT when I was getting my PhD, and he was everyone's favorite. Technically, the department frowned on teacher-student relationships, but I was never in any of his classes, so he wasn't *my* professor, which stupidly made it easier for me to fudge the rules. Justin also had this air about him—like he just... I don't know, thought he was special enough to do whatever he wanted. He was much too old for me, but either way, we were both adults and he was the darling of the department. If the dean cared, he turned his head whenever he saw us together."

My skin suddenly feels hot. It's not just jealousy I feel, but a surge of protectiveness. Sadie may have been an adult, but I am also very aware of power imbalances in relationships. And a fresh out of college student and a professor really toes that line.

I'm also suddenly very aware of the seven years between Sadie and me.

She continues, "Looking back, I see things differently. But Justin was brilliant and funny and thoughtful. It was very easy to get swept up in his charm. I honestly couldn't believe he found me interesting at all."

I ache to tell Sadie how interesting I find her. I want to fold time in half so I step through the wrinkle just to tell *that* Sadie she didn't need some older, fascinating douche to see her as interesting.

Again, I stay quiet. It's the hardest thing I've done in a long time.

"At first, he made me feel seen. *Really* seen. But then, the longer we were together, the more he…" Sadie trails off, and I swear, I feel her tremble the tiniest bit.

I pull her closer, pressing a quick kiss to her temple, longing to do more.

"He wasn't *mean* to me. Not directly, anyway. But eventually, he started making little comments about the kinds of clothes I should buy. About how I should wear my hair—straight, never wavy. He paid for me to get regular manicures and to shop in the nicest stores in Boston. Don't get me wrong—the pampering was nice on the surface. It made me feel … important. At least at first. But eventually, it started to feel like he was molding me into this very specific kind of woman. A woman who was not me."

Now I just want to punch the guy. I want to find him, tell him he should have known better than to try to manipulate a student—even a PhD student—when he was a professor, and then sock him right in the jaw.

"Justin's entire family was wealthy. Very Boston elite. They sailed every weekend, attended the fancy charity events where everyone just stood around and talked about how much money they had. It was important to him that I also fit the image."

Okay, now … I'm starting to feel a whole new kind of

uncomfortable. Older man with family money and a boat —*perfect*.

"Ah," I say. "I see. So, Justin and I have some things in common."

"Logically I realize that you aren't anything like him," Sadie says quickly. "But … I think there's some muscle memory that's triggering my fear. Just because of the parallels. The whole experience made me not want to give myself over to anyone, not to lose myself in a relationship again." She pauses. "It also made me wary of … "

"Rich boys?" I ask when her words trail off. "Maybe even billionaires in boat shoes?"

"Little bit." She pauses. "I mean, I didn't really know who I was as a person when I was with Justin. And I liked him so much, I let him try to mold me into this picture-perfect society girlfriend. The most terrible part is that I knew it was happening. I could see it, but I ignored it, thinking I was in love with him. I just got lost."

"You were young," I say.

"Not *that* young. But I was just repeating the patterns I knew. I saw my mom do this same thing a dozen different times when we were growing up. Every man she dated, she morphed into what version of herself she thought he'd like best. She became a cross-country skier for a few months, which was totally ridiculous because she'd never even been on skis. Another guy loved Nascar, and suddenly Mom was memorizing the names of every guy who ever won the Daytona 500. She was only defined by the man standing beside her, and I hated it. I swore I would never do the same thing, and then as soon as I was old enough to leave the house, that's exactly what happened."

"Sadie," I say, lifting one hand to stroke her cheek. I wish I could see her right now. But maybe this is a conversation best had in the dark. "In all seriousness, I'm so sorry that happened to you."

"Thank you," she says stiffly, and I can hear the but coming. "But it wasn't just something that *happened* to me. I wasn't passive. It was my decision too. If I became who Justin wanted, then I didn't have to decide who *I* wanted to be. It was like a game, you know? Like playing dress up. I wasn't the *real* Sadie. I was *Justin's* Sadie. Which was fine, because then I didn't have to decide who the real Sadie was."

"You seem sure of yourself now," I say. She might be one of the most self-assured people I've ever met. And this vulnerability, knowing this story, doesn't change that.

"Thank you," she says quietly. "It's taken work."

"Do you feel like a relationship would put that at risk?"

We both tense when the boat makes a sudden movement. My stomach dips, and I tighten my hold on Sadie. Lightning flashes, and the rain pounds as the wind picks up, giving a long, low howl. The weather suits my mood a little too perfectly.

"Yes? No? I'm not sure I know. I haven't had to ask myself that question because I've worked so hard to keep everything casual. But now you're telling me you want something real, and I like you enough to want to give you that," Sadie says. "But that means I have to *be* real, which I'm sure I can do on my own. But I'm not so sure I can do it with another person."

"I think you feel pretty real." I pinch her side lightly, but this time, she doesn't giggle. She flinches. I drop my hand to rest on the curve of her waist.

"Ben, we're currently in a bubble. In the middle of the Atlantic Ocean, trapped on a yacht with no phones, totally separated from our normal lives. This isn't real life."

I know she's right—this *isn't* real life. It is like a bubble.

But that doesn't mean it will pop the moment we set foot back on the dock at Oakley.

"So, let's take this outside the bubble. See what happens. Just because this has all happened in the midst of unusual circumstances doesn't mean it can't work in real life."

"Doesn't it?" Sadie asks.

My fingers flex, tightening on her waist, tugging her closer. "No. It doesn't."

Sadie sighs, lifting her hand to trace my jaw with her fingertips. It almost feels like she's memorizing the contours of my face before saying goodbye.

"I want to believe you," she says quietly. "But you know what? There might be actual people out there who want to harm me, and that doesn't scare me half as much as you do."

"Why?"

"I like my walls, Ben. You make me want to take them down."

"And how are those walls serving you?" I ask. "Will you keep them up forever? Be alone forever?"

She's quiet for longer than she should be, and I swear, it's like I can hear the loud thoughts banging around in her head.

"A week ago, it would have been an easy yes," she says. "I've genuinely believed I'm better off alone because then I can just *be* me and not worry about it."

"Sadie, the last thing I would ever want to do is change you," I say, trying to keep a frustrated edge out of my voice. I feel like the longer we talk, the more she opens up, yet somehow the higher her walls are actually getting. Like I'm losing her moment by moment, even when she's in my arms. "The reason I like you is because you're *you.*"

"*That's* why I'm so scared, Ben. You're taking away all my reasons to keep up my walls."

There's a knock, and we both startle. I peel myself away

from Sadie and fumble my way through the dark to the door. German hulks in the hallway lit by small, generator lights along the floor.

"Is Sadie with you?" he asks, and I want to snap that it's none of his business.

Except, in a very literal sense, she *is* his business. "She is. And she's completely safe and secure."

German nods. "Let her know we'll be heading back to Oakley as soon as the storm dies down. The situation has been resolved."

"Resolved?" I ask, crossing my arms as relief wars with sudden panic in my gut. "Explain."

"Resolved," he repeats. "As in, we believe there is no longer a threat against Ms. Markham."

"You *no longer believe*?" I ask. "Or you know for certain?"

"We believe it is safe for her to return home," German says, and the look on his face, even in the dim light, tells me I'm not going to get any more out of him.

With a quick nod, he disappears down the hallway, and Sadie steps up next to me. My stomach falls. Because the theoretical return to the real world we weren't done discussing just stopped being theoretical. A whole lot sooner than I anticipated.

"You heard?" I ask, and she nods, the shadows on her face making it difficult to read the expression in her eyes.

I want to close the door. I want to grab Sadie in a hug, pull her to my chest, assure her that I'll be patient, that I believe this is worth fighting for. But I don't do this. I don't know that she *wants* me to do this.

"I'm glad you're safe," I say.

"Me too. It's a relief." She sounds anything but relieved. She sounds more like one of those automated voice messages.

"Well," I say, just as Sadie says, "I should—"

We both laugh humorlessly. "You first," she says.

"This really brings us full circle," I say. "Should we talk about where this leaves us? About what's next?"

I sound desperate. I feel desperate. And I already know what Sadie's going to say—or some version of it—before she says it.

"I need some time, Ben. This whole conversation was … a lot. And I guess I need to pack."

It's a thin excuse, and we both know it. But I'm not going to push anymore, even though I want to tell her she doesn't need to do that right now. She also doesn't need to get off the boat the second we dock.

Instead, I open the door wider and step aside. I watch Sadie walk across the hall, allowing her the space she asked for, hoping like hell this isn't the biggest mistake I've ever made.

SIXTEEN

Sadie

I'VE NEVER DONE a walk of shame. But that's exactly what it feels like when I decide to leave Ben's yacht when the sun is barely peeking over the horizon. Hurriedly grabbing all my bags and tiptoeing out of my room, I can only hope Ben's door won't pop open to reveal the man whose words and smile and everything are making me rethink my life.

If I see him, I might crack.

It works. His door does not open. And I am just about to disembark, accompanied only by the two agents who were up and ready before I was, when Leandra calls, "Off so soon, Sadie?"

I freeze, just like a cartoon character—one leg poised in the air and my eyes wide. Clearing my throat, I lower my leg like a normal person and turn, giving Leandra the best smile I can manage.

"Good morning," I call brightly. "I didn't know anyone else was up."

She arches a brow, clearly not buying it. What's more, I can read the disappointment clearly written on her face. "Where's Ben?"

"Still sleeping." I wave a hand. "I didn't want to disturb him."

"Is that right?"

No, it's *not* right. It's wrong in every sense of the word. Wrong not to wait for Ben to get up before leaving. Wrong to leave things between us as unfinished as a half-crocheted sweater. Wrong to lie to a woman I truly enjoyed getting to know.

I am all-too aware that I am currently sprinting away from my fears rather than facing them head-on. I'm doing dirty the man who did so much for me this week. Yet even knowing this, even seeing Leandra's disappointment, even thinking about Ben waking up and realizing I'm gone doesn't make me want to stay. If anything, I'm itching to put some distance between me and this yacht.

I wait for a lecture. For a rebuke. For Leandra to tell me I'm making a mistake—which, I probably am. I know she'll be Team Ben in this situation. Even if she didn't have an established loyalty to him. I'm the person sneaking away without so much as a thank you.

Instead, Leandra's eyes soften, and she strides over, wrapping me in a hug. I don't move for a second, my arms pinned to my body and my brain shocked into nonaction. Then, I manage to wiggle my arms loose so I can hug her back.

I need a hug, even if I probably don't deserve one. Leandra smells homey, like maple syrup and sunshine, and somehow, this only makes me sadder. She smells and feels like a mom, and it's been a very long time since I've felt like I *needed* a mother.

"Go easy on him," Leandra says. As tears prick my eyes, she adds, "And go easy on yourself, too."

Unfortunately, I suspect it's a little too late for both.

With a last squeeze, she quickly lets me go and strides away, disappearing down the stairs. This is *almost* enough to make me change my mind. To drop my bags on the deck and sprint back down to Ben's room.

But what would I say?

What can I promise?

What, exactly, do I want?

I have no idea. Which is why I pick up my bags, force back my tears, and walk onto the dock, German and Daniels trailing behind without a word.

THE FACT that I have a snuggly raccoon sitting on my lap eating Fruit Loops with his tiny hands does nothing to soften the matching menacing glares my sisters are giving me.

"You just *left* Ben?" Eloise asks. "Without even saying goodbye?"

"He was *sleeping*," I say.

It's been less than twenty hours since I snuck off of Ben's boat and walked myself over to the inn. (Seventeen and a half, actually. But who's counting?) Every new hour, guilt wormed its way just a little deeper inside me. Pretending it's not there hasn't lessened the squirmy feeling, but for now, I just keep ignoring. There are plenty of other things on my mind.

When I stepped into Gran's house, Eloise ushered me into the kitchen, where she presented me with a mug of coffee, a new iPhone—apparently someone let her know I'd been missing mine—and a hug I didn't know I needed until I collapsed into my sister's arms. I'm usually not much of a hugger, and that's two in one day that made me teary.

It took twenty minutes for German to fully debrief me with Eloise fluttering nervously around the kitchen like a mother hen and Daniels being his usual, silent self. Merritt appeared halfway through his explanation, piercing me with a dark glare, clearly unhappy I hadn't been more forthcoming with the two of them about why I fled to Oakley. And why I had government agents shadowing me *and* them.

The good news is that the man whom I had outed as a first-class criminal with my apparently not-so-surreptitious digging has been apprehended. Along with his known associates I identified through my hacking. He is no longer a threat to my safety or to the countless people he harmed before.

Despite Merritt's glares and Lo's obvious worry, I still don't regret my choices.

Unless I think about how my choices led me to Ben. And I don't regret that, not exactly. I feel … I don't know. I can't pinpoint or identify one singular feeling. They're more like a tangled ball of yarn, and I'm afraid if I try to tug on one strand, the whole thing will tighten and knot into something far messier than what it already is.

"So, that's it, then?" I asked German in the kitchen this morning. "Time for you to thank me and say goodbye?"

German did not thank me. Nor, as it turns out, did he say goodbye.

Instead, he told me, "When you lift a rock and all the bugs start squirming and trying to hide—that's where we're at now."

Gross analogy. But I got what he was saying: they want to

be totally *sure* before they leave me. Probably more for insurance purposes than anything else.

I can't argue with extra safety. Especially now that my sisters know exactly what kind of trouble I'm in. I didn't miss the way Eloise's hands shook until she stuffed them in the pockets of her blue dress patterned with pink flamingos.

Maybe German didn't thank me for unearthing the information that led to the arrests, but his lip curled up the tiniest bit when he spoke. And I'm interpreting that to mean *You're a genius, Sadie. Thanks so much for sharing your brain and saving the world from the lowest of lowlife scum.*

When German and Daniels left the kitchen to take posts outside, that's when I faced the Inquisition. After listening to both sisters yell at me for several minutes, talking right over each other about my stupidity, I held up a hand and said, "I need a nap and a shower. Not necessarily in that order."

Merritt shuttled me off to her house, which is where I managed to hide all afternoon, feigning sleep and actually sleeping, until my sisters forcibly dragged me from my bed—okay, more like lured me with promises of food and raccoon cuddles.

Which quickly soured as it turned into the Inquisition, part two.

"I can't decide which is stupider: what you did for your job or what you did with Ben," Merritt says.

"Equally stupid, maybe?" Lo suggests, and I roll my eyes.

"How was the opening week for the bed and breakfast? And the Flower Festival?" I ask, desperate for a subject change. I'm not sure what I expected when I finally unloaded everything to my sisters. Guess I should have expected THIS.

At least now, I have Banjo. I scoop up another handful of Fruit Loops, and he holds out his grabby hands. I want a raccoon. Too bad it's not exactly legal. At least not in Georgia. But as it turns out, a full rehabilitation wasn't possible for Banjo, so Hunter was given a special license to keep him.

Lucky.

Knowing my uptight older sister is now a raccoon mom will *never* not seem hilarious to me. I'll have to see if I can get a t-shirt made. She'd never wear it, but it would make me happy all the same.

"Stop trying to change the subject," Lo says. "We're not done scolding you."

"It's weird. I guess I hoped maybe I'd get some version of, 'Well done, Sadie! Way to shut down a whole ring of human trafficking with your efforts!' Not telling me I'm stupid."

"We *are* proud," Lo says. "You are a rockstar, Sadie. A brave, brilliant rockstar."

"Thank you," I say.

"But it doesn't mean you're not stupid," Merritt adds.

Sisters are so fun. Everyone should have at least two!

Under any other circumstance, I might be happy to see Lo and Mer united on a topic, as I spent much of my life playing the mediator, the go-between, the bridge between my older and younger sisters. They are North and South on a compass, two opposing ends of a magnet. And unlike yin and yang, this did not mean harmony.

Maybe living together on Oakley has shifted things between them. I wonder briefly if now I'm the odd sister out, and I don't like the idea at *all*.

I mean, yay for Merritt and Eloise getting along! Boo if it's at my expense or leaves me hanging.

Guess I could change that if I moved from Atlanta to Oakley …

I shut down that thought immediately. It comes too close to thinking about moving here to be closer to Ben. Which dances too near the realm of being like my mother, to making changes for someone else. Shedding my skin to put on someone else's.

But also: practically speaking, I signed a two-year lease. One I could break, but it would be costly. Given the way I blew up my last government task, those might be scarce moving forward. I'm certainly not expecting a medal if German's reaction is anything to go on.

"So, back to Ben," Lo says. She pauses to take a bite of a saltine cracker from the sleeve of Saltines she's holding in her lap. "I can't *believe* you just snuck out while he was sleeping."

"I believe it," Merritt says.

Man—it's been a while since I've found myself on the receiving end of Merritt's ire, and I forgot how unyielding she can be.

"It's not like I fled the state," I argue. "Also, aren't you supposed to take my side? Isn't that sister code?"

"Sister code involves taking your sister's side when she needs it. And calling her out on her crap when she needs that. And you definitely fall into the latter category."

I roll my eyes at Merritt's ability to work a word like *latter* into this conversation.

"Maybe I was just in a hurry to see my sisters. Which was a perfectly natural thing to do when I came to Oakley to see you and instead spent a week in yacht prison with government agents breathing down my neck and throwing my phone into Davy Jones's locker."

"Oh, whatever," Merritt says with a roll of her eyes. "You came to Oakley because a government agent said you *had* to. We both knew you weren't really planning to come to the opening."

She pauses, letting this uncomfortable truth settle over the room, like a foul mist. Eloise won't look at me, and for the first time, I realize how much I might have hurt my sisters by not making it a priority to be here. I can't seem to escape my mistakes today.

"And leaving Ben's boat at butt o'clock in the morning had nothing to do with you wanting to see us," Merritt says. "That was about you. You and your inability to handle any relationship that progresses past surface level."

"Mer," Eloise chastises, but she doesn't argue that Merritt is wrong.

I mean, how could she? Merritt *isn't* wrong. I'm self-aware enough to see the patterns in my own life. And to know exactly how cowardly and wrong it was to leave Ben like I did.

My older sister doesn't apologize or back down. Instead, she sets her jaw, picks up a colorful throw pillow from the couch, and pulls it onto her lap.

My pride still stinging from this nonstop assault on my actions, I take a moment to channel my breathing and take in Merritt's living room. I need to focus on something for a moment that isn't my very obvious list of shortcomings as a human.

This is my first time back at Merritt's since she and Hunter got married, and she's done a lot to make his house feel as much like her as it does him. There are vibrant splashes of color everywhere, from Mer's paintings hanging on the wall to the throw pillow she looks like she's trying to murder. Better *it* than me.

But the house is also spotless, neat and orderly and very Merritt. I love the juxtaposition of her two halves. The order she craves, and the artistic expression that keeps her sane *despite* that order. Hunter, who is currently sleeping in their room down the hall, has softened Merritt's edges. At least, some of them. Clearly, she's still got some that are quite sharp, all currently directed my way.

"Sadie," Eloise says, forcibly dragging me back to the conversation at hand. "I just want you to think about how it looked to Ben. Maybe you didn't mean to leave for good. Maybe you did want space and planned to talk to him later." Merritt scoffs at this, and Lo flinches. "But what *you* were thinking doesn't matter because you didn't say any of this to Ben. To him, it looks like you ran. It looks like rejection."

Her voice is much softer than Merritt's but the words cut more deeply. I *did* run. I know it. Even if I'm not admitting it out loud to them.

Running has always been my go-to. When our parents fought. When I went through a breakup. When I was feeling alone or upset about anything at all. At some point, running away shifted to running and hiding. Not the typical kind of hiding, like in a dark corner, but staying in the shadows to watch. I may have taken some inspiration from *Harriet the Spy*, still one of my favorite books. Then, my running didn't feel so cowardly.

Not like it feels now.

I hate that at almost twenty-seven, I'm still turning to unhealthy coping mechanisms I used as a kid. I've been through therapy, for crying out loud! Shouldn't I be better about things like this?

And I know Eloise is completely right. I have to close my eyes when I picture Ben, waking up and probably walking across the hall first thing, barefoot, shirtless, and sleep rumpled. Wearing that smirky, self-satisfied grin—the one I give him a hard time about but secretly love.

I didn't think about hurting him. I only thought about myself.

The longer we talk, the more disgusted I feel with myself.

As though he agrees, Banjo hops off my lap and scurries off to sit by Eloise's feet, where he begs until she laughs and hands him a saltine cracker from her stash.

Thanks for having my back, pal. Can't even count on a raccoon these days.

Just like Ben couldn't count on you.

Argh! It's totally not fair when even my internal monologue turns against me.

"You told him you needed space," Eloise continues, clearly not done putting me through the wringer. "And then you disappeared without an explanation." She pauses, purses her lips, then continues, almost apologetically. "You do know his mom died, right? And his dad only cares about the possibility of getting some of that family money. Ben has dealt with a lot of abandonment."

"Wow. Sounds like you two got close this year."

Right now, my sarcasm is not making very good armor. It's thin and ugly and full of holes. It makes me sound mean. Uncaring. Like Lo's words aren't tearing me apart inside. Like I don't want to steal one of my sisters' car keys and break all of Oakley's speeding laws to get back to Ben. To explain.

But I can't bring myself to shed my sarcastic suit of armor in exchange for healthier, more emotionally mature responses. Not yet.

What would I even say to Ben? Would he even want to see me after this? Or did my running away make it super clear how unfit I am to be in a relationship? He's probably lounging by the pool thinking he sure dodged a bullet with me.

"For all you know, he doesn't even know if you're still on Oakley," Merritt says. "He could think you're already back in Atlanta."

I shift, sitting up a little taller. "Does he not know I'm here? Your husbands both talk to him on the daily, so don't pretend like you don't know if they told him."

Hunter's and Jake's friendship with Ben is why, in the back of my mind, I assumed that Eloise or Jake would have let him know I'm still here. Relying on them to tell him is pretty cowardly, but then we've already established how good I am at the whole running-in-fear thing.

Eloise's eyes dart to Merritt, and she shrugs before saying, "I don't know. Honestly. But even if he *does* know, he still needs to hear from you, Sadie. Being here and *not* talking to him is almost worse than leaving."

I sink back onto the cushions with a weary grumble, disturbing Banjo enough that he leaves Eloise and her crackers, scurrying over to a basket of blankets next to the fireplace. He burrows under the top blanket, then pulls it over himself in a gesture that looks uncomfortably human.

And it feels distinctly familiar. Because am I not doing exactly that in a figurative sense? You know you're in a bad place when you're drawing parallels between yourself and a raccoon.

There are a million questions running through my brain. Ones I just have no answers to. What would it look like to be in a relationship with Ben?

There's my two-year lease. My lack of desire to leave a city I just got to. The lack of security about my job after what I did. That's a whole lot of uncertainty right there.

If I were in a relationship with Ben, would I stay in Atlanta? Would he be willing to move or do long-distance stuff, or would he rather I live on Oakley full time?

There's something nostalgic and hopeful about that thought, buoyed by the very real fact that both of my sisters are already *on* Oakley, happily married and settled. I moved away from DC because I wanted to be closer to them, but to be on the island itself full-time?

Of course, if I'm with Ben, I wouldn't even need to work. If the numbers I dug up on the internet are even close to correct, he probably makes what I make in a year in a single afternoon, just in interest. Men with megayachts don't need their wives to work.

But that's exactly how I *don't* want to be thinking. *You won't even need to work* was Justin's line, smoothly delivered in a way that somehow didn't feel patronizing at the time, even though now, looking back, I can't imagine how I didn't see it —see him—for what he was. Also, how little he knew me if he thought I wouldn't *want* to work, even if I didn't *need* to.

Of course, you should finish your PhD, Justin said more than once. *But there's no reason to make plans beyond that. It isn't as though you'll have to work.*

But I have a feeling Ben wouldn't ask me not to work. He wouldn't pressure me into moving to Oakley. For the last time: Ben isn't Justin. They don't exist in the same space. Period.

I may not have answers to any of these questions, but I do know I should probably not be deciding them alone. These are questions and decisions to make *with* Ben. Or else I'm being just as awful as Justin, making executive decisions for us both by myself.

"What am I supposed to do?" I say, my gaze shifting from one sister to the other. "I barely know Ben. It hasn't even been a full week we've spent as a … couple-ish *thing.*"

"You can't even say *relationship*, can you?" Merritt asks, the twitch in her lips the first sign of amusement I've seen all night.

"Shut up. I can say it."

"So, say it. Re-la-tion-ship."

"*Relationship.* There—said it." I cross my arms. Eloise's head swings back and forth between us, like she's not sure if she should laugh or jump in.

"Try saying it in relation to yourself. Repeat after me: *Ben and I are in a relationship.*"

"I don't need to say it," I say.

"Because you can't," Merritt says.

"Stop being ridiculous. Seriously, though—how will this work? I can't just uproot my life because we had some fun making out on his yacht."

Eloise's eyes turn wistful as she smiles. "It *is* fun making out on that yacht."

"Lo, that's not the point," Merritt says. She waits a beat. "Though I *also* concede that making out on the yacht is fun."

Lo and I exchange twin expressions of shock. "You, Merritt Markham, made out on Ben's yacht?" I ask.

Merritt arches a brow. "You know I'm married, right? And that married people do kiss. As well as many other things, which are also fun to do on yachts—"

I gasp, and Lo bursts out laughing, thankfully cutting off Merritt giving us both a talk about the birds and the bees. I find myself smiling, forgetting for a few seconds about the gnawing ache inside me.

"The point," Merritt says, bringing us back to order like the quintessential big sister, "is that it's time to grow up and stop running. Especially when you're running away from your own happiness."

Lo hops up and moves so she's sitting next to me on the tiny loveseat I've been occupying—and enjoying—all by myself. But this is Lo's way. Confident. Comfortable in her own skin. Positive that everyone will be better off with a little bit of her sunshine in their life.

Which, despite my own love of snark, I can absolutely say I am.

Eloise reaches over and takes my hand. "Sadie, I know you said you've only known Ben for a week, but that's not true. You've been getting to know Ben for almost two years. Since that very first time he snatched the phone out of my hand when I was on a video call with you. Do you remember?"

Of course, I remember. I made fun of what he was wearing, and we spent twenty minutes sniping back and forth, something that left me in such a great mood. A mood that lasted until a date I had that night with a guy who could hardly carry on a normal conversation, much less one that lit me up inside.

I remember how it felt to be in Ben's arms while the storm raged and we simply ... existed. It was something special, something unexpected. Something I could really get used to.

The talking and the kissing aren't so bad either.

"Every time you come to Oakley, the two of you gravitate toward one another," Lo says. "Everyone but *you* suspected you'd eventually stop fighting and start kissing, so don't go acting like this hasn't been in the works for a long time."

"You *all* suspected?" I ask. "Really?"

"He's kind of perfect for you, Sade," Merritt says. "And look, just because you say you want to have a relationship doesn't mean you have to pack up your apartment in Atlanta right now. You aren't *that* far away. You guys can do long distance for a bit. Figure stuff out. You can commit without uprooting anything at all."

I drop my head back onto the cushions and think about their words. Logically, I know they're right. And they should know because both of them did exactly what I'm so scared of doing myself. They uprooted their lives and relocated to Oakley to be with their husbands.

Except that isn't how it really feels for either of them. Eloise came to Oakley because she was in the middle of a transition period after college. Something tells me she'd still be living here running the inn even if she hadn't fallen in love with Jake. Jake is a bonus, but this island has clearly given her the life she was meant to have all along. And she didn't have to give up on her dreams—she just finished her master's in a low residency program.

Talk about cake and eating it too.

As for Merritt, she talks about moving to Oakley like it was her homecoming. A return to the person she was before she got too scared and too closed off to realize what she actually wanted. Which is, apparently, a house on the edge of a marsh with a bunch of rescue dogs, a raccoon, and a quiet, bearded man who loves her exactly as she is.

Me? I've always felt a connection to Oakley, but I'm not sure it's in my blood quite like it is for my sisters. I've never even tried to imagine a long-term life living in a very sleepy beach town.

I *could* work from anywhere. And if Ben were in Oakley, well ... maybe I could get used to it if I really tried. Maybe I'd even like it.

But at what point does this kind of compromise become losing myself?

I don't realize I've said this out loud until Eloise grips my hand tighter, giving me a squeeze. "You aren't Mom, Sadie. Never have been. Never will be. You don't need to worry that making compromises or choices for another person means giving up yourself."

When did my youngest sister grow up and get so wise?

Apparently when I was sitting around being stubborn and running away from all my problems.

"You don't have to have all the answers now," Merritt says, ever logical. "All you need to know is whether or not you want to see if a relationship with Ben will work. You need to know if it's worth giving a chance. Then you have to commit to the effort. If it doesn't work, it doesn't work. And you'll figure out what happens next, then. But if it *does*?"

She lets the question hang in the air. I close my eyes, allowing myself to consider what a life with Ben might look like. The billionaire thing is a perk, for sure. But it isn't the first thing that comes to mind. The first thing I think of is the way it felt to have Ben taking care of me.

Then there's the way he listens to me and anticipates how I might feel, working in advance to make sure I'm comfortable. It's his love of history and the annoying way he's committed to preserving Oakley's old-school charm. It's the way he treats his staff and gives back to his community.

He has some walls up, too. I'd rather he confront his father head-on than hide behind some silly image that doesn't come close to reflecting the man he really is, but I also understand those walls. What are we all if not a complex mix of easy and complicated, good and bad, confidence and insecurity?

"I'm so scared," I say more to myself than to my sisters. "I already like him so much."

Eloise grins. "It's a fun feeling, huh?"

I glare at her. "No."

"Just lean into it," Merritt says with a shrug. "Learn from my mistakes and stop running right now. Unless you're running *to* Ben, in which case, get the hell out of here and go find your man. I mean, there are worse things than marrying a billionaire."

Eloise's smile hasn't dimmed the slightest bit. "One who has a yacht we can all agree is perfect for kissing."

I snort. But the ache in my chest has eased. My brain is firing on all cylinders instead of flying at half-mast. Okay, so maybe my ability to make good analogies and avoid mixing metaphors is broken, but whatever.

My heart starts pounding in my chest. I *do* want to give this a chance. I *do* want to see what could happen. I *do* want to stop running away for once.

And I want to find Ben. Right this very second.

I sit up a little taller, and Eloise squeals. "She's gonna do it!" she says. "What do you need? What can we do to help?"

"I just need to find him," I say. "I need to apologize for leaving." I throw a hand over my face. "Oh man, why did I leave him? What was I thinking?"

"You were just scared," Merritt says. "It's normal. You're human. Stop worrying about it and just go fix it." She yawns. "But in the morning."

"No way! I'm not waiting for morning. I'll go now."

Eloise looks at her watch. "Sadie, it's two o'clock in the morning. Don't go right now."

"Just wait a few more hours," Merritt says. "He's probably asleep. And no one wants to have a rational relationship talk at this hour."

"Um, we literally just did that," I point out.

"You've made him wait this long," Eloise says with a shrug. "A few more hours won't hurt. Plus, you could use a shower."

"Thanks for that," I say drily. "Will one of you take me in the morning? This not having a car thing is for the birds."

Eloise nods, her face totally serious as she says, "We ride at dawn."

SEVENTEEN

Ben

WHEN YOU HAVE GOOD FRIENDS, it turns out you can't even mope on your yacht in isolation. Not without them sticking their intrusive noses in your business.

In Hunter's case, he also comes with dogs who stick their noses in my *actual* business.

"Hey, now," I say, gently redirecting the two dogs who seem intensely interested in greeting me by way of aggressively sniffing my crotch. "What happened to a good, old-fashioned good morning?"

Sunbeam, Hunter's shepherd mix, gives a low woof, sitting back on her haunches, but the Great Dane, Lilith, flops down on the rug with a groan. She takes up practically the whole room.

Hunter chuckles. "There you go. They said hi. Your face looks like a frat house after a weeklong rager."

"I don't understand the analogy," I say. "But thanks?"

Jake steps into the room, glancing around with a frown, though the only thing really out of place in the lounge is me, sprawled out on the couch in yesterday's clothes. I discreetly give myself a sniff. Not *that* bad. I'm not sure why my friends are acting like I'm some kind of charity case. I'm not surrounded by a thousand beer cans or dirty dishes. And sure—maybe that's because I'm not into beer when I'm already sad and because Leandra cleaned up all my dirty dishes.

But I'm really doing just FINE, thank you.

"What Hunter means to say is it looks like we got here just in time." Jake takes a seat in a chair across from me, his crisp suit and sharp eyes giving me all-business vibes.

I should have known I couldn't just wallow in peace. But then, I did text both of them last night, pumping them for information. Things like: is Sadie still on the island, and did she say anything to her sisters that they, in turn, said to their husbands that they could, in turn, say to me. But I guess when you're married, you don't always give up your wife's secrets.

I set down the book on World War II submarines I've been reading—more like staring at the pages—and remove my reading glasses from the top of my head.

"Just in time for what?" I ask.

"To save you from making a stupid mistake," Hunter says. He takes the seat next to Jake, which means now they're both directly across from me like some kind of committee, ready to weigh in on my actions.

I roll my eyes. "Ah. So, this is the part where you judge my life choices, find me lacking, and give me your sage and unsolicited advice?"

"Precisely," Jake says. He's not smiling.

Hunter, however, chuckles again. "Glad you're amenable to the idea."

"*Amenable*, huh? We're breaking out all the big words today. It must be serious."

"You should go take a shower," Jake suggests. "And shave."

"Personally, I like the stubble," Hunter says.

"Of course, you would, lumberjack."

"And he doesn't smell *that* bad," Hunter tells Jake.

"I don't smell at *all*," I say.

"My dogs disagree."

I glance at Hunter's dogs. Lilith is already snoring softly, but Sunbeam is still sitting at my feet, tail swishing along the floor.

"Maybe they just like me."

"Maybe we should stop beating around the proverbial bush and ask you why you're here alone instead of going after Sadie?" Jake asks.

I drag my hands down my face, feeling the extra growth of stubble from my lack of showering and personal hygiene over the past twenty-four hours. Is that all it's been? It feels like so much longer from the time I woke up and realized Sadie had already gone, taking her things and her agents without so much as a note.

Which, to me, sure seemed like a very firm period at the end of our conversation the night before.

Am I really so surprised she chose to leave? To run?

After everything she told me about her previous relationship and all the things I apparently have in common—on the surface, anyway—with her rich, older ex, I get it. Kind of.

But I'm also deeply hurt. I laid it all on the line, and she decided I'm not enough. Or not worth the risks. Or she just doesn't share the same feelings I do or the same hope I do that we could figure out a way to make things work.

This is what I get for having hope at all. For thinking

there might be a chance, that maybe I should attempt something I've never tried in the past. Instead, this just seems like confirmation I'm not built for serious relationships.

The one time I put myself out there, the woman runs off without saying goodbye. Seems like a pretty blatant sign to me. The sign reads: *Give Up! Committed Relationships Are Not for You!*

"I'm not really in the mood for a jaunt to Atlanta," I say. "I prefer the ocean."

Jake and Hunter exchange a glance. "She's not in Atlanta," Jake says. "She never left."

I let this information settle over me, testing out how it feels. Sadie hasn't left. She's still on the island. A tiny bubble of hope rises fast and then, just as quickly, pops.

She may not have left Oakley yet, but she still left my boat—left *me*—without a word.

"Just ask me about the Markham sister sleepover at my place last night," Hunter grumbles. "They talked all night long."

I put my reading glasses back on, then pick up my book. "I hope they had a lovely time. But it still doesn't change anything."

"What exactly happened?" Jake asked.

I shrug. "Nothing all that interesting. We kissed. Went on a date. Talked about our feelings. I told her I was looking for something real. Then she left without saying goodbye the moment she had a chance. As one does," I say.

I read the same sentence about a U-boat five times before the silence gets to be too much. I push my glasses down my nose and glance up at Hunter and Jake, who are watching me with two of the creepiest smiles I've ever seen.

I frown. "What?"

"Were you this dumb with Eloise?" Hunter directs this to Jake.

"Dumber," Jake says. "You?"

Hunter nods. "About as dumb. Twice over."

"Is this some kind of effect the Markham sisters have, or is it something about *us*?" Jake asks.

"Maybe men in general," Hunter says.

"Don't put me in the same category as you two," I say. "I'm not the one who snuck off a boat before dawn to avoid an awkward *it's not me it's you* conversation."

"No," Jake agrees a little too reasonably. "You're just the guy too stubborn and prideful to put things on the line for the woman you want."

"I already put things on the line," I say, tossing my book and glasses next to me on the couch. "I already told you—she gave me her answer when she left."

"Hm," Hunter says.

"Don't *hm* me! I told her how I felt! I said I thought we could make this work! That I was willing to try!"

"And are you?" Jake says with the most annoying smile. He leans back, casually crossing one leg over the other. "Trying?"

"From where I'm sitting, your attempt at *trying* looks more like wallowing in self-pity," Hunter says.

"Your *trying* definitely doesn't include showering," Jake adds.

I throw up my hands. "Just because things worked out for the both of you blockheads doesn't mean it will work for me. Getting married to a Markham sister also doesn't make you experts on love or on Sadie. She isn't Eloise," I say, pointing at Jake. I switch my finger to Hunter. "Or Merritt. Sadie said no. The end."

"I thought you said she didn't say anything before she

left. Isn't that what he said a minute ago?" Hunter asks, running a hand down his dark beard.

"He definitely said she left without saying a word," Jake says.

"Maybe he's a mind-reader?" Hunter says.

"Must be. That sure must be a good skill to have. You'd think he would have better luck with women, knowing exactly what they're thinking at all times," Jake says.

"You guys are really funny. Regular comedians. Or are you trying to pretend you're both experts on love?"

"I'm only an expert on recognizing a prime example of male pride and stupidity," Hunter says. "Especially after living it out myself first. Did you know I almost lost Mer because I was so busy trying to placate my ex and keep the peace for Izzy's sake? I was living in the past, too afraid to move on to the future." He pauses. "Are you sure you're not doing the same?"

I'm honestly not sure of anything. Well, anything more than the fact that it feels like someone dug into my chest with a garden trowel, leaving me aching and hollowed out.

I fix my gaze on the floor. "I don't know."

"I may not be apprised of the specifics, and I know Eloise and Sadie are very different people. But if you're at all interested in a future with her, don't let her go now," Jake says. "Find her before she leaves Oakley. Lay it on the line *again*. Clearly. And if you didn't tell her you love her—"

"Who said anything about love?"

The idea has my heart thrashing around in my chest so loud I can hear the blood rushing in my ears. Jake smiles, while Hunter gives a low chuckle.

"Oh, he's got it bad," Hunter says.

Jake clucks his tongue. "Still in a state of denial. That's

unfortunate. I think Eloise said Sadie planned to head back to Atlanta later today—"

I'm on my feet before I've even finished processing. The dogs, catching my excitement, react instantly, Sunbeam runs in circles while Lilith gives three deep woofs, then trots toward the door, glancing back at me as if to say, *Hurry up, idiot.*

"Is she still at your house?" I ask Hunter.

He shrugs. "Can't say. Guess you'll have to go looking."

"Y'all are both some help," I grumble, striding toward the door with a renewed sense of purpose.

Jake and Hunter follow, the dogs running circles around our heels. On deck, I find John, Leandra, Tao, and Danny, looking as though they were waiting for me to emerge. As though they fully expected this. Maybe everyone in my life knows me better than I know myself.

I roll my eyes. "You too? Is this whole island trying to help me pull my head out of my ass?"

"I think Frank even made a series of TikToks, waxing on about shipping you and Sadie," Jake says.

"You're watching TikTok now?" I ask. "What kind of lawyer are you?"

He smirks. "The kind who likes to keep up with the everyday events of his clients by way of Frank's posts."

"Whatever you need to tell yourself," I say.

Leandra beams and holds out my shoes—the worn boat shoes Sadie has made fun of on more than one occasion. "I'm proud of you," she whispers, kissing me on the cheek.

As I move to walk past Danny, he hands me a clean shirt. "I'm not saying you need this but …"

"Oh, he definitely needs it," Jake says.

"You really should pay your crew more," Hunter says.

"We might make more than you, big man," Tao says with a laugh, and Hunter feigns thoughtfulness.

"Let me know if you ever need a handyman on your yacht."

"Boat," I correct. "And no, I don't."

Though I really think I smell *fine,* this is like the third reference to my hygiene. Might as well not risk it. I pull off my shirt and exchange it for the one Danny gave me. It can't hurt to *not* smell like I haven't showered since the day before yesterday. Although this one stinks like he hosed it down with cheap cologne. I sneeze.

John gives me a nod, and Tao smiles widely as I pass him. "Tell Sadie she's welcome to lose to me in poker any time," he calls.

I only wave a hand as I disembark, a man on a mission now, Jake and Hunter right on my heels, the dogs now running ahead. They circle back when Hunter whistles, then fall into step beside Hunter.

"Are you guys going to follow me the whole way?" I ask, not bothering to turn around. I don't need to when I can practically feel them breathing down my neck as I stride across the dock.

"Maybe," Jake says. "Hey—isn't that Sadie?"

I blink, slowing down as I realize Sadie is coming toward me on the dock with just the same speed and intention, which makes my chest warm. I don't even care that German and Daniels are trailing fifty yards behind her like her stupid government shadows.

I grin as Hunter bumps into me from behind.

"Are you just going to stop and let her come to you?" he demands.

"No," I say, giving him a big shove backward. "And maybe you two should just stay here."

I pick up the pace, hustling across the mostly empty dock toward Sadie. She looks fierce and beautiful, her hair a little wild and windblown—just the way I like it.

Though I suspect she may apologize for sneaking off my boat, I can also see a fire in her eyes that tells me she might have a few choice words for me too.

Good. I wouldn't have it any other way.

We're about two boat lengths away when she passes a man sitting on an overturned bucket, reading a newspaper that covers his face, a tackle box at his feet. A man I wouldn't have noticed had he not tossed the newspaper aside and hopped up just as Sadie passed.

Some instinctive part of me sounds an alarm even before I see German and Daniels take off at a sprint, before the man grabs Sadie in one hand, pulling a dark object from the tackle box with the other.

A gun.

Sadie starts to thrash, but then the man presses the gun under her chin, and she goes completely still. So do I. German and Daniels keep running, as the man turns, looking between the agents on one side and me, Jake, and Hunter on the other.

"Everyone stop moving now," he says.

I'm already frozen, panic and adrenaline warring within me as I stare helplessly at Sadie.

She's practically limp, eyes wide and her hands hanging by her sides. I can see her fingers trembling as her fists clench and unclench.

My brain is leaping all over the place, touching on and casting aside possible solutions. Nothing I can think of wouldn't put Sadie at greater risk. It's also hard to think at all when she's being held at gunpoint.

This is totally surreal and yet acutely visceral. Every breath seems weighted, every moment lasting a lifetime.

I have to assume this guy is willing to use his weapon. And he's currently trapped between my friends and me and two agents, both with hands on their guns. Which seems like it will only escalate things.

Behind me, one of Hunter's dogs growls softly. I wish they were trained guard dogs, not simply loyal rescues. I'd happily set either of them loose if I thought it would help.

"Here's how this is going to work," the man says.

His voice has the slightest accent, though I can't pinpoint it. I find myself memorizing every detail I can. The thin, white scar on his cheek. The dark eyebrows and lined forehead. The silver ring on the hand holding the gun.

"You two are going to toss your guns in the water," he says, calmly, like this is something he does every day. He fixes German with a look. "Now."

As German and Daniels slowly reach for their weapons, the man turns slightly so his back is more to us, keeping Sadie like a shield between him and the agents.

I take the smallest step forward, then another, glad I know this dock well enough to know where it will creak. I only hope when the man turns back, he doesn't notice I'm a few feet closer

"Ben," Hunter warns, in an almost inaudible whisper.

I ignore him, taking one more step before the man says, "Now, you go in too. That's right—just step right off the dock and stay down there."

German and Daniels jump in the water, leaving a clear path for the man to leave with Sadie. I take one more big step. The man turns back, and I freeze.

Sadie no longer looks terrified. More ... resigned. Calm.

She thinks there's no way out of this.

As the man starts to back away, I worry Sadie's right. My stomach drops.

"The three of you," the man says, tilting his head toward the water. "Hop in."

No one moves. I feel a surge of pride even as I hope we're not being stupid.

But right now, the man has Sadie. He didn't just shoot her and run the way he could have.

Which may mean he's not supposed to, that he is planning to take her somewhere else. From the little I know, you never let someone take you to a secondary location. But if he has plans to do so, it means he's less likely to hurt her *now*.

"I can't swim," I say. "Sorry."

"Does it seem like I care?" the man asks. "In."

Still, neither Jake nor Hunter obeys, probably taking their cues from me.

"Whatever they're paying you, I'll pay you more to walk away now," I tell him. "Double. Triple. Whatever."

I doubt this will work, but I'm stalling, hoping German has some backup plan or that I can think of something —*anything*—to get Sadie away from this guy.

I meet her gaze, and she gives me a sad smile. Then she blinks, deliberately and dramatically, three times.

What does *that* mean? It's too short to be Morse code. We don't have some kind of secret messaging thing between us either.

Sadie does it again and I rack my brain trying to figure out what she could be trying to tell me.

Behind her, I see German quietly climbing a ladder back up to the dock. Maybe stalling wasn't such a bad plan. A dark car pulls up to the lot and two men jump out. From their dress and movements, I'm guessing they're the other agents who have been on Oakley watching over Merritt and Lo.

"What do you say?" I ask, wanting to keep the man's attention on me. "More money to walk away."

The man gives me a sharp smile. "Tempting. But I won't live to spend it if I don't follow orders."

I take a step forward. "What if the man who hired you is no longer a threat?" The man's eyes narrow, so I keep pushing. "From what I understand, the whole thing is over. Done."

I don't really know that. I only know German said it was safe, that the main players were gone. If this is some hired gun, maybe he simply took an assignment and doesn't know the men who hired him have been arrested.

This is my best hope, and I'm banking on it.

"Just name your price. Anything."

He hesitates and his eyes narrow, but then he shakes his head. "I can't walk away. Bad for business."

He starts to back away again. But with his eyes on us, he doesn't see German reach the top of the ladder, crouching along the side of the dock, waiting. The man also doesn't see the two agents creeping forward, staying low, likely in case the man turns.

This still seems so very risky. I wish I could swoop in and save Sadie. That I had Jason Bourne or Jack Reacher skills and could figure out the best way to take this guy out without Sadie getting hurt.

She keeps up the blinking as they move away.

Blink, blink, blink.

Blink, blink, blink.

What is she trying to say?

And then, as I'm seriously debating taking my chances and rushing the man, she stops blinking, her eyes going wide as they shift to my right. I see a large, dark shape and movement just before a massive pelican dive bombs the man holding Sadie.

For a moment, all I can see is feathers. The only sounds are a yell from the man and a thud as Sadie drops to the deck and starts to scramble away. I'm running before I even realize it, tugging Sadie into my arms and running back toward the yacht. My only thought is to get her away, to get her safe.

We pass Hunter and Jake and the dogs, and I hear running footsteps and shouts from the other direction.

Glancing back, I see the man down on the dock, German pressing a knee into his back. Sunbeam is yanking at the man's pant legs, and Jake holds the gun loosely with two fingers. Above them, on one of the dock's wooden posts, the massive pelican looks bored.

I stop, letting Sadie slide down to her feet, though I don't let her go. I can feel her shaking, and I'm not sure that she could stand.

Dropping my forehead to hers, I squeeze my eyes closed, breathing heavy. Her hands clutch my shirt, and I can feel her heart racing where our chests press together. Mine matches hers.

"I thought I might lose you," I say.

"I'm so sorry I left," she says breathlessly. "It was cowardly and selfish and I'm so, so sorry, Ben."

I lift one hand from her back, reaching up to cradle her head. "How about we make a promise—no matter how hard things get or how uncomfortable, we don't leave when things are unresolved. We can take time, we can hit pause, but we don't leave."

"Yes," she says. "That is … if you didn't change your mind about me."

"I didn't. I could never."

And then I'm done with talking. I don't care that a man is

being zip-tied a few yards away, or that we have a whole audience now—my crew on the boat and half the island gathered at the end of the dock.

I forget all of it and unleash every feeling I have into kissing Sadie.

She kisses me back with a desperation only matched by my own. Our mouths make promises as I deepen the kiss, wanting her to feel every vow I'd like to make in the way my lips claim hers.

We pull back, breathless, and a round of claps and cheers erupts behind us. Glancing up, I see my entire crew standing on the deck of the *Oakley*, wide smiles on their faces. Leandra is wiping away tears, and it appears Tao is also crying. There's a first.

Down the dock, German and the agents are leading the man away. Jake and Hunter stand watching me and Sadie, smug looks on their faces that I don't even mind. At least for right now.

Later, I'll find a way to get them back for being such jerks. Even if they were *correct* jerks.

I fix my attention back on Sadie. "You okay?" I ask, brushing a strand of hair off her cheek.

She nods, then shudders. "I think so. When the adrenaline wears off, I think I may crash."

I grin. "I happen to know a safe place for you to crash. How do you feel about boats?"

"Boats? Or yachts?"

"Whatever you want, Sadie girl. Anything you want."

She leans up, pressing a kiss to my lips with a sigh. "That sounds perfect, Mr. King."

"Hey," I say, remembering, "what do the three blinks mean? What were you trying to tell me?"

Her cheeks go pink, and she bites her lip. Then she grins and blinks once. "I." *Blink.* "Love." *Blink.* "You."

There's a deep rending sensation in my chest, a deep aching the way growing pains hurt, like my body is making room for new growth.

"You do?"

"Maybe it's too soon," she says quickly, suddenly looking unsure. "But something about facing imminent death—"

I can't help it. I growl. A purely animalistic, feral sound that makes her grin.

"Did you just growl at me?" Sadie demands with a crooked grin.

"I don't want to hear you talking about death. You're here. You're safe." I press a soft kiss to her lips, then whisper against them, "And just so we're clear, I love you too, Sadie girl."

EIGHTEEN

Sadie

APPARENTLY, the residents of Oakley Island need very little reason to have a party. Genevieve's Bed and Breakfast is finally opening? Let's have a party! Jake's nephew Liam got a ninety-five on his spelling test? Definitely have a party!

Sadie Markham escaped being kidnapped and killed by a hired hitman? Party time!

I appreciate the sentiment. I really do. But a part of me just wants to hide out on Ben's boat, wrapped securely in his arms, and sleep until next week. Maybe next month.

Harriet pushes through the door of Ned's bar with an enormous tray of sandwiches and I hurry to meet her, lifting the tray out of her arms and carrying it to the tables that have been pushed together. Merritt sees me coming and shifts platters around to make room.

There's already an impressive spread of food—casserole dishes covered in foil, chips and dips, heaping bowls of potato salad and other sides. It's been humbling to see so many people—some I barely know—filing through the door, giving me warm smiles of support as they drop off the food and settle into the booths and tables and stools at the bar.

I shouldn't be surprised. This is Oakley, after all. But I get the sense that all this love really has to do with how much everyone loves Ben. He belongs to these people, which I guess means I belong too. The thought warms me.

"Where's that man of yours?" Harriett asks as she unloads a selection of condiments from the bag hanging over her shoulder.

That man of mine. I smile at her words. Because she's right.

Not-so-playboy billionaire, Benedict King, might belong to Oakley. But he also belongs to *me*.

"He'll be here soon," I say. "He had a few things to take care of this afternoon."

A few things … which he refused to discuss with me even a little bit. When I pushed, he kissed me on the nose and told me he'd see me soon.

"What about Eloise?" Harriett says. She pulls out a six-pack of ginger ale and sets it on the bar. "These are for her. Picked them up from some fancy grocery store over in Savannah. The lady told me they're twice as strong and might help her feel better."

Eloise is dealing with nausea? She didn't seem sick when we were together at Merritt's the other night. She was snacking on saltines the entire time and …

Oh. OH MY GOSH.

My baby sister is pregnant.

Or *maybe* she's pregnant?

If she is, I have no idea how she managed to keep it a secret. We talked almost all night at Merritt's. How did she not scream it out?

But then, we really only talked about *me*. Knowing Eloise, she didn't want to diminish the gravity of my situation by bringing up her very happy news.

"Eloise is in the back with Ned and Jake," I say.

Harriett nods and picks up the ginger ale. "I'll just take this back to her."

"You're good to us, Harriett," I say, and she smiles, pulling her long white braid over her shoulder.

"Sugar, the three of you make it easy."

The minute she disappears through the swinging door that leads back into the kitchen, I practically run to Merritt, who has moved to the opposite end of the bar where she's opening and stacking up the paper plates and utensils.

"Merritt!" I whisper yell. "Harriett just brought special ginger ale for Eloise. To help with her *nausea*."

Merritt looks up, dropping a handful of plastic forks that clatter all over the bar top. "What?"

"And she was chowing down on saltines when we were at your house the other night." I lean forward. "Is our little sister pregnant?"

Merritt presses her lips together, and I might be crazy, but it looks like there are tears collecting in her eyes. I have no idea what Hunter did to soften up Merritt and all her prickly edges, but he has my unending gratitude. It's sweet to see her like this.

It also gives me endless fodder to tease her later.

"Has she said anything to you?" I ask.

Merritt shakes her head. "No, but there's been so much going on. It feels like all we did was stand around and hold our breath the whole time you were gone. That and running the bed and breakfast. But yeah—she's been acting differently. Taking more naps. Eating constantly—" Merritt pauses and shakes her head. "I should have known. I can't believe she didn't tell us today! But then, tonight is about you. I'm sure she doesn't want to steal the moment from you and Ben."

"Whatever. We don't need a moment. We don't even need a party. I'm tired of things being about me. And I don't think I can be around her all night without saying anything."

"Let's go find her, then," Merritt says. She picks up the last of the forks, then heads toward the kitchen. I scramble around the bar to follow her. We barrel into the kitchen side by side and freeze when we see Eloise and Jake in an embrace, their foreheads close together. Harriett and Ned are nowhere to be seen, but the ginger ale is sitting on the steel counter.

Lo and Jake turn and see us, and … oh man, is Jake *crying*? He smiles widely—a rare sight—then takes Eloise's face in his hands, kissing her soundly once more.

"Go ahead and tell them," he says.

Eloise nods and Jake moves past us, wiping his eyes with his shirt sleeve. Instead of stepping around us, my very grumpy brother-in-law wraps his arms around me and Mer and gives us a bone-crushing double hug. He's laughing when he lets us go and heads back into the bar.

Merritt and I exchange a wide-eyed glance, then look at Eloise who is also laughing, wiping tears from her own eyes. "So, Jake and I are having a baby," she says. "If you couldn't guess."

And then, we're all wrapped up in a three-way Markham sister hug. One of many in the last forty-eight hours. But this one feels somehow even weightier. I swear, I can almost feel Gran smiling down at us. This is what she always wanted for us.

Probably exactly what she hoped for when she left the three of us her big house with its stipulations that one or more of us live here to fix it up. It took almost two years, but now we're all here. And though I'm not ready to make a decision yet about leaving Atlanta, I cannot deny the siren's call Oakley seems to have on me.

Or maybe it's the call to be near my sisters.

Or Ben.

By the time the three of us make it back to the party, the room is packed full, and people are already lined up, filling their plates with sandwiches and sides.

My eyes immediately pick out German and Daniels, who have plates in hand. German looks slightly less frowny than usual, and I wonder if the magic of Oakley is finally rubbing off on him.

Ned's big, booming laugh echoes across the bar, and I find him in the corner with Jake. By the look in his eyes, I'm guessing he's just gotten the news that he's on his way to having a second grandbaby. Naomi and her now-official boyfriend, Camden, are at a table near the trusty wooden mermaid that welcomes patrons into the bar, Liam between them. Frank is—as always—filming. And Bard the bird is bobbing his head, every so often quoting what sounds like centuries-old poetry. Shakespeare? Donne? Eloise would know. I don't care.

There's only one person I care about right now, and he's not here.

I force myself not to worry. Ben said he would be right back. I'm sure he will be.

As German nears the end of the food, his plate piled high, he looks up and makes eye contact. He clears his throat as Daniels steps up beside him. "I have news."

"Yeah?" I ask.

"The man from the docks was the only one with a contract."

I try to keep my expression neutral. *Contract* as in, contract to kill me. No biggie. Who *hasn't* had a hitman hired to kill them?

"Communication was cut off, so he had no way of knowing everyone else had been taken into custody. It's over."

"You thought that before," I say.

"Yes, but we weren't sure of something like this. If there were any other players outside of those we knew. We're sure now. Sure enough to head out tomorrow."

I want to feel happy about this. I *do* feel happy. But it's going to be a while before I don't also feel a knot of dread in my stomach every time I think about those moments on the dock.

I was so certain my life was over. That I was saying goodbye to Ben. That I would never see my sisters again. The only thing that lessened the anxiety was Ben's presence.

Ben's solid arms wrapped around me afterward. His whispered reassurances in my ear.

My being in love with him has nothing to do with him being a billionaire. But I'm not sorry he's capable of paying for a little extra security.

I believe German when he says I shouldn't still be a target. But I also believed him when he said it was over the first time, before I was grabbed and held at gunpoint.

Ben already contracted with a security firm. The man works fast. I'll have protection with me here, and when I'm in Atlanta. At least for a while.

I considered fighting him on it. Then decided I didn't mind in the least.

"I'm glad to hear that," I tell German. "And I'm glad you were there. Even if you *did* destroy my phone."

He shrugs. "Be glad for the rogue pelican. All my years in this business, I've never seen anything like that."

I'm not able to hold back my smile. "You've probably never been anywhere like Oakley."

"That's the truth," he says. German, unlike me, sounds like he can't wait to get out of here.

Daniels eyes Bard the Bird on his perch. And then, lo and behold, the man speaks.

"I used to hate birds," he says thoughtfully.

I wait for more. But that's it. I'm laughing as the two agents walk away, taking a seat with Leandra, John, Danny, and Tao. More people I need to speak to. When I'm not so overwhelmed. And maybe once I finally find Ben.

Finally, the only man I want to see appears in the doorway of the bar, a loud cheer erupting as he does. He waves, but his smile only widens as his eyes scan the bar until they land on me.

I hurry toward him, weaving my way through the tables, then pull him down for a very long, very intentional kiss. The cheers get louder, shifting to include some catcalls and whoops of encouragement.

I'm not exactly sure what came over me. But I'm safe, I'm loved, my baby sister is pregnant, my older sister is happy enough to cry over it, and I have to do *something* with all these emotions.

When I finally pull away, Ben's eyes gleam with warmth and appreciation. "What was that for?" he asks, his hand slipping around my waist.

I shrug. "Nothing. I just love you."

He kisses me again. "I'll never get tired of you saying that. I have something for you." He tilts his head toward the door. "Come outside with me?"

When we reach the door, he shifts so he's behind me, and

covers my eyes with his hands. "All right," he says, his breath close to my ear. "Now take a few steps forward."

I hear the door open, then let Ben help usher me over the threshold into the muggy Georgia air.

"Okay. Stop right here. Annnnd … open your eyes."

Ben's hands fall away and I blink, my eyes adjusting to the bright afternoon light. At first, I can't figure out what I'm looking for. Cars line the street outside the bar. A few golf carts too. Seagulls swoop and glide through the air. The palm trees in the square across the road sway in the breeze.

"Sadie, look *right* in front of you," Ben says through a chuckle.

Right in front of me … there's a car. A very pretty, very shiny, very *new* car. More like a small SUV painted a bright blue.

"Is that …" I look at Ben. "Wait—what?"

"Do you like it?" he asks.

I just keep staring. "You bought me a … car?"

He bites his lip like he's nervous, and a surge of emotion for this man makes my chest tighten. "The thing is, I couldn't stand the thought of you driving around Atlanta in a clunker without working air conditioning. Or having to fly every time you come because you can't trust your vehicle. And I know you well enough to know riding in the SUV with a security detail is the last thing you would want. So … yeah. I bought you a car."

The man bought me a car. I know for someone with a whole island and a megayacht this is chump change. But for me, it's huge. It's also so very thoughtful.

Ben runs a hand through his hair. "Do you like it?"

So many thoughts are running through my brain. One: Ben is giving me the resources I need to *stay* in Atlanta. He isn't asking me to move. He isn't demanding that I uproot my life for his. He's giving me the means to go back and forth safely. If I want.

The reality is I probably *will* eventually move to Oakley. I don't like to be away from Ben for an afternoon. I don't see that changing. And I can't imagine spending entire weeks away from him.

But I love that he's giving me the room to make that decision on my own time. Whenever I feel ready to do it.

Two: this is a *car*. An entire freaking CAR. I'm going to have to wrap my head around what it means to have a boyfriend who makes as much money as Ben does. My instinct is to think this is too much. But for him? It really isn't.

Also, I really, really love the color. I kind of want to reach out and pet it. Is that weird? Probably. I want to do it anyway.

"Please say something, Sadie," Ben says, his voice wavering and uncertain.

Instead, I turn and kiss him, my hands moving to cup his jaw. I can't believe he's real. That he loves *me*. That I spent so long resisting this man. That now, as soon as I stopped resisting, things are moving forward so quickly.

And that it doesn't scare me in the least.

"It's perfect," I say. "Thank you."

"I have to admit, I worried you might refuse," Ben says. "I know it's a lot. But I just want you to be safe. And I want you to have your independence, Sadie. Of course, I'll drive to Atlanta too. I'll come see you as often as you come here. Whatever it takes to make this work."

"I know you will," I say. "And I love that so much. But we won't have to drive back and forth for long," I say.

His eyebrows go up.

"Atlanta is just a city. I don't have ties there. This is your *home*, Ben." I look through the windows of the bar, where quite a few faces are close to the glass, watching us, including Frank. "And you are my home."

I can see the impact my words have in the way Ben's eyes go a little glassy, the way he works to swallow, the brusque way he nods.

"Okay?" I ask him, my voice rough.

"Okay," he says. "But only if it's what you really want. I would walk away from all of this to be with you."

He would. I know he would. But the thing is—I want to be where he is. And as I think of the bar packed with smiling faces, I want to be here too. Oakley is more home than anywhere I've ever lived. It somehow worked its way into my blood through all the summers spent here, through my connection to Gran, through my sisters, and now, through Ben.

I shake my head, shaking off his words. "No," I say simply. "Our life is here. It's what I want. *You* are what I want."

We kiss one more time, and a comfortable warmth settles into my heart. All that resisting, and here we are.

Who would have thought that the most infuriating man I *ever* met would finally be the one to capture—and heal—my heart.

EPILOGUE

NINE YEARS LATER

Ben

"I DON'T KNOW if I can do this."

Sadie bites her lip, and I remind myself this is not a time to be thinking about her lips. I smile and run a hand over her braid, which hangs halfway down her back now. I love the length—but then, I liked it short too.

Over the past nine years, Sadie has tested out just about every look she could think of, and she pulls off every single one. I even loved the pixie cut she sported for a year, and I never thought I'd be into hair that short.

Turns out, with the right person, I can be into just about everything.

"You can do it," I tell her, keeping my voice level. This is ultimately her choice, so I'm not going to influence her either way unless she asks. "If you want."

Technically, all of her choices affect me and vice versa, but she and I learned early on that it works best for us when we discuss things together. In situations like this, we give the other person freedom to make the final call.

It might not work for everyone, but then, every marriage is different. This is what works for ours.

It's how we decided she should leave Atlanta with a year and a half left on her lease and stop all the long distancing, which almost killed me for the few months it lasted.

How we decided to get married, then how we decided to make the wedding tiny—just family in a surprise ceremony on the yacht when they thought they were just coming to dinner.

And how we decided to have a second wedding ceremony, inviting pretty much every resident of Oakley to watch us repeat the same vows on the lawn of Genevieve's bed and breakfast.

Mostly so they wouldn't hold lifelong grudges for being excluded.

It's how we decided to repurpose my mother's mansion into a luxury boutique inn and build our own house on Hunter's side of the island. Quiet, away from people, but close enough to walk over to Hunter and Merritt's.

I stroke her cheek, then trace the laugh lines around her eyes as she smiles. "You can do this, but you also don't *have* to. Up to you, Sadie girl."

We've practically beaten this topic into the ground. She brought it up a year ago, and since then, we've had multiple conversations, spent late nights making pro and con lists, and she's even made spreadsheets and plugged numbers into a mathematical equation. She wouldn't be Sadie if she didn't.

She beams at me. "Have I ever told you I love when you call me Sadie girl?"

"Only a few dozen times."

"Make it a few dozen and one," she says. Then, she lifts her hand, fingers hovering over the laptop. "I'm doing it."

"Need me to hold your hand?" I tease.

She scoffs, but then looks up at me with *the* look—the one I can never say no to. I used to call it her Puss in Boots look after I saw the Shrek movies while babysitting for Lo and Jake's kids. "Maybe you could rub my head though?"

"Of course."

I shift in the bed, propping the pillows up behind her so she's comfortable, but I can still reach her neck and head easily. Since that first time I rubbed her head through the migraine on the boat, I've done this countless times. The feel of her hair under my fingertips, the sounds she makes when I use just the right amount of pressure—all of this is familiar. And I love it.

I start to undo her braid while she continues to stare at the email in front of her. I watch her eyes move across the screen, her lips moving as she reads over her email again. I get the braid undone and begin combing my fingers through the long strands before I press my fingertips into her scalp.

"You know," she says, her eyes fluttering closed, "if this billionaire thing doesn't work out, you could pursue a career in this."

"What—head massages?"

"Yup. They'd pay you the big bucks. It's not a skill with you—it's an art form."

"Do you have much experience to compare it to?" I ask. "I mean, how many male head masseuses have you tried, Sadie?"

She snorts. "Enough to know you're a master."

"Ten? Twenty? A *hundred*?"

Sadie slams her laptop closed and turns, grinning. "There. I did it."

My fingers still in her hair. "You did?"

"I did." She draws in a breath. "I quit my job. I mean, it's more like shutting down my own business but—"

I cut off whatever she was going to say by pulling her into a tight hug, then rolling us both across the bed, almost to the edge, making her squeal.

"Ben! What are you doing?"

I bury my face in her neck, kissing her as my hands find those ticklish spots by her ribs. Her giggles turn to full-on belly laughs.

"I guess this means you approve?" she says through her laughter, breathless and smiling.

"It means I'm happy *you're* happy," I tell her, rolling us again until she's on top of me, her long hair tickling my bare chest. "Also, that's a very big thing to have done, and it's not even nine o'clock in the morning. What*ever* shall we do with the rest of the day?"

Her grin starts mischievous, clearly following the same line of thought I am when it comes to ideas for how to pass the time, but then it fades into something softer.

"Speaking of how to spend our time, I have a confession to make."

As much as I love the wildness of Sadie, I'm a man who thrives on order. Sometimes, her surprises throw me for a loop and require some time and thought before I can get on board. A confession sounds particularly ominous.

"Okay ..."

Sadie drops down until her mouth is by my ear. For a very long moment, she just hovers there, breath hot against my neck. Then, she whispers, "Let's try for a baby."

I go still, unsure I heard her correctly. "Wait—what?"

"You heard me, Mr. King."

Sliding my hands from her hips to her shoulders, I gently

push her up until I can see her face. I need to see her expression, to know if she's being serious. And she absolutely is. Not that I thought she'd tease me about something like this, but this is so unexpected I almost don't believe her. I can see the sincerity in her expression.

But she's also still Sadie, so she props her elbows on my chest and drops her head in her hands, looking down at me with a smirk.

"Well?" she asks. "What do you think?"

"I ..." Swallowing, I search for the right words.

Despite not having the kind of family that made me want to establish my own—at least in terms of children—sometime after Sadie and I got married, the idea started to appeal to me. Probably because of how many kids are around all the time. Hunter and Merritt have Izzy and are hoping to adopt, Naomi is around with Liam and Ezra as much as her hockey-playing husband's schedule allows, and Eloise has three kids, the latest one born just a month ago.

It's chaotic and loud, and all of the relationships have shifted to accommodate all the kids. Something about this appealed to me. But Sadie has been steadfast in not wanting children. She told me this before we even got engaged—and back then, child-free by choice sounded great to me. I wasn't about to pull a bait and switch and suddenly tell her I changed my mind.

Though she does know I'm open to the possibility of kids. We talk about everything, and I told her while reassuring her I was okay if we didn't.

I never tried to change Sadie's mind, and I was never disappointed. Not exactly. There were simply times that I longed for what my friends have. The full, loud chaos of a house with kids.

But as I told Sadie, it didn't feel like anything was *missing*. She is exactly what I want and need. *All* I want and need.

And yet …

"I thought you didn't want to have children," I say. "You're not doing this just for me, are you?"

She shakes her head, a smile overtaking her face. "I don't know what changed. Just that something did. I don't know if you're still even interested, so I guess if you're not—"

"I am," I say quickly. "But only if you're sure. Are you sure? Because I need you to know—you are enough for me, Sadie girl. Only you."

"Some might say I'm too much," she teases.

"Not me."

"We might not even be able to get pregnant. Merritt can't, and sometimes these things are genetic. I don't want you to be disappointed."

"I won't be." I pause, letting my gaze rove over her face, looking for signs. "You're really serious? I need to know you won't regret this. That you've thought about it and know it's what *you* want. It has to be what we both want. Are you completely and totally positive?"

Sadie rewards me with a huge smile. "I stopped taking my birth control last week."

"You did?"

"I did." She tilts her head, studying me. "Are you sure you still want to try for a baby?"

"Yes."

The answer is fast. No hesitation. Because, though I would have been content with Sadie alone, this feels like an added blessing. An expansion of an already perfect life.

"I had to ask because … you're kind of getting up there in years, Mr. King. Basically a grandpa already."

I'm so shocked by her teasing that my laughter practically bursts out of me. "Forty-four is *not* old."

"It is when we're talking about becoming a father for the first time," she says with a cluck of her tongue. "Grandpa Ben. It has a nice ring to it."

I flip us over so quickly she gasps, then giggles as I pin her arms above her head. "I'll show you grandpa."

I kiss her through her laughter, kiss her so thoroughly the laughs become pants, then a soft groan. I pull back, grinning. Sadie smiles back.

"You know what the best part about this is?" she asks.

"What?"

"All the *trying*."

I don't disagree with her there. And as I bring my mouth back down to hers, I hope that whether or not we're successful in our trying, we'll not only enjoy the process, but each other.

Always, every moment—each other.

Almost the end! Keep reading for a super epilogue…

SUPER EPILOGUE
THREE YEARS AFTER THE EPILOGUE

Eloise

"LEELEE! Don't drag your towel in the—never mind."

I shake my head, giving up on the idea that my three-year-old cares even a little bit about how much sand she's collecting as she drags her pink, flowered towel right over the dunes.

To be clear: she won't care. At least, not until later tonight when she's fighting me off as I try to rinse off all the sand in the bathtub. She will *absolutely* care then and be sure to let me know all about it with her very strong lungs.

"I got it, Mama." Genny brushes past me, scooping her little sister up in her arms, making Leelee squeal, her two blond ponytails bobbing as they spin.

I take this opportunity to grab Leelee's towel from her chubby hands and shake it off. As I do, an arm snakes around my waist, and I smile, immediately leaning into the touch.

I drop my head back onto Jake's shoulder. "Hey, handsome."

His lips find my ear. "What if I'd been a stranger?" he murmurs, his warm breath sending a shiver through me.

This man has never stopped affecting me this way. Not even twelve years after our encounter on this very beach when I had a wardrobe malfunction and he rescued me.

"I could smell you," I tell him with a laugh.

Not true. But now that he's practically wrapped around me, I definitely *can* smell him, and he smells *amazing*. Almost amazing enough to send the girls on up ahead while we duck back into the house and—

Jake growls and gives my earlobe a little nip, interrupting my derailed train of thought. I laugh, hearing Genny mutter, "Gross," from up ahead.

Nothing like a tweenager to keep you humble. Genny reminds me *so* much of Merritt. Which, in most ways, is a good thing. She is eleven going on thirty-five. She's absolutely wonderful with her little sisters, though she's far too bossy for Natalie, who at seven, has decided she doesn't want to be babied. Nat ran ahead of us all, carrying her skimboard. It's the latest in a series of athletic pursuits she has more than enough ability to handle—ability that she absolutely did not inherit from me.

"Kiss! Kiss! Kiss!" Leelee chants, the very opposite of her oldest sister, who makes a gagging noise.

I grin, tilting my face back to Jake's, letting him plant a kiss on my lips. A little too quick of a kiss if you ask me.

"No more PDA," Sadie calls, sounding almost as disgusted as Genny.

She's walking over from the carriage house, a baby on one hip. We haven't had people actually living in the carriage house in years, but we sometimes use it for overflow guests when the inn is full. It's a great place for everyone to change and get ready when the family gathers for beach days at the bed and breakfast.

I should know *which* baby Sadie is carrying, but I still can't tell the twins apart. And Sadie doesn't like it when I put a marker dot on their hands or feet, so I'm flying blind with the six-month-old boys.

"You're one to talk," I fire back, and Jake chuckles. "Speaking of, where's *Benjy?*"

Sadie smirks. "David had a diaper blowout. Straight up his back."

So that makes the baby on her hip Daniel. His tuft of blond hair atop his head is like duck fuzz, blowing a little in the ocean breeze. I want to snatch him out of her hands and snuggle him up, smelling that new baby smell I miss so much. It feels like just yesterday, not three years ago, when Leelee was that small, with a similar downy head of blond hair.

I really, really hate the phrase *time flies*. So cliché! And yet so very true.

But if it's flying, at least I can say I'm enjoying every moment. Okay—not *every* moment. Anyone who tells you to enjoy every moment deserves a nice smack. While in the throes of post-baby blues, I started to understand you can't enjoy every moment, but each day, it's possible to intentionally enjoy *some*. On the hardest days, maybe just one moment. But I always strive to at least have that.

It isn't easy managing a bed and breakfast and also three girls and the occasional academic research when I can make the time. The one thing I did give up and don't miss at all: social media.

"You got *Benedict* to change a diaper?" Jake asks. "Seriously? I'm impressed."

Sadie's smirk turns into a full-on grin. "He lost a bet. I won't say what about."

The look on her face tells me I definitely do NOT want to know what it was about. Despite Sadie complaining about PDA, she and Ben are hands-down, by far the absolute worst out of all of us in terms of being over-the-top with physical affection and talk that most of us do not find appropriate for public consumption. And they're proud of it.

"When I left, Ben was getting out the garden hose."

Jake grins at this. He looks really cute when he grins. Even—no, *especially*—with the laugh lines around his eyes. "That's a pretty ingenious solution, actually."

"Too bad you never thought of it," I tease, but I cannot picture my husband using a garden hose to clean off a baby.

Jake handled—and *still* handles—parenting like a task needing to be done totally by-the-book. Garden hoses as washing apparatus are decidedly *not* in the parenting books.

Though at times I tease him about his rule-following nature, more and more as we've gotten older, I appreciate his steadiness. Especially when it comes to balancing out my tendency to land in chaos despite my best efforts to avoid it.

I decide I need my baby fix, so without even asking, I steal Daniel away from Sadie, who stretches her empty arms overhead and cracks her neck.

"Thanks," she says. "I swear, I'm going to throw my back out one of these days with these two."

The twins might have been born a little small, coming early as many twins do, but they made up for lost time and are now almost the same weight as Leelee, wearing 2T clothing at six months old.

"You're just a little chunker," I tell him, nuzzling into his neck and inhaling that baby smell. "An adorable little chunky monkey."

"Where's Mer?" Sadie asks.

"Late again," I say, glancing out over the beach just in case she and Hunter arrived with their kids and dogs and bypassed the main house. Nope. Other than a few locals enjoying the unseasonably warm November day, Merritt's crew is not here.

"It feels weirdly gratifying to see her running late for everything after bugging us about it for years," Sadie says. "I love the way having a little one has ruined her sense of timeliness and perfectionism."

I agree. Mostly.

But not fully. Because I also know that since she and Hunter started fostering Charlie, an eight-month-old pulled out of a truly abysmal home situation, Merritt has been struggling with legitimate anxiety. Something she might not have told Sadie yet. I'm shocked Mer told me, but she had something of a breakdown a few weeks ago, and I think she took me seriously when I suggested she see a professional and consider some anti-anxiety meds. If not holistic things. Or both. *All* the things.

Whatever she wants to do—I want her to do *something*. Mental health is hugely important. And I know, to someone like Mer who likes to control all the things, it can be hard to ask for help. To admit that she needs it in the first place is huge.

I make a mental note to ask her how she's doing today, if we manage a minute of privacy. Maybe I'll swing by this week, even if not.

Ben catches up to Sadie before we reach the sand, handing David to her before he and Jake move ahead, probably to set up the tent that will shade us from the sun. Even though it's November, sun is sun. Between the babies in the group, and Merritt's efforts to keep her skin wrinkle free until she's seventy-five, shade is non-negotiable. Also, it's hot.

I toss another look over my shoulder, hoping Merritt gets here soon if only so I can put eyes on her and make sure she's okay. I don't see her, but I do spot a mop of curly brown hair zooming down the path like a rocket.

"Coming through!" Ezra, Naomi's youngest son, flies past, sand kicking up behind him as he runs toward the water.

"Ezra, wait up!"

Liam moves up beside us, his arms laden with bags and beach chairs. He's even got one of those fancy Yeti coolers strapped to his back. Naomi's oldest son is only a few semesters away from graduating from college, and his shoulders are broad enough to handle the load, but seeing him haul so much so easily suddenly makes me feel *ancient*.

"Sorry about Ez," he says as he hurries past. "You know how he gets."

"It's good to see you, Liam!" I call, and he spins around, taking a few backward steps as he offers me a charming grin. "You too, Aunt Lo."

"That boy has always had a soft spot for you," Sadie says when he's out of earshot.

"As he should." We slow and wait for Naomi and Camden, who are coming up behind us. Their two-year-old daughter, Mandy, is sitting on Camden's shoulders. "Liam looks like a full-grown man, Naomi. What happened to him?"

"Tell me about it," she says as she leans in for a hug. "I can hardly stand it." When Naomi pulls away, she takes Daniel with her. It's always like this when we're all together. Kids are passed around and loved on, as comfortable with one aunt as they are with another. I love it so much it should be illegal.

Naomi and Camden live with their crew across the bridge in Savannah, but the rest of us are right here on Oakley, giving us every opportunity to turn the "it takes a village" mentality into an everyday reality. I never imagined I'd raise my kids with both my sisters close enough to see them multiple times a week, but now that I am, I can't imagine doing it any other way.

Something tells me our scheming grandmother knew exactly what she was doing when she wrote her will in a way that required us to spend time on Oakley. She wanted us to love this place like she did. She wanted us to have the home she knew we deserved. I wish—not for the first time—that she could have lived long enough to see it.

"That smile is going to wreck some hearts," Sadie says, tilting her head toward Liam who has dropped all his bags and is chasing his little brother toward the surf. Nat and Genny are running too, Leelee close behind.

"It already has," I say, thinking of Izzy, who has harbored the biggest crush on Liam for years now.

Liam stops and drops onto the sand, letting his brother, along with his cousins dogpile him. He laughs as they take him down, disappearing in a wiggling mass of kids. Only Genny stands back, watching with hands on her hips instead of climbing all over her older cousin like she used to do.

Something stretches and tugs in my heart. Genny is growing up. It's an unusual sensation to be both excited about something and terrified to see it happen all at the same time.

"Does he look more like Jake than he used to?" Sadie asks, shifting David from one hip to the other.

"The older he gets," Naomi says. "Though he smiles a lot more than his uncle."

"Everyone smiles a lot more than his uncle," I joke. It's true, but Jake smiles a lot—for *me*.

We finally reach the tent, and I drop into the beach chair Jake has just set out for himself. "Why, thank you, darling," I say, and Jake rolls his eyes. I pull out a bottle of sunscreen and hold it up. "Can you get the girls? They'll fry if we don't, and if you go now, you'll catch them before they get wet." When he doesn't look enthused, I add, "I'll let you get me next."

"On it," Jake says quickly.

"I'll help," Camden says. "Ezra needs it too, even if he doesn't think so."

"Mandy, you go with Daddy, okay?" Naomi says. "He'll put some sunscreen on you. Camden, don't forget the tops of her feet!"

Camden lifts a hand in acknowledgment, then Naomi and Sadie drop into chairs next to me, a twin in each of their laps.

"How is it having Camden home?" I ask. "Are you used to it yet?"

Naomi's husband just retired after years of playing professional hockey, so his busy work and travel schedule basically stopped overnight.

Naomi smiles. "Is it terrible if I say it's ninety-five percent great and five percent *oh my word, Camden, please go find something to do?*" Naomi snuggles Daniel—or did she switch him for David when I wasn't looking?—a little closer. "Maybe even ninety-nine percent great. But yeah. He's a little like a lost puppy right now, which is making it incredibly hard for *me* to get work done, because he's home all day, and he just wants to ... hang out."

I grin. "*Hang out*, huh? Is that what we're calling it these days? The new Netflix and chill?"

Naomi smirks. "Okay, the *hanging out* part has been really great."

"I bet it has," Sadie says. "If we didn't *hang out* in the middle of the day during nap time, we never would. Once seven p.m. rolls around, I'm good for nothing but sitting on the couch and nursing babies."

"Seriously, my heart's breaking for you both," I say. "All that time with your husbands just lounging around the house. It must be so terrible."

Sometimes it feels like Jake and I are hardly in the same room until we're collapsing into bed, too exhausted to do anything but kiss each other goodnight and pass out. Between running the inn, and maintaining Jake's law practice, and keeping up with the girls, we're both running ourselves ragged.

Daytime sex? I can't even imagine it.

Sadie nudges my knee. "Hey," she gently says. "Just plan something. Put in on the calendar."

"I didn't say we never *hang out*. Just not in the middle of the day."

"Whatever works for you," Sadie says. "You know the girls are always welcome to stay with me and Ben."

"Or us," Naomi says. "Just say when."

"Help?" a voice calls from behind us. We all spin and see Merritt approaching, her arms full of bags and towels and a very squirmy baby boy.

I'm the only one not currently holding a kid, so I jump up and rescue Merritt, lifting Charlie out of her arms. "Oh my gosh, Mer," I say, as I snuggle the baby against my chest. "Has he gotten bigger since I last saw him? You're trying to catch up with your cousins, huh?" Charlie grins a toothless grin and lifts his slobbery hand to my cheek.

"It's amazing what a little consistency can do," Merritt says. "Are we the last ones here?"

"Barely," Naomi says. "And you haven't missed much. Just a conversation about Eloise's sad sex life."

"It isn't sad. It just takes place at more normal hours. Now, can we stop talking about my sex life, *please*? We're going to scar the babies."

Merritt spreads out an oversized beach blanket under the tent and drops her stuff on top. "Sex? I don't even think I remember what that is."

"If you want to walk back to the carriage house with me, I'll remind you," a deep voice says.

Merritt spins around to see her husband standing at the edge of the tent, a wide smirk on his bearded face. After more than a decade of having him as a brother-in-law, Hunter rarely surprises me. The man is as steady and unflappable as any man I've ever known. But every once in a while, he says something that is so uncharacteristically bold, it makes me think there must be a whole side to him that I don't actually know.

I have a feeling it's a side only Merritt knows. My sister wakes him up like no one else can.

Mer takes a few steps toward him and presses a long kiss against his mouth. The kind that *almost* makes me have to look away. "Are you flirting with me, Hunter Williams?"

Charlie lets out an ear-piercing screech from my arms, and Merritt's shoulders drop. "Man, that kid has impeccable timing." She turns to me and takes Charlie while Hunter sets up a beach chair next to their blanket. "Where's Izzy?"

Hunter tilts his head toward Liam, who is in the water now, Leelee dangling from one arm, and Mandy dangling from the other. Liam doesn't come to our beach days nearly as often as he used to since he's in college, but whenever he does, he's always a good sport about all the kid-wrangling his younger cousins expect.

"She's primping," Hunter says with a grunt and a dark look. "She knows Liam's here."

Merritt tosses me a knowing glance, and I chuckle. We've been calling Liam and Izzy cousins since I married Jake and Merritt married Hunter. But the two aren't related by blood and they aren't *technically* cousins. The older Izzy gets—or maybe it's the more handsome Liam gets—the more she seems to be aware of that fact.

Minutes later, Merritt is stretched out on the blanket feeding Charlie, and Hunter has moved down to the beach to join Jake, Ben, and Camden, who are working together with Nat and Ezra to build a sandcastle. I will never get tired of seeing these good, good men playing with their kids, looking at their nieces and nephews with patience and tenderness.

Soon, the men will get tired of the sun, and they'll make their way back to the tent where they'll dig into the coolers looking for drinks and five minutes to relax without a kid asking for something to eat. Or to have a turn on the boogie board or to play a game of spike ball.

They probably won't get five minutes to themselves—none of us usually do—but most of the time, they'll get up anyway. Just as we all would, and all do, for each other and each other's kids.

It's not lost on me that it's nothing short of magic that we're all here, that our marriages are solid (for now) and our kids are all healthy and whole (for now).

But this magic we found on Oakley—it's more than that, too. It's not just my relationship with Jake or Sadie's with Ben or Merritt's with Hunter. It's also the friendships we've built—the relationships I have with my sisters that I never would have found had Gran not brought us here. The relationships all of our children have with each other.

Her house changed us. This *island* changed us. Gran's legacy changed us.

Down the beach, an enormous pelican drops onto the sand not far from where the kids are still working on their sandcastle, a little pink ID tag wrapped around his leg. Steve must be close to twenty years old now, but it always makes me smile to see him around the island. They switched to green tags the year he was rescued, so we always know it's him. As impossible as it seems, we realized he was the bird following Sadie and Ben on the yacht, the bird who took out a paid hitman—someone should really make a movie of this. Except … no one would believe it.

Ever since then, Steve seems to love dropping in on us. At the bed and breakfast sometimes, but especially when we're on the beach. Maybe because he knows we'll feed him—even if we shouldn't.

"Mom!" Nat calls. "Look! It's Steve!"

I wave in response, but then I'm distracted when Hunter stands up, dropping the tiny yellow shovel he's holding as he glares across the sand.

"Um, Mer? Why does Hunter look like he wants to kill someone?"

She sits up, following my gaze to her husband, then tracing *his* gaze to … Izzy.

Izzy, who is walking across the sand with bold confidence, wearing a pair of cutoffs and a teeny, tiny string bikini top I'm guessing she was *not* wearing when she left the house with her dad.

"Oh geez," Merritt says, hopping up off the blanket. "I better go stop him from saying something stupid."

"I think she looks great," Sadie says. "Gotta rock what

you got while you got it. I mean, if she *wants* to rock it."

"Hey," Naomi calls after Merritt. "Remind Hunter that she's nineteen, not thirteen!"

I move to the blanket to sit with Charlie while Merritt is gone, my eyes drifting to Genny, who has moved to a towel beside the tent. She's stretched on her belly, reading a book, her knees bent and her ankles kicking the salty sea air.

"I don't know if I'm ready to see her grow up like that," I say to Naomi, feeling the unwanted prick of tears. I've been *way* too emotional the last few weeks.

"Don't sweat it," Naomi says. "It's a wild ride, but you and Jake will do great."

I'm sure we'll do great ... *sometimes.*

I'm also sure we'll make mistakes and stumble and have moments where we feel like the world is conspiring against us. Heaven knows we've had enough of those times already.

But I'm also sure we'll be okay. That when life gets really tough, because I know it will, we will have the support network we need to get through it—one day at a time.

We have our family.

We have *Oakley*.

And that's more than a girl could ever hope for.

"Picture time!"

Naomi claps her hands and shouts through cupped hands, which has the added effect of saving Izzy from Hunter's overprotective grumbling. Now, we're *all* grumbling, but half-heartedly. We might not love the act of taking a photo every time all of us are together, but we're always glad to *have* the photos. I have a whole series framed on the wall of the inn, showing the expansion of our family over the last thirteen years.

Ned has a matching set on the wall of the bar. Even though he no longer runs it day to day, he's insisted on keeping the pirate decor and these photos. And Bard—because parrots live even longer than pelicans.

"Get closer together," Naomi orders, bending to check the settings on her camera.

Genny, who has taken a sudden interest in photography, adjusts the tripod and asks Naomi a question I'm too far away to hear. The cousins all sprawl at the front, arms around each other, the bigger ones holding the babies. Finally, Naomi shoos Genny over with the other kids and then scurries over herself, folding in beside Liam.

Jake curls a hand around my shoulder and leans close as we wait for the self-timer to activate. "You okay?"

I nod, my throat suddenly too tight to speak.

"Because you've got that look," he continues.

"What look?"

He pulls away a little, giving me a once-over before breaking into my favorite smile. "The look that says you're thinking about having more babies."

I laugh, and of course, that's when the camera starts snapping away. I'll probably have five chins and a too-wide smile. *Worth it.*

As Hunter shouts at Naomi to hurry up, I curl into Jake. "I'm not thinking about it," I tell him as the camera starts taking the next round of photos. "Because we already are."

At that, Jake's mouth falls open, and I can already imagine this last set of pictures, where my husband's shocked face and my tearful laughter will mark the further expansion of the wild and perfect chaos of our perfectly imperfect family.

THE END

WHAT TO DO NEXT

You've finished the Oakley Island series! What*ever* shall you do next?

Keep reading, of course! If you loved Jenny & Emma's styles, don't miss their co-written Appies series.

The first two books are actually part of the Sweater Weather series, *Just Don't Fall* by Emma and *Absolutely Not in Love* by Jenny.

You can find more of the Appies HERE: https://emmastclair.com/appiesbooks

---

And as for where to start with Jenny's books, head into the How to Kiss a Hawthorne Brother series for smoking hot brothers, small town/farm setting, and baby goats. Find the Hawthornes here- https://jennyproctor.com/hawthornes/

For a freebie from Jenny, go to: https://subscribepage.io/S933oF

If you're wanting to dive into more of Emma's books, you might want to start in the fictional town of Sheet Cake, Texas with the Graham family. Read about Sheet Cake here- https://emmastclair.com/sheetcake

- For a freebie from Emma go to: https://emmastclair.com/ante

A NOTE FROM EMMA & JENNY

Hey, lovely readers!!!

Writing this last book in the Oakley series was so bittersweet for us. On the one hand, it's always nice to tie up a series, and we've been SO excited about Sadie from the start.

But on the other hand … it's saying goodbye to Oakley!

And for now, it's saying goodbye to co-writing books. Writing together was SO much fun, and I think we really perfected the blending of our voices and the bringing together of our strengths. We definitely will still be working together, but our upcoming series we'll be writing each book separately. (While still being critique partners.)

We finished the series out with a bang—or a splash?—while writing this during a tropical depression in Florida that flooded the streets and blew our television straight off the TV stand. Because OF COURSE we'd have a tropical storm while on a writing retreat!

Hopefully, you caught our nod to the Appies! We are super excited to bring you more hockey books together in 2024.

We love all of our readers and have loved partnering up for these books!!! How I wish we could all meet up on Oakley for some talking parrots and a little raccoon snuggling.

Maybe one day...

Until then, happy reading!!!

All the heart-eye emojis,

-Emma & Jenny

PS- Thanks so much to Teresa, Rita, Devon, Micah, Megan, Marsha, and Ruth for sending typos from the early copies! And sorry if I missed anyone who sent them after we read this. <3

ABOUT EMMA

Emma St. Clair is a *USA Today* bestselling author of over twenty books. She loves sweet love stories and characters with a lot of sass. Her stories range from rom-com to women's fiction and all will have humor, heart, and nothing that's going to make you need to hide your Kindle from the kids. ;)

She lives in Houston with her husband, five kids, two covid-decision cats, and a Great Dane who does not make a very good babysitter. She earned her MFA in fiction at University of North Carolina at Greensboro writing literary fiction, but for now is focused on LOLs and HEAs.

Let's connect!

Newsletter signup: http://emmastclair.com/ante

Instagram: https://instagram.com/kikimojo

Facebook Reader Group: https://www.facebook.com/groups/emmastclair/

Facebook Page: https://www.facebook.com/thesaintemma

BookBub: https://www.bookbub.com/authors/emma-st-clair

Website: http://emmastclair.com

ABOUT JENNY

Jenny Proctor grew up in the mountains of North Carolina, a place she still believes is one of the loveliest on earth. She lives a few hours south of the mountains now, in the Lowcountry of South Carolina. Mild winters and of course, the beach, are lovely compromises for having had to leave the mountains.

Ages ago, she studied English at Brigham Young University. She works full time as an author.

Jenny and her husband, Josh, have six children, and almost as many pets. They love to hike and camp as a family and take long walks through the neighborhood. But Jenny also loves curling up with a good book, watching movies, and eating food that, when she's lucky, she didn't have to cook herself. You can learn more about Jenny and her books at www.jennyproctor.com.

Let's connect!

Newsletter Sign Up: https://subscribepage.io/S933oF

Instagram: www.instagram.com/jennyproctorbooks

Facebook: www.facebook.com/jennyproctorbooks

Facebook Fan Group: www.facebook.com/groups/jennyproctorbooks

Bookbub: https://www.bookbub.com/authors/jenny-proctor

Website: www.jennyproctor.com

A GROOM OF ONE'S OWN

He always dreamed of getting married--but for love, not to avoid deportation.

Eli Hopkins has it all--almost. A hockey career with the

wildly popular Appies. Teammates who are like brothers. The only thing he's missing is someone to share it all with.

Oh--and correctly filed visa paperwork.

Due to administrative error, Eli is about to lose everything.

Unless he can find someone to marry him in the next thirty days.

And he might have the perfect woman in mind. The only problem? He'd like to marry her for real, not simply for legal purposes.

Now Eli faces the challenge of winning over a wife who thinks the marriage is in name only ...

FIND IT HERE!

https://emmastclair.com/groom

ROMANCING THE GRUMP

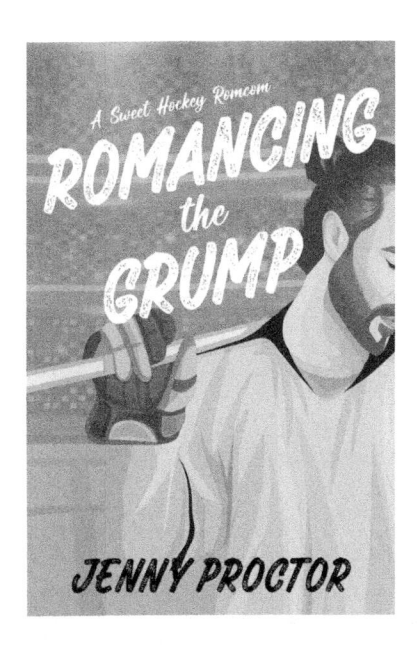

He's a grump and happy to stay that way. But can her sunshine melt the ice around his heart?

Nathan Sanders didn't earn his reputation as the grouchiest player on the Appies minor league hockey team by chance. So when Summer Callahan breezes into his life with her flirtatious smiles and endless charm, he responds like he always does: he completely ignores her.

But Summer is intrigued by the surly center, and she won't be deterred quite so easily. She's convinced that the ones with the hardest shells on the outside are often the softest underneath. And she's determined to prove it.

FIND IT HERE!

https://emmastclair.com/jennygrump

A Free Sheet Cake Novella from Emma!

Get a special FREE Sheet Cake novella! This takes place between books three (The Pocket Pair) and four (The Wild Card) but acts as a standalone.

READ IT NOW! - https://emmastclair.com/ante

Two Free Novellas from Jenny!

When you sign up for Jenny's list, you can grab not one but TWO free novellas!

Grab them here- https://jennyproctor.com/freebies

Printed in Great Britain
by Amazon